# NOT
# BY
# BLOOD

# NOT
# BY
# BLOOD

## A THRILLER

## CHRIS NAROZNY

CROOKED
LANE

NEW YORK

Published in the United States by Crooked Lane Books, an imprint of The Quick Brown Fox & Company LLC.

Crooked Lane Books and its logo are trademarks of The Quick Brown Fox & Company LLC.

Library of Congress Catalog-in-Publication data available upon request.

ISBN (hardcover): 978-1-63910-333-1
ISBN (ebook): 978-1-63910-334-8

Cover design by Kara Klontz

Printed in the United States.

www.crookedlanebooks.com

Crooked Lane Books
34 West 27th St., 10th Floor
New York, NY 10001

First Edition: July 2023

10 9 8 7 6 5 4 3 2 1

# CHAPTER

# 1

THE DRIVER PULLED up in front of a shuttered bodega and tapped his GPS.

"No such address," he said. "But it's got to be this block."

His look told me I had one last chance—he'd gladly drive me back to that quaint little cobblestone street where I'd flagged him down.

"Here is fine," I said.

"Suit yourself."

He started peeling away before I had both feet planted on the sidewalk. I took a second to get my bearings, then turned and headed down a dim corridor of crumbling rowhouses, my brother's SOS call playing on a loop in my head:

*"I swear, Teen—it's bad this time."*

*"It's always bad, Bill."*

*"Not like this."*

*"So hang up and dial 911."*

*"Teen, please . . .:*

He kept hammering at me with his nasal junkie twang.

*"Just give me the goddamn address,"* I'd said.

Of course, he wouldn't tell me what kind of trouble he was in—not over the phone. *"Shit's that bad, Teen."*

The driver had guessed right—I found Bill's squat near the end of the block, sandwiched between a vacant lot and a burned-out brownstone. At a little after midnight, a half-dozen men crowded the stoop—some with brown paper bags, some sucking on joints, their voices loud and relaxed—like a summer block party in late October. Bill wasn't one of them, and he wasn't waiting at the curb like he'd promised. I dug out my phone, stepped behind a delivery van, and called his latest prepaid number. Straight to voicemail.

The old rage came charging back. I'd dragged my ass out of a warm bed. I'd lied to Tom, my husband, told him I'd been called in to cover the graveyard shift (lately, all our fights were about Bill). I had to be at work for real in six hours, yet here I was again, upending my life on a dime. For what? So that ungrateful shit could leave me dangling out here like murder bait? How many times can you rescue a man who just keeps hurling himself back in the water?

It was the old fear that kept me from storming off. Visions of Bill writhing on the floor, choking on his own vomit. No time to call 911—do something quick, or your big brother dies. Maybe he was up there now in that grimy, off-books shelter, locked in a bathroom stall or hidden under a blanket, gagging and changing colors, having his deathbed epiphany—the moment that could actually turn him around if only he lived through it.

I checked my pocket to make sure the Narcan was still there.

\* \* \*

The men on the stoop let me pass without so much as a glance. Inside, I found a kind of reception desk—a card table flanked by red plastic chairs—but nobody keeping watch. Off to the side was a doorway with a black bed sheet hanging from the molding. I walked over, drew the sheet back a few inches. What had once been a sprawling parlor now looked like a Civil War pest tent—malformed rows of cots and bedrolls and air mattresses, belongings lying ad hoc on the floor, slumped male bodies shuffling here and there with no purpose or conviction. I asked the nearest of them where I could find Bill Morgan.

"Three flights up," he said. "Room with a real door."

There were more men congregating on the stairs, leaning against a wall on one side, the remains of a banister on the other. A skeletal kid in his late teens drank spaghetti from a can. An old man poked around inside a broken transistor radio. Others just sat there. This crew gave me a hard look but didn't say anything.

More sheets hung from doorframes all along the poorly lit second-floor hallway, marking a series of dormitories that I imagined residents graduated to after time served downstairs. I heard rustling and dragging feet and snoring and an occasional voice. The curtains did little to lock in the stench of sleeping men who drank and smoked far more often than they bathed.

The fourth floor was a loosely converted attic with the rafters and insulation still exposed. A plywood door with a hook for a handle stood between sagging columns of cardboard boxes. No light here save what filtered up from the floor below. I stepped forward, gave the door a few gentle taps. Nobody stirred. I knocked harder, then grabbed the hook and pushed. The door swung open. There wasn't any lock—just a chain and plate on the inside.

Bill wasn't there. I switched on the bulb hanging from the ceiling, then reached back and pulled the door shut. The room stunk like bleach and stale cigarettes. To the left was a thin mattress lying on a built-in bed frame. No bedding, no pillow. To the right, a small sink with dark yellow stains running up from the drain. Faded synthetic carpeting covered what little floor there was. I guessed the bed and the sink and the door made this the luxury penthouse suite. Standing with a knee on the edge of the bed and one foot on the floor, I could palm both walls.

I went over to a small window and opened it, then stood gulping air and taking in the view: a half-dozen tiny yards and the backs of other brownstones. No fire escape. Not even a tree branch to grab onto.

And no trace of Bill.

I told myself he'd show up any minute. Nothing to worry about. Maybe the bleach was a good sign. Maybe he'd been cleaning to keep the cravings at bay. He must have stepped outside for a smoke with the guys. Somehow, I'd missed him on my way in. This was probably a twelve-step thing. He'd called me here to apologize for his many sins. Bill wouldn't know how else to summon me. He wouldn't know how to be Bill without his little sister dragging him off a ledge.

Ten minutes passed. Then twenty. I heard fighting coming from the floor below. Neither voice was Bill's. I wondered if the bleach fumes were poisoning me. Just for something to do, I lifted the mattress and looked underneath. There was dust, grime, a Canadian penny, and a sketchpad—a black, soft-covered, pocket sketchpad with the seams fraying through the spine.

I knew then that something was very wrong. There were only two things my brother couldn't do without, two things he needed to make it through the day: heroin and a little black book. The first, he knew how to get at a moment's notice; the second, he never let out of his sight.

# CHAPTER

# 2

SINCE WE WERE little, since before child services split us up, Bill had a gift: making three-dimensional objects appear on a flat surface came naturally to him. So naturally, he took it for granted, couldn't understand why everyone didn't draw as well as he did. I still have the first sketch he sent me from reform school—a pen-and-ink rendering of a porcupine some kids had trapped in a garbage can behind the cafeteria. I hung it on the wall in my bedroom. The Davidsons, my new adoptive parents, said he must have traced it out of a book, but I knew they were wrong: he'd sat up late in his bunk with a flashlight and drawn it from memory, same as when we shared a room.

It was a teacher at Stony Brook Academy who first convinced Bill to keep a "journal in pictures." She thought it might help him open up. Not that Bill was shy—he'd just stopped talking. Total, round-the-clock silence. It lasted long enough to scare a few counselors, but not long enough to land him in a psych ward. The journal, however, stuck. Twenty-plus years later, he still went everywhere with a pencil in one hand and a sketchpad in the other. He drew while he ate, while he talked,

while he rode the subway. I imagined he kept on drawing with the needle in his arm—right up to the moment
he nodded off. Once the last centimeter of a pad was
filled, he tossed it. It wasn't about posterity for Bill. It
was about getting from one hour to the next.

I dusted the pad off on my jeans, then stood with
it by the window. For a while I just stared at the cover,
afraid of what I'd find inside. I thought maybe Bill had
left it behind on purpose—maybe there was something
in it he wanted me to see. A clue or a confession. Some
truth he'd been unwilling to share until now. The question was, did I want to know Bill's truth? Maybe Tom
was right—maybe decades of junk had worn Bill's cere-
bral cortex down to nothing. Maybe he was too far gone
to ever come back. I'd open his sketchbook and see . . .
what? Jagged lines veering off the page? Deranged fan-
tasies? Goat heads and hexagrams? Baby skulls on pikes?

So many maybes. I opened the damn book.

The early drawings were all wispy spirals and bil-
lowing shadows, like he'd been teaching himself to draw
the wind. Sketch by sketch, the spirals morphed into
barbed wire; the shadows turned into smoke rising from
industrial chimneys. Then came a series of portraits—
page after page of the same man's face. He looked to be
in his mid-fifties, with gorge-like smile lines and close-
cropped hair. The drawings—maybe a dozen of them—
were identical save for a detail here and there. Bill must
have spent hours stabbing in the five-o-clock shadow
with a razor-fine pencil point. The shading under the
eyes appeared blue and purple, even in black and white.
Whatever else the drugs had done to Bill, he still had his
motor skills.

The rest of the pad was blank. I flipped through the
empty pages, hoping for a more personal and direct message, but there wasn't one. There was, however, a phone

number written on the inside back cover. No accompanying name or information, but I figured I knew who it belonged to—or at least I knew what he looked like. I pulled out my phone, typed in the digits. Any friend of Bill's was likely to be up at this hour. Before I could hit "Call," the door to the room flew open.

"Oh, I'm sorry, miss. Didn't mean to startle you. I saw the light was on and thought Billy'd come back."

The man stood in the doorway, holding one hand out in front of him, palm upward. A proper New York City cockroach was using the hand like an obstacle course, crawling over and between the splayed fingers, its slick body contracting and then expanding with each pass.

The man was old, but not elderly. He wore a flannel shirt, unbuttoned, no T-shirt underneath. I couldn't tell if he had six-pack abs or was just malnourished. Maybe he was one of those homeless who spend their days doing pull-ups at the park. If he'd been drinking, I couldn't smell it over the bleach.

"Who's your friend?" I asked.

He smiled down at the cockroach like it was a newborn puppy.

"Henrietta," he said. "I was going to introduce her to Billy."

"Henrietta the cockroach?"

"They make better pets than you'd think. Low maintenance and easy enough to replace. This one's a real beauty. Quick-witted too. If they had a Westminster for bugs, she'd get first ribbon."

"I'm sure she would," I said. "My name's Tina. I'm Bill's—Billy's sister."

He grinned.

"Samuel—Samuel, not Sam."

"Nice to meet you, Samuel."

"Billy ain't here no more. Unless maybe you come to see his other friend?"

"Other friend?"

"Dumb Jake. I'm looking after him. I promised Billy I would."

"Dumb Jake needs looking after?"

Samuel nodded.

"He ain't dumb like that, though. He just don't say much. He and Billy are real close. I wouldn't let nothing happen to Dumb Jake."

"It's strange that Billy never mentioned him."

"Well, Jake's the shy type. He don't like folks talking about him. But deep down he's good people. You want me to take you to him?"

"I'd like that," I said. "I'm always curious about Billy's friends."

"All righty, then. Time to say goodnight, Henrietta."

He bent forward like he was going to kiss the cockroach on its glistening back. Instead, he flung it to the ground, mashed it into the carpet with his bare heel, and shuffled away from the corpse.

"I'd best put on my slippers," he said. "It's chilly outside."

# 3

THE ODOR OF bodies and dope and liquor was somehow more suffocating on the descent. Samuel
walked heel to toe, like he'd learned the hard way not to
wake anyone. When we reached the bottom, he turned
and whispered:

"We'll have to take a detour. Given the hour."

He moved behind the card table and opened a small
door I'd assumed led to a closet.

"Hold tight now," he said. "It gets real dim down
here."

The railing was a long metal pipe bolted to the concrete wall. I felt chips of paint flaking off on my palm.
Samuel waved his hand in the air to break up the spider
webs. He missed as many as he caught.

We passed through a second door and into total
darkness.

"Isn't there an overhead light?" I asked.

"Not with a bulb in it."

I dug my phone back out of my pocket, swiped on
the flashlight and handed it to Samuel.

"Try this," I said.

He held the screen up, facing him, then jerked his head away.

"Shit's purple now," he said.

He guided me in baby steps down a kind of aisle cutting through a large open space with a low ceiling. Every now and then I'd have to duck under a pipe or a wooden beam. The vent windows on either side were painted black. Samuel's slippers smacked against the concrete floor.

We walked past busted cots leaned up against columns of water-damaged boxes, a wheel-less shopping cart bedded with newspaper, the shells of an old washer and dryer. At the end of the aisle was a thick wooden door. Samuel opened it, and we kept going up a short flight of steps, into a decent-sized yard cluttered with stripped bicycles and more gutted appliances.

"Almost there," Samuel said.

He kicked aside a wooden plank and squatted down.

"I'm here now, Dumb Jake," he called. "Brought you a visitor."

Hunching forward, he muscled two anvil-shaped bricks out of the way and pulled back a long swath of blue tarp. The air around us filled up with flies.

"Now, Jake," Samuel said, "I told you I wasn't gonna make you no more food until you finished what I already brought."

If Dumb Jake said anything back, I didn't hear it. Samuel looked at me over his shoulder.

"Don't be shy, girl. Come say hello."

I went into a crouch and sidled forward. As an EMT, I'd been called to enough crime scenes to know what I'd find. Dumb Jake hadn't been dead long. The rats hadn't turned up yet, and the blood running from his mouth was still damp. He lay atop the blanket he must have been wrapped in when he was transported here. He'd been shot in the stomach, then posed with his hands covering the wound. Beside the body were a fly-covered liverwurst sandwich and a porno mag.

Bill hadn't been lying—not this time: the trouble was real.

I gently retrieved my phone from Samuel and pointed the light at Dumb Jake. He was in his mid-to-late fifties, well fed, well dressed, thinning hair slicked to one side, aftershave still potent. He wasn't the man in the sketch-pad, and he didn't look like anyone Bill would know by choice. Parole officer, maybe? Plainclothes Vice?

"Hello there, Dumb Jake," I said.

"Save your breath," Samuel said. "He don't converse worth a damn."

"It's late. He must be tired. We should let him rest."

"Yeah, okay. You come back tomorrow in the day-light. Maybe he'll be more lively then."

He took out a grease-stained handkerchief, spit into it, leaned over and wiped at the blood on Jake's face.

"Good night now," he said. "You sleep good. In the morning, you'll tell me your dreams."

I lowered the tarp. Samuel set the bricks back in place.

"So, it was Billy who asked you to look after Dumb Jake?" I asked.

"That's right. Until he gets back."

"Did he say when that would be?"

"Never does."

"Billy's stayed here before?"

"Oh yeah. That boy's a comer and a goer."

I thought: *Maybe, but this time he'll stay gone.*

I'd had plenty of experience dealing with mentally broken patients. It didn't matter if they were psychotic or just slightly delusional—you had to play along, make them feel important. The trick was to keep them talk-ing, then filter for the truth. Deep down, Samuel knew

Jake was dead; get him the right medication, and he'd be as reliable a witness as anyone else. Which was probably why he went off his meds in the first place.

"I'm going to be honest with you, Samuel," I said. "Billy's in danger. A lot of danger. If I find him in time, I can save him. But I can't do that without you. You were the last person who saw Billy."

Samuel looked suddenly very sober, like he was corralling his faculties, preparing for the enormous effort it would take to cut through whatever had gone wrong in his wiring.

"How do I help?" he asked.

"Just tell me everything you remember about the time before Billy left tonight. Start at the beginning. Did you meet Dumb Jake out here, or up in the room?"

"Up in the room. I was lying next door, reading my magazines. I could hear them talking—Billy, Jake, and a third guy, who split before Billy called me over. Sounded like they was having a real interesting conversation, or at least all three meant what they said."

"Could you make it out?"

"Not much. They was shouting, but hushed like. Like they was trying to shout without anybody hearing."

"Did you catch any of what they said?"

"There was something about a letter."

"A letter?"

"A love letter, I think. You know, a rivalry-type scenario."

"Were Billy and Jake still arguing when you went over to Billy's room?"

"I didn't go over there like that. Billy called for me later, after they'd gone quiet. Said he needed my muscle."

"For what?"

"Dumb Jake had passed out drunk. He was lying on the bed, wrapped up like a mummy. Billy always keeps a lot of bedding. He gets real cold at night, like he has no blood in him. Anyways, he asked if I knew someplace where Jake could sleep it off. Somewhere private, 'cause Jake was real shy, and he'd be embarrassed by the state he was in. He liked getting drunk, but he didn't like no one seeing him drunk or seeing him wake up from being drunk.

"I thought of this tarp straight off. Truth is, I'd been planning to make a tent out of it for myself, as a kind of getaway—a place to be alone when the mood struck. So, me and Billy carried him down here."

"When was this?"

"Three, four hours ago? Not too early to be drinking, but early for him to be so drunk."

"The two of you carried him straight down the stairs?"

"People don't ask no questions around here."

"But you said Dumb Jake didn't want to be seen?"

"That's why Billy swaddled him up. No telling who he was, covered like that."

"Smart," I said. "You have any idea where Billy might have gone? Where else he sleeps?"

Samuel shrugged.

"We ain't friends like that. We don't talk much about life outside of here."

The thought seemed to depress him, or maybe he was just getting tired. Either way, I doubted there was much more he could tell me. What I needed now was a moment alone with the deceased.

"Did you hear that?" I asked. "My stomach's growling. I haven't eaten since lunch. Any chance you'd make me one of those sandwiches?"

He smiled, glad to be facing a problem he could solve.

"Come along, now," he said. "I'll fix one right up."

I hesitated.

"Would you mind bringing it to me out here? The air helps me think."

"No problem. Just stay where you are. Mustard okay?"

"Perfect."

"Maybe I'll throw in some canned peaches."

I watched him disappear into the building, counted up to ten-Mississippi, then tipped over one of the bricks and rolled the tarp back. I did what I'd seen detectives do with more than one DOA: I went through his pockets. Whatever else happened, he hadn't been robbed. I laid his keys, wallet, phone, money clip, and vape pen out on the tarp beside him. The money clip was stretched to capacity, the top bill a crisp-looking hundred.

One item was clearly missing: his gun. An empty black-leather holster remained strapped under his left arm.

I looked inside the wallet. My guess hadn't been far off. Jake Bickert was a private detective. He'd worked for a midtown firm called Empire Investigations. According to his driver's license, he was fifty-four years old, five eleven, lived in Queens, and wouldn't be donating his organs.

*Stop while you still can,* I told myself. *Stuff his shit back in his pockets and call the cops.*

I should have started dialing the second Samuel introduced me to Dumb Jake, but 911 hadn't been so much as a whisper in the far reaches of my mind. Why not? Probably because I'd decided a long time ago that no one would ever take Bill from me again. Bill wasn't just my brother—he was the only person I'd always known. Every other familiar face disappeared twenty years ago, the day our father killed our mother. There were new faces for a while—lawyers, journalists, cops, social workers—but none that lasted, and then the state packed Bill off to Stony Brook Academy because his "juvenile record" made him "unfit for adoption." A bullshit vandalism charge—twelve-year-old Bill drawing with spray paint on the side of a liquor store.

I'd stood with my brother through some of his darkest hours, but I'd never seen him hurt anyone. Not physically. He'd snatch the last dollar from your purse to score his next fix, but he wouldn't take it by force. Beneath the addiction, he cared about other people. There were times when I thought he got hooked because he cared too much. If he'd pulled the trigger, then there had to be a story. Self-defense, an accident, mistaken identity. Something. Call the cops now, and the only story I'd have to tell would sound very, very bad. Bill arguing with the dead man. Bill disposing of the dead man. Bill the ex-con, the junkie, the orphan who'd spent his life bouncing between institutions on the taxpayer's dime. Why not toss the key?

I scanned the surrounding windows. Most of them had gone dark. No prying eyes that I could see. I took up Bickert's phone, then used his thumb to gain access. An alert said he had a half-dozen missed calls. No voice-mails. I swiped over to his text messages, hoping for an exchange that might explain what he wanted with my brother. But Bickert hadn't been much of a texter. There was a note from his pharmacy asking him to pick up his prescription, another from Delta asking him to rate his recent flight. Both were more than a week old.

I hit the phone icon and tapped on "Recents." I saw it right away. The number behind those missed calls. I'd dialed it myself that morning. Tom's number. My husband.

I went a little numb. Then I felt like I was on one of those rides where the floor drops out from under you while you're spinning at hundreds of miles per hour. I couldn't tell if I was plummeting through space or sitting still while the world imploded around me.

The spinning stopped when I felt my own phone buzzing in my pocket. I pulled it out. The screen lit up with a text from a private caller. The message was just two letters, one of them repeating:

*SHHHHHH . . .*

# 4

*D*ON'T RUN, DON'T RUN, *don't run* . . .

The blocks leading from the squat seemed extra deserted. No chance of getting a Lyft or an Uber to come fetch me in this neighborhood at this hour. No cabs in this neighborhood period, and no way I'd let myself get cornered on a subway platform. I kept one eye on Google Maps as I walked straight down the center of the street. If the author of that text was going to jump out from behind a parked car, I wanted to give myself as much space as possible.

*Shhhhhh . . .*

Who? Not Bill—not from a private number. On his best and calmest day, he wouldn't have the foresight or know-how to arrange a ghost text. That third voice in the room? The bleach, the way every scrap of Bill's belongings—from the Salvation Army wardrobe to the cigar-box heroin kit—had been carted off, the fact that he'd left behind the sketchpad I now carried in my pocket . . . all of it suggested that someone had either helped or forced Bill to disappear post killing. All I could come up with was the mystery subject of those portraits. Maybe Bill had found a mentor. Maybe Bickert had paid the price.

But then where did Tom fit in?

*Tom.* The name went tearing through my skull. Six missed calls to a gut-shot private detective, all from my husband. Could it have been Tom who sent that warning? Had he slipped out of the house, followed me? Was he lurking in the shadows now?

Ridiculous. I gave myself a brush-up lesson on the man I'd married. Harvard pedigree. Westchester childhood. Heir to a real-estate fortune. An architect who designed and funded the construction of schools, hospitals, and community centers in neighborhoods like the one I was skulking through now. A father who'd actually earned the "World's Greatest Dad" moniker scrawled across his coffee mug. Not the type to kill anyone. Not the type to have anyone killed. Besides, he was burning the midnight oil in his study when I left, too absorbed even to look up when I told him I'd been called to the station.

But then why had he been hounding the man who turned up dead in my brother's backyard?

I wasn't running, but I was walking pretty damn fast. Fast enough to be sweating during the coldest hours of a late-October night. I nearly went tumbling when the toe of my shoe caught on a crater in the asphalt. I righted myself, looked around, saw there weren't any witnesses. There wasn't anyone at all. No people, and no light save for a faltering streetlamp in the middle of the block.

I kept walking. Gradually, and then all at once, the city that Con Ed forgot morphed into the city that never sleeps. The traffic picked up. I heard voices and car horns. On Atlantic Avenue, trucks were delivering the day's supplies to early-bird shopkeepers. There were customers exiting the all-night diner. A subway rumbled under my feet. I was back on familiar ground, but I didn't feel safe—more like a steady-state danger was settling in for the long haul. Because something told me tonight was just the beginning for everyone but Jake Bickert.

* * *

It was nearly four AM by the time I reached our stoop. My feet were dragging, but my pulse was stuck in over-drive. What would I say to Tom? Should I confront him now, march into our bedroom, flip on all the lights, rip the pillow from under his head and demand an expla-nation? The truth was, I didn't feel angry so much as baffled.

And then there was the question of how much to share. Could I tell Tom that Bill had been involved, one way or another, in killing a man? Or that I'd used the dead man's thumb to gain access to his cell phone? Made myself an accessory after the fact? On the other hand, there was the question I had to ask: *What was it you hired Jake Bickert to do?* Because why would Tom be speed-dialing a private detective if he wasn't on the payroll?

I lingered outside, looking around, like maybe some-one really had been following me. Our apartment was three flights up—the top floor of a brownstone Tom had refused to buy outright. His guiding principle: no conspicuous consumption of any kind. The bulk of his inheritance was tied up in the Foundation. I knew that when I married him. It was one of the reasons I fell in love with him.

As soon as I stepped into our living room, I sensed something was off—like when you pick up a suitcase and know instantly that it's too light, that the thing you'd needed to bring with you is lying on your bed, a thousand miles away. I switched on the overhead, half expecting to find someone—Bill? Bill's mentor? Bickert's ghost?—lounging in the recliner, smiling and maybe smoking a pipe, the way TV villains always seem to materialize without having tripped the alarm or busted the dead bolt.

But everything was exactly as I'd left it—Tom's back-log of *Architectural Digest* magazines scattered across the couch, our son Aiden's LEGOs making a lopsided fortress in the middle of the area rug. I headed straight for his room, stuck my head in, found him tucked safe and sound under his brand-new Spiderman blanket. I moved down the hall, opened the door to our bedroom, and whispered, "You awake?" as I flicked on the light. No Tom—just an angry heap of linen at the foot of the bed. I checked his study. I checked both bathrooms. Gone.

I went into the kitchen, searched the counters for a note, but there wasn't one. I took out my phone, called the number Jake Bickert had failed to answer six different times. Two short rings followed by a notification of a full mailbox.

I sat at the kitchen table, with my head in my hands, and tried to think. My best guess: Tom called the station, found I wasn't on duty, then went out looking for me.

But that didn't make sense. Tom would have phoned me before he did anything else. He didn't have a suspicious bone in his body. There were times in our marriage when I'd tried to make him jealous just to see if it could be done. It couldn't. No way he'd go creeping around in the dead of night, hoping to catch me in the act.

More importantly, Tom would never leave Aiden alone. Not even for the time it takes to empty the trash. Not since we'd come home from a summer weekend in the Poconos to find our furniture overturned, our drawers in disarray, my laptop gone (Tom had brought his with him—no such thing as a full day off for my husband). They'd torn the safe from the wall in Tom's study and carted it away. It was a week before we could get Aiden to sleep in his own bed. Tom had iron grids fitted over every window, including the two-by-four pane of frosted glass in the master bathroom. He strung surveillance cameras at four-foot intervals and installed monitors in the kitchen, the living room, and our bedroom. We could watch each other watching each other from opposite ends of the apartment. He even talked about converting our walk-in closet to a panic room.

I wasn't on board with the beefed-up security. It felt more paranoid than cautious, more claustrophobic than comforting. But Tom, who almost never puts his foot down about anything, insisted. It wasn't the loss of property that scared him—it was the notion that whoever took our stuff might come back for Aiden: a rich-kid-for-ransom scenario. Not so farfetched. Tom and his foundation make the papers. The local news is there to interview him at every ribbon-cutting ceremony. He's as close to famous as any developer gets.

When Tom said *someone* might take Aiden, he meant Bill—or friends of Bill. That's what our recent battles had been about. Street cameras caught two heavyset men in overalls and green baseball caps—neither of whom looked a thing like my brother—loading our belongings into the back of a moving van. Tom was convinced Bill had sold us out, made a copy of my keys, then traded the duplicates for dope. I told him that was insane (it wasn't)—it could have been any of the charity cases he hired through his foundation. He wanted to turn Bill in, said I was putting our son at risk for the sake of my junkie brother.

"You always choose him over us," Tom said.

*   *   *

No chance of sleep, so why bother trying? In a few hours, I'd have to start getting Aiden ready for school. Until then, nothing to do but wait and hope for Bill to reach out, for Tom to come home. Meanwhile, I gave my anxiety free rein. I stood at the kitchen window, squinting down at the street through narrow iron bars, begging Tom to appear, keeping an eye out for a shadowy Mr. or Ms. *Shhhhhh* . . .

I moved into the living room, sat perched on an arm of the sofa, listening, telling myself that on the count of three, the front door would swing open. I squatted in the hall outside Aiden's door and speed-flipped through Bill's sketchpad, willing my eyes to settle on some buried clue.

*Breathe* . . .

Tom and Bill gone in a span of hours, connected by a dead private detective. No such thing as coincidence. No way to explain it given the little I knew. I glared down at my phone, ordered the fucker to ring. When it finally did—just as I was about to go wake Aiden—I held it out in front of me and cocked my head like a suspicious dog. The rings kept coming, but my thumb wouldn't budge.

I stepped back to the kitchen window. The sun was almost up. A handful of type A's were already marching toward the subway. I hit "Talk" but didn't say anything.

"Hello, is this Mrs. Evans?"

I recognized the voice. Not the specific voice, but the genre it belonged to. I knew it by the deliberate slowness, the artificial calm. A first responder, like me. Or else a priest or a doctor. Someone who'd been trained to switch himself off when news was bad.

"Yes," I said.

"I'm Sergeant . . ."

The name and precinct blurred by. A cop. That meant it had to be Bill.

Except it wasn't.

"I'm sorry to have to tell you this, but your husband's been in an accident."

"An accident?"

"He was hit by a car."

In that weird twilight before the horror settles in, I started mentally picking at his diction. *"Sorry to have to tell you . . ."* meaning he was sorry to have been tasked with breaking the news; *"hit by a car,"* as though it had happened in a vacuum, as though the car had been driving itself.

At least he didn't make me ask for the essentials.

"He's in surgery now. Critical, but stable. They took him to Brooklyn Methodist."

*Which parts of him are critical, and which parts are stable?*

"That's on Sixth Street in—"

"I know where it is," I said.

I don't remember ending the call, only kneeling on all fours to retrieve the phone after it slipped from my hands and ricocheted under the refrigerator.

# 5

I LIFTED AIDEN OUT of bed, planted him on his feet,
tousled his hair until his eyes looked ready to stay
open. He mumbled something I didn't catch—the last
bit of dialogue from an unfinished dream.

"Come on, champ," I said. "Rise and shine. This is
a special morning."

He looked extra small, extra gangly, extra handsome:
a dead ringer for his father at that age. I stroked his peach
fuzz with the backs of my fingers and pushed away a
sudden flash of me raising him on my own, watching
the fuzz turn to stubble, the stubborn curiosity (once, I
clocked him asking thirteen questions in a minute) give
way to hormonal brooding. In my first memories of Bill,
he couldn't have been much older than six or seven. No
hint yet of who he'd become—no way of knowing who
Aiden will be.

"Why is it special?"

"Because Uncle Paul's making chocolate chip pancakes for you," I said.

"Is he bringing them here?"

"We're going there. After breakfast, he'll take you to
school. I have to be at work early today."

Paul, my adoptive brother. The one I didn't meet until I was twelve. Steady, reliable, eager to help. The eye in any storm. Lucky for me, he lived just three blocks away.

"Now get a move on," I said. "Uncle Paul will be sad if we let his pancakes go cold."

*   *   *

The fifth-floor hallway smelled like melting chocolate. Paul stood outside his door, rubbing his hands against a denim apron. There were splotches of flour in his curly black hair. Aiden got a running start, then threw himself into his uncle's arms.

"Whoa there, little man," Paul said. "Can't wait till we get some sugar in you."

He gave me a concerned look over Aiden's shoulder.

"I brewed coffee," he said.

"I can't stay."

"I figured. Just let me dump it in a thermos. Soy creamer, right?"

"You're a godsend."

*Godsend*—not a word I could remember having used before.

On a normal day, Paul's railroad two-bedroom made me jealous . . . of Aiden. It was a child's paradise. The kind of place that gets adults thinking about what childhood might have been like. Clay models and plastic action figures lined the wall-to-wall built-ins. Goblins, trolls, wizards, astronauts—a gamut of superheroes and villains—all characters from video games Paul created: he's a top-notch designer specializing in K–12 educational entertainment. Thanks to my adoptive brother, kids can learn basic algebra while shooting down alien spacecraft, master grade-school geography by racing a pirate to the buried treasure, conjugate Spanish verbs while chasing a car thief through the streets of Madrid.

"You hungry, buddy?" he asked Aiden.

"I could eat a horse."

Paul smiled. There was no telling where Aiden had heard that one.

"How about pancakes instead?"

Paul hoisted Aiden onto an eggcup chair at the island separating his kitchen and living area, then slipped around to the stove and stacked more pancakes than I thought a forty-five-pound boy could handle onto a gremlin-covered plate.

"Dig in," he said. Then, to me, "Coffee coming right up."

"I want chocolate milk," Aiden announced.

"Hey," I said, "you've got a mountain of chocolate right there. How about thanking your uncle for the incredible breakfast he went out of his way to make for you?"

It was an adrenaline-and-instinct scolding: my mind was already at the hospital.

"Thank you, Uncle Paul."

"Any time."

Paul stood with his back to us, pouring a full pot of coffee into a NASA-worthy thermos. When he turned around, I almost did a double take. The low-slung track lighting didn't do him any favors. He looked like a hollowed-out substitute for the wiry, athletic man in his prime who could have been a contender for any most-eligible-bachelors list—even in a field as crowded as New York City. Sallow cheeks, eyes like road maps, sweat trickling down his forehead. The baggy gray sweatshirt made him appear flat-out skinny. For a second he reminded me of Bill.

Then it dawned on me: he and Tom were close. They played chess and went on the occasional pub crawl together. The only time I'd seen Tom literally stagger was after a night with Paul. Neither of them had a wide circle of friends. They probably meant more to each other than I'd realized. I felt a quick surge of guilt. Since the call came, I hadn't once thought of Paul as anything but an emergency babysitter. I wanted to say something reassuring, but Aiden was sitting right there, and I had to get to the hospital.

"Should stay piping hot all day long," Paul said, passing me the thermos.

"I'll call you," I promised. "Soon as I know more."

*And I'll try not to ask for another favor when I do.*

# CHAPTER

# 6

I WAS NO STRANGER to the Methodist ER. A nurse I'd become friendly with over countless patient handoffs gave me what details she could. We stood toe to toe in the hall outside the waiting area while she fast-talked through her surgical mask, and I tried to remember her name. Something with an L. Lisa? Lois? Louise? It seemed so important, like everything depended on my getting it right, on my being able to say, "Thank you, So-and-So," when it was my turn to talk again. Meanwhile, she kept on listing the conditions that might kill or maim my husband: head trauma, internal bleeding, broken femur. "Too soon to know," she told me. He'd be on the table (my words) a while yet.

"Thank you, Laura," I said.

Just like that. As soon as I stopped trying, it came to me.

\* \* \*

I'd passed through the waiting area before but had never lingered long enough to absorb the atmosphere. Metal-mesh benches, fiberboard drop ceiling, nicotine-colored walls. No paintings or prints. Not even a fire-code poster. The kind of space that would never look clean, no matter how long you scrubbed.

This early in the morning, the population was thin— a handful of weary faces, all of them alone, none of them here for Tom. At first that angered me; then I realized I hadn't told anyone but Paul. Not that there were many people to tell. Tom was the only child of two only-children parents, both dead, and he worked too damn hard to have much of a social life beyond Aiden and me. His staff at the Foundation would need to know, which meant I'd have to talk to Desmond, Tom's right-hand man and the closest thing he had to a best friend. Desmond, who'd made a very drunken and determined pass at me during the waning hours of the Foundation's last ribbon-cutting party. I'd come within an inch of smacking him. He phoned the next day, contrite and mostly sober. Neither of us had seen the need to upend Tom's world.

I took a seat with a clear view of the doorway through which a surgeon would eventually enter and call my name. The clock on the wall showed it was still just eight AM. Desmond could wait a while longer.

Nothing to do now but think. Not the kind of situation where you can lose yourself in a crossword puzzle or an airport paperback. Any attempt at distraction just reminds you of what you're distracting yourself from. Best to let your mind go. Mine, wired on caffeine and lack of sleep, sped along multiple tracks at once. There was the Tom track: images of my husband lying unconscious on an operating table, monitors spitting out zigzag lines, a stranger's blood tubing into his veins, a dog-tired surgeon bellowing commands. There was the Aiden track: How do you tell your six-year-old son that, best-case scenario, his dad isn't invincible? There was the Bill track: What had my brother done; where had he gone to; who had he gone there with; why hadn't he called?

And then there was the obvious and glaring echo of the past: what Tom and I called *the incident*. Not a tragic incident, in the end, since it brought us together, but so very nearly tragic. I hadn't been waiting outside an ER then—I'd been wheeling Tom into one. I didn't know who he was. Nothing about him said borderline-celebrity philanthropist. He'd been riding in the passenger seat of a yellow cab, on his way to JFK. The cab was lying on its side when we got there, top wheels spinning. Not a scratch worth mentioning on the driver, but Tom was trapped, unconscious, bleeding from the head. Faulty airbag. It was my first time using the jaws of life.

I thought about Tom afterward in the same way I thought about anyone I'd worked on, which is to say hardly at all. No time to look back with all the fresh trauma piling up. He was the one who tracked me— and my partner, Dan—down. He wanted to thank us. Reward us, actually, with a generous cash infusion. Dan had no qualms. I might have been insulted if Tom weren't so damn attractive. Skin and bones from a month in recovery, but attractive, nonetheless. Thick red hair, broad dimples, full lips, a chin that looked like it could take a punch, an even smattering of freckles under each eye. Last time I'd seen him, he'd been all blood and swelling. I looked at him in the light of day and thought, *I didn't know I had a type until now.*

"You've recovered nicely," I said, then felt my face turning colors.

Eventually, I talked him out of the bounty and into dinner—at the Russian Tea Room, so I wasn't letting him off cheap. A month ago, we went back for the tenth anniversary of that first date.

I would have thought Tom had met his quota—one near-death vehicular experience allotted per lifetime. Maybe he'd agreed to take someone else's turn: that would be just like him. It would also explain what he'd been doing out in the world during the wee hours while our son lay home alone.

A rush of distraught voices somewhere close by brought me back to the here and now. I unscrewed the lid to Paul's thermos, then drank straight from the mouth. Paul hadn't been lying: the coffee was third-degree hot. I puffed out my cheeks and shook my head. When my eyes stopped watering, I noticed a dour-looking man in a windbreaker, standing in the center of the room, staring straight at me.

*Great,* I thought, *I'm making a spectacle of myself.*

Then I spotted the gun on his hip. Plainclothes, but not undercover. He started toward me.

*Oh my god, Tom . . .*

But that news wouldn't come from a detective. Bill, then? Everything always seemed to boil down to those two names. I gave the detective a weak smile just to test his mood. Nothing came back in my direction. Then I hit on the name that most scared me: Jake Bickert.

*I'm going to jail, and I don't even know if my husband will live or die.*

THE DETECTIVE SAT down next to me without asking if he could. I took that as a good sign: cops don't generally cozy up before they slap the cuffs on.

"Mrs. Evans?" he said.

"Yes?"

I had the absurd thought that I should offer him some coffee.

"I'm Detective Knowles. I'd like to talk to you about your husband's accident."

"Okay."

Looking at him up close, I thought he really should work undercover. If I saw him an hour from now wearing anything but that windbreaker, I'd have no idea who he was. Average height, average weight, average build. Early middle-age. Generic male haircut. The guy you sat next to on the bus yesterday and the day before that. Tailor-made to blend in.

"The last thing I want is to make this more difficult for you," he said, "but we don't believe it was an accident."

He paused while I tried to make sense of the words: *If not an accident, then . . .?*

"There's footage," he told me. "Street cameras show—"

"A drunk driver?"

He shook his head, then gave me the baseline facts in an up-tempo monotone: the car didn't have its lights on, didn't have any plates, had pulled onto the block and remained hidden between cameras while the driver waited. The incident itself wasn't caught on film, but the same plate-less car was picked up driving full bore down Conover Street a few minutes later, this time with a visible dent in its hood. No clear image of the driver's face. Knowles sat back, gave me space to paint my own picture.

"Conover Street," he said. "Out by the piers. Isn't that where your husband has the headquarters for his foundation?"

I nodded. Tom had redesigned an abandoned warehouse, made the headquarters itself a centerpiece in his urban revitalization portfolio.

"Do you have any idea why he was going to work at one in the morning?"

One in the morning—roughly same time I was emptying Bickert's pockets.

"No," I said. "All kinds of emergencies crop up. He probably didn't want to wake me."

"Considerate," Knowles said. "Unfortunately, the incident occurred on a nonresidential block. Desolate at that hour. We don't even have any doors to knock on."

"Tom's a saint," I said.

The words flew out of my mouth—pure reflex. I could see where Knowles was going, what he was insinuating. Tom mixed up in something illicit.

"That's his reputation," Knowles said. "But isn't it possible he made enemies along the way?"

"Along the way?"

"Think of it like this: the poor loved Robin Hood—the rich, not so much. Your husband has outbid some powerful people."

My first thought: *If this is you digging for your career-making case, then you've broken ground in the wrong spot.* My second thought had to do with security cameras and iron bars on the windows and a would-be panic room. It had to do with Jake Bickert and six missed calls. Something was going on. Something bigger than a burglary. Tom had left Aiden alone because he was going out to meet the threat. He knew where it would be. Was that why he'd been calling Bickert? To let him know there'd been a change of plans and he was needed elsewhere?

But then why had Bickert ever been needed at Bill's squat? What kind of scenario involved my brother killing a man hours before someone tried to murder Tom?

"Mrs. Evans," Knowles said, "can you think of anyone who might want to hurt your husband?"

"No," I said. "No one."

His expression told me I'd hesitated a beat too long. "Are you sure?"

*Come clean, Tina. Walk him through the last eight hours. Every minute. Whatever this is, it's more than you can control.*

But then I saw Bill in a jail cell. I saw myself in a jail cell. I saw the letters *Shhh* framed in a small purple box on my phone's screen. And I thought, *Who will protect Aiden?*

"I'm sure," I said.

He wasn't buying it. He shifted his weight, gave what looked like a very practiced sigh.

"I have to ask this, Mrs. Evans," he said. "Where were you at roughly one AM this morning?"

"At home. Asleep."

*No turning back now. Not an omission, not a lapse of memory—a straight-up lie. A lie he'll be able to disprove in a heartbeat. Your cell phone was pinging off towers all over Brooklyn. No more slap on the wrist. Hard time. We'll find out just how tough you really are . . .*

"All right," Knowles said, standing. "I'll be in touch."

He handed me his card. It seemed like a deliberately cold way to break the conversation. No well wishes for Tom? No vague and all-encompassing apology or platitude? *"I'm sorry this happened . . . I can only imagine what you're going through . . ."* He might as well have said it out loud: *"You're in my sights."*

He was halfway to the door when I called him back.

"What's your department?" I asked.

I thought maybe we knew some of the same people. People who could vouch for me.

"I work homicides," he said. "Attempted, in this case."

His slight grin filled in the rest *". . . At least for now."*

# 8

"You might as well go home for a bit, hon. Get some rest. We'll call when there's news."

Not Laura—a different nurse. Older and calmer. I hadn't been asleep, but I felt like she'd woken me up. There were people on the benches I hadn't noticed come in. Across from me, two women I took for mother and daughter were sharing a meal—something charbroiled and slathered in red sauce—out of a Styrofoam container. I hadn't noticed the smell before, either. I looked at the clock, saw it was a little after noon. I wouldn't have guessed more than fifteen minutes had passed since Knowles left.

"I should stay here," I said.

"It's going to be a while. Then, once he's out of surgery, they'll take him straight to ICU. Visiting hours don't start until six thirty."

"Six thirty?"

"Six thirty to eight thirty, AM and PM."

She smiled down at me.

"We'll call you," she repeated.

"Thank you," I said, working the base of Paul's thermos back into my handbag.

I wondered if I was getting special treatment, either because I was Tom Evans's wife or because I was part of the tribe, a kind of advance scout for the men and women of the Brooklyn Methodist ER. Whatever the reason, I didn't mind.

Home was a short walk away, but the blisters from last night's hike made it tough going. I stopped at a small public square, sat on a bench, and pulled out my phone. Either I was lucky or, more likely, Desmond was screening. My message made the situation sound less urgent than it was. Next, I called the station, extended my sick day to an indefinite absence. Chief Vetrano already knew about Tom. He passed on the squad's thoughts and prayers. Soon to be followed by sheets of baked ziti and tins of homemade cookies. Maybe even flowers. We look after our own—and everyone else too.

\* \* \*

Tom's idle security system should have been proof enough that I was alone, but still I went room by room, looking under beds, poking around in closets, pulling back curtains. Not even a mouse . . .

I had one more call to make—the number at the back of Bill's sketchpad. I gave myself a minute to regroup, then walked into Tom's study, stood on tiptoes, and pulled the pad out of the gaping hole where the safe had been. In hindsight, hiding a junkie's picture diary seemed like overkill, but I couldn't shake the notion that Bill had left it for me on purpose, that there was something in it he needed me to find.

Sitting at Tom's drafting table, I opened the pad to the inside back cover, typed those digits into my phone. This time I hit "Talk."

Another recording:

"You've reached Jeff's Automotive. This is Jeff. I'm either busy or I'm not here, but . . ."

I ended the call without leaving a message. Jeff caught me off guard. If I'd had to guess, a repair shop would have been near the bottom of the list. Bill was a dyed-in-the-wool public-transit man. He'd never owned so much as a scooter. As far as I knew, he didn't have a driver's license. I tried the number again just to be sure I'd got it right. Same result.

*What the hell are you playing at, Bill?*

I turned back to the last and most detailed portrait of that face I didn't recognize.

*Are you Jeff?* I asked. *Of Jeff's Automotive?*

I ran my eyes over every line. There were crags and crow's feet, but no abscesses or pockmarks. None of that mostly-deflated-balloon look common to addicts who've outlived their expiration date. Maybe Jeff the Mechanic was a good guy. Maybe he moonlighted as a substance counselor or community activist. Maybe he was helping my brother find the straight and narrow.

Maybe, but I doubted it. I knew from experience that dark angel was far more likely. Dangle the right dose, and you can get an addict to do just about anything. In Bill's case, you might get him to rob his sister and her rich husband. You might even get him to kill someone, though I found that hard to believe.

I slammed the little book shut and collapsed forward onto Tom's table, head buried in the crux of one arm—the high school student's fetal position. When I sat back up, I locked eyes with the subject of another portrait: Tom's father.

The painting used to provide cover for Tom's safe; now it stood leaning against the far wall. The fake two-man moving crew had stolen other paintings, prints, photographs—mostly reproductions from museum giftshops—but they'd left Tom's dad behind. I couldn't blame them. Words like *austere* and *foreboding* didn't come close. Steel-gray eyes, veins popping in his forehead, an expression that said the world and everyone in it had fallen short of his expectations. No wonder Tom never talked about his childhood—not even when I pressed. I asked him once why he kept the portrait hanging where he couldn't help but see it every day, and he said, *"To remind me of who I'm not."*

Which made me wonder again about who Aiden might become.

*He got the gene.* That's what people said about Bill, as though *the gene* were some kind of autonomous command center. No need to go looking for explanations once you know someone has the gene. According to his confession, our old man stabbed our mother in the throat because she'd "smoked his last dime bag." Was that the gene at work? Was the gene dormant in me right now? Had Bill soaked it all up, or was there some left over for my son?

*Worries for another day.*

Right now, there was Tom and Bill, Bill and Tom. There was Private Detective Jake Bickert lying dead between them. All three unavailable for comment.

But Tom's laptop might have a few things to say.

I spotted it sticking out from under a blueprint on the hardbacked chair he kept for guests. I should have thought to look for it earlier. If Tom had hired Bickert, there'd be a contract, an invoice, a progress report. Something to explain *why* he'd had a PI tracking my brother.

I fetched the computer, carried it back to the drafting table. A minute to boot up, and then there was Aiden, wearing an outsize yellow hardhat and standing atop the roof of a newly constructed rec center, the Manhattan skyline for backdrop. The box telling me to enter a password or use Touch ID looked like Aiden's thought bubble.

I felt a sudden swell of anger, as though Tom were deliberately shutting me out. No chance of guessing the password: jumbled birthdays and baseball stats weren't good enough for my husband. He practiced a kind of bibliomancy. He'd open a dictionary, shut his eyes, and stab the page with his finger. Then he'd dress up the nearest entry with numbers and ampersands. I knew this because he reset the passwords on all our joint accounts every couple of months. I had to keep track of concoctions like Ex1c0is&b419lE and sO121L&r444ium.

What I needed now was a computer whiz, someone who could circumvent the password altogether. Only one name came to mind. An MIT grad with a passion for programming. So much for not going to Paul with another favor.

\* \* \*

Twenty minutes later, Paul and I were sitting across from each other in his futuristic living room, me on a sleek black futon, him on an aerodynamic metal throne straight out of the gaming world. Tom's laptop lay on the coffee table between us. Paul looked more like himself now—alert and composed, sporting what could have been the same Marvel Comics T-shirt and blue jeans he wore all through high school. His hair was damp from a recent shower.

"I can do it," he said. "It won't even be that hard. It's just a question of getting the right software."

"But?"

"I wish you'd tell me what's really going on."

I started to double down on a story about Desmond having lost some contract the Foundation desperately needed. Paul waved me off.

"Detective Knowles called," he said. "He's calling everyone Tom had contact with in the last twenty-four hours."

*Everyone.* As in Private Detective Jake Bickert. Six hang-ups to the man Bill likely shot dead. I had to remind myself to breathe.

"I didn't want to scare you," I said.

"Scare me? I'm your brother."

His tone was more pleading than angry. He leaned across, put a hand on my shoulder.

"I'm sorry," I said. "The truth is, I don't know much. Only that Tom hired a private investigator and didn't tell me about it. Then last night happened."

Paul looked up at the ceiling while he thought it over.

"You don't know *why* he hired a private investigator?"

"That's what I'm trying to find out."

"Tom's a developer. He could have hired a PI to research a real-estate deal. Or any other number of things."

"Maybe."

"But you don't think so?"

"He was run over a block from the Foundation at one in the morning. Something's very wrong. He was keeping something from me, and now that he might . . ."

I couldn't make myself finish the sentence.

"I get it," Paul said. "But shouldn't you be taking this to the police?"

"I can't."

"Why not?"

"Because Tom didn't go to the police."

Paul looked at me like he knew I was withholding.

"Tom wouldn't get involved in—"

"He could have been protecting someone. Maybe things spiraled. I don't know. That's the point."

Paul nodded.

"All right," he said. "Give me a day. I should have it unlocked by then."

I stood, picked up my handbag. Paul stood with me.

"You really are a godsend," I said.

We hugged.

Over my shoulder, he said, "Have you told Mom?"

As if by reflex, I thought, *My mother's dead.* Mrs. Davidson didn't count. If we talked twice a year now, it was a lot. She'd put her house on the market when Aiden was a month old, then followed her best friend to a retirement community in Tempe. The move confirmed a suspicion I'd had ever since Mr. Davidson died: adopting me had always been his idea.

Mr. Davidson was everything his wife wasn't: warm, caring, patient. And he didn't expect me to cut ties with my past. He knew from experience how painful it could be when people disappeared. He'd grown up a foster kid, but unlike me, he'd never found his forever home—just bounced from family to family. He wanted his adopted daughter to feel grounded. He used to take me to Stony Brook on weekends to visit Bill. He'd drive us to the beach and buy us crab cakes at a restaurant in town. More than once, he read Bill the riot act, laid out a clear vision of the future he was speeding toward. Mrs. Davidson never laid eyes on Bill. Anytime I mentioned him, she turned to stone. She'd never been overly invested in her birth child either, but that didn't stop Paul from hoping—even as an adult.

"I'll call her," I told him. "As soon as I know something more definite."

## 9

IT WAS ONLY TWO PM when I left Paul's. Time seemed to be standing still. I walked to the corner, leaned against a lamppost, and checked my messages. No word from the hospital, no word from Bill.

So long as I couldn't be with Tom, finding my brother was the priority. I tried to think of who Bill might confide in besides me. Like most junkies, my brother didn't have the kind of friends you kept for very long. With one exception: Jerry, his bunkmate from Stony Brook.

Post-juvie, Jerry had blossomed into a low-profile dealer with a steady clientele. Now and again, he'd hire Bill to make a special delivery. Payment came in the form of dime bags. The last time I saw Jerry was at a Fourth of July barbecue. I had a can of lighter fluid in one hand and a match in the other and was threatening to set him on fire if he didn't leave my brother the fuck alone. Bill stepped between us, dragged me away.

*You're embarrassing me, Teen,* he said.

If anyone knew where my brother had disappeared to, it would be Jerry. He might even be harboring Bill, which is why I decided to drop in unannounced.

\* \* \*

When Jerry wasn't a ward of the state, he lived with his aunt in her Sunset Park brownstone. I'd only been there once, but the directions were easy enough to remember: half a block uphill from the subway, one door down from the funeral parlor. Convenient for the aunt, who'd inherited the parlor from her parents. For a while, there'd been talk of bringing the newly rehabilitated Jerry and his sidekick Bill into the fold, training them up as undertakers. Neither the offer of an apprenticeship or the rehabilitation stuck.

The doorbell sounded like porch chimes on a blustery day. A few beats later, the aunt was staring at me from the other side of a grade-A security door. I wondered whose business the door was meant to protect: hers or Jerry's?

"Sorry to bother you," I said. "Is Jerry here?"

Both her eyebrows shot up: I didn't look like the sort of girl who'd come calling for her nephew.

"And you are?"

"Tina," I said. "Bill's sister. Bill from Stony Brook."

She broke into a wide smile.

"Oh, right," she said. "You were gonna douse Jerry in gasoline and burn him to a crisp if he so much as said boo to your brother again."

I'd forgotten she'd been there.

"That was a long time ago."

"Not when you're as old as me. The more you have to look back on, the shorter time gets."

She didn't seem all that old—early fifties, tops, with airtight posture and a toned physique, the type who'd look elegant and refined if only she cut back on the blush and Botox.

"Bill hasn't been by here, has he?"

She shook her head.

"Haven't seen him in a number of years. He in trouble?"

"Always," I said. "But this time it's bad. I was hoping Jerry might know where he is."

She gave me a sympathetic look, as though Jerry and Bill made us members of the same sisterhood. But Jerry was predator, Bill prey. Not the same thing at all.

"Jerry just stepped out. He should be back—"

She cut herself short.

"Now," she said, pointing.

I turned and looked. For a second, I thought he was going to run. Instead, he came as far as the curb, then nodded for me to climb down off the stoop.

"I got this," he told his aunt.

I'd forgotten how little he was—almost child-sized. His fade haircut and cuffed jeans didn't make him look any more grown-up. He stood there, staring at me, like he couldn't decide if I was dangerous or just disgusting.

"Won't take long," I said. "Promise."

I started down the steps, glanced back when I heard the aunt say it was nice to see me. Jerry seemed to think seeing me was anything but nice.

"Lucky you're Bill's sister," he muttered.

"Oh, yeah," I told him. "Luckiest girl alive."

We sat side by side on the bottom step, Jerry scooting as far away as space would allow. He was carrying an extra-large to-go cup in one hand and a white paper bag in the other. He set them on the sidewalk at his feet, opened the bag, and pulled out a sugar-dusted turnover.

"Chasing something?" I asked.

"Nah, I'm done chasing. Shit comes to me now."

"King Jerry."

"Damn right."

Up close, he smelled like a dozen warring aftershaves.

"So, what the fuck do you want?" he said.

He bit off a man-sized chunk of pastry, swallowed without chewing.

"Have you seen my brother?" I asked.

"Like, recently?"

I nodded.

"Nah."

"Talked to him?"

"Nope."

"Any idea where he might be?"

Jerry wiped cherry-colored goop from his chin with the heel of one palm, then licked the palm clean.

"Probably hiding from you," he said.

"Me?"

"Or your better half. Same thing, right?"

"Why would Bill be hiding from Tom?"

"Better ask Tom."

There was a hint of a smirk, like maybe Jerry knew Tom was out of commission. Could it have been Jerry's foot on the gas? Only if Bill were sitting next to him. I felt a sudden jolt of paranoia. What if Bill had called me to that squat in order to make sure Tom showed up at the Foundation alone? Then I remembered Bickert. Bill wouldn't avoid one murder charge by setting himself up for another.

"I'm asking *you*," I said.

"Not sure I'm at liberty to—"

I smacked the top of his head. Not hard—more like a glancing blow—though the edge of my hand still came away coated in gel.

"You want the neighbors to witness you getting your ass kicked by a female?" I said.

He grinned.

"Neighbors know I like it rough."

One of life's unsolvables: Why does a pissant drug dealer get to be so comfortable in his own skin while the rest of us lie awake at night, raking ourselves over the coals?

"Listen," I said, "this is serious. I think Bill's in real shit here. Like, felony-level shit. So I need you to tell me—why would he be hiding from my husband?"

"Damn, you really don't know?"

"Know what?"

"I gotta hand it to your better half. That's cold."

"What's cold?"

"Sending your brother away without your say-so."

"What do you mean, 'sending my brother away'?"

"To that dry-out place upstate."

"Detox?"

Jerry nodded.

"Bullshit," I said. "Tom can't just send people away. He's not a judge."

"Yeah, but he's rich as fuck, and he knows people. You got that, you can turn gangster anytime you want."

"Turn gangster?"

"As in, get your ass clean or catch a bus to Rikers."

I hit him with my blankest stare.

"I gotta spell it out?"

"The burglary?"

"Bingo. Except Bill didn't have shit to do with that."

"You're sure?"

"No way he would've cut me out."

That much was probably true. The rest was easy enough to picture. Tom stepping in to fix my biggest problem once and for all. Not telling me because he knew I'd put up a fight.

"Did Bill ever mention someone named Jeff?" I asked. "A mechanic?"

That won me Jerry's blankest stare.

"Never mind," I said. "What did Bill tell you about the place upstate?"

"Real swank. Only high-tone fiends need apply. Gourmet breakfasts. Indoor swimming pool. But they tortured him up there."

"Tortured him how?"

"Fucked with his head. Worse than any drug. Had him seeing shit, like, from when he was a kid."

"What kind of shit?"

"Wouldn't tell me. Just said he couldn't take it, so he split."

"And that's why you think he's hiding from Tom and me? Because we might send him back?"

Jerry nodded, slurped some coffee. A thin line of brown liquid dribbled down his chin.

"What else did he say?"

"I don't know, man. I only saw him the one time since he's been back."

"When was that?"

"Like, ten days ago?"

"Where?"

"My place of business."

"He came by to score?"

"Nah. I offered, but he wasn't taking. Clear-eyed too, as far as I could tell."

"Bill was clean?"

I thought back to that SOS call. Bill's voice was as wobbly as ever, but he'd found his words without stammering, and his answers to my questions were direct and on point.

"I need you to think really hard, Jerry," I said. "What was the name of the clinic?"

"Clinic?"

"Rehab. The place upstate."

He started to answer, then stopped himself. His mouth fell open like he'd been gifted the revelation of a lifetime.

"Tom hurt Bill, didn't he?"

"What are you talking about?"

"That's why you're asking me and not him. Bill's AWOL, and you're thinking your old man had him—"

"Tom's in the hospital," I said. "Car accident. I'm not asking him because he can't talk."

Judging by Jerry's reaction, no way he was behind the wheel.

"So where's Bill?" he asked.

It had taken this long to convince Jerry I wasn't playing some kind of game.

"The rehab, Jerry. What's it called?"

"Fiends call it Betty Four Seasons. I don't know what it says on the brochure."

"Thanks," I said. "If you hear from Bill—"

"I'll tell him you're looking."

I was pretty sure he meant it.

# 10

"YOU'VE REACHED JEFF at Jeff's Automotive . . ."
I was sitting at the window of a café across
from the subway entrance, twenty ounces of Americano and a warm guava turnover on the counter in front
of me. I needed a moment to think, catch my breath.
Outside, the sky had split open, hailstone-sized drops
bouncing off the sidewalk, then bursting apart an inch
aboveground. Umbrellas shot up. Pedestrians scam-
pered. The sudden deluge made a shabby avenue appear
even shabbier, all that water only proving the grime was
here to stay.

I tapped the internet icon on my phone, thumbed
*Betty Four Seasons* into a search engine. The first hit took
me to, of all things, a Yelp review. Marissa H. of Princ-
eton, New Jersey, wrote:

> *Hawthorne Wellness Retreat (aka Betty Four
> Seasons—lol) gave me my life back. Was it easy?
> No (although the mud baths and deep-tissue mas-
> sages made it a little easier . . . lol). But now I have
> the tools I need to move forward without looking
> behind me.*

No doubt about it: BFS was a real place, beyond the scope of anything Jerry's brain could invent. It was too much to hope he'd borrowed someone else's story—that someone other than Tom had forced someone other than Bill to make the trip upstate, and Jerry had repurposed the episode just to torpedo my day. In short, whether or not he'd gotten all the details right, Jerry had told the truth.

Still, I had trouble making it real. I couldn't form a clear image of Tom and Bill alone together in a room, Tom laying out his ultimatum in no uncertain terms: Hawthorne or hard time. The scene became slightly easier to picture when I replayed arguments from the last few months: Tom calling Bill my "blind spot," my "albatross," my "Achilles' heel." He went so far as to say Bill was "destroying" me. My response: "Get a grip, Tom."

Even when we weren't arguing, Tom's resting face had become a grimace. When was the last time he'd stroked my hair or let his hand rest on the small of my back? When was the last time we'd had sex? Not since that pre-robbery weekend in the Poconos. Was our dry spell Bill's fault too? Had Tom, in his convoluted way, confronted my brother for the sake of our marriage? If so, Tom must have reached deep into a part of himself I'd never seen in order to scare Bill silent, because Bill, for all his guile, had never been able to keep a secret from me. Not for long, anyway.

I turned back to my phone, scanned the dozen or so remaining reviews, every one of them gushing. The words "healing" and "awakening" were repeated ad nauseam, probably lifted from that brochure Jerry had mentioned. One name figured prominently: Dr. Whitney Alden—more often, just Whitney. Whitney was a "pioneer," a "maverick," a "genius," and a "gentle soul, despite it all." I didn't know what "despite it all" meant, but I figured it had something to do with the alleged torture.

I followed the website link. The welcome page showcased a mansion set atop a hill overlooking the bucolic Hudson Valley, river included. It struck me as the kind of place you'd want to visit once you'd *finished* detoxing, once fresh air and scenery mattered again. I opened the drop-down menu and clicked on "Staff." A yearbook-style screen full of well-coiffed, happy faces appeared, most of them counselors, though there was also a yoga instructor, an acupuncturist, a massage therapist, a chef, and a nautical aerobics trainer. Then there was Dr. Whitney Alden, alone in her row at the top of the page. Harsh black glasses, hair a sunset shade of red, face narrow and angular. A bit goth for a shrink. Her smile looked like an exercise meant to stretch her lips as far as they'd go without showing any teeth.

I clicked on her thumbnail, and a bio popped up. Harvard, then Yale, then a residency at Mass General. Ten years of private practice in Manhattan. She was the founder and leading practitioner of post-traumatic addiction therapy, a treatment she began developing in grad school. The description of this therapy was kept vague, though the gist matched what Jerry had told me: it involved "freeing repressed memories." Alden touted Hawthorne's completion rate at ninety-eight percent. Count Bill among the remaining two.

At the bottom of the "About" page was a link to an interview Alden had given the *Hudson Times*. I opened it, then zoomed in on the tiny font. The article was titled "Wellness on the Hudson." Beneath the headline was a photo of Alden standing, arms akimbo, in front of the retreat's Cathedral-like double doors. A brief introductory paragraph called her a "visionary in the field of addiction therapy." Hawthorne Wellness Retreat was the "pinnacle of her vision."

**HT:** Let's start with how Hawthorne differs from other rehab facilities.

**ALDEN:** First and foremost, it's our approach to treatment.

**HT:** Post-traumatic addiction therapy?

**ALDEN:** That's right.

**HT:** Tell us about it.

**ALDEN:** Well, it begins with the premise that trauma and addiction are inextricably linked. There are two kinds of trauma: there's the trauma we know about—the trauma we remember and consciously relive—and then there's the forgotten trauma.

**HT:** You're talking about childhood trauma?

**ALDEN:** Yes, though the forgotten trauma remains lodged in the adult unconscious. Often, it's what holds us back; left unattended, it can cripple us emotionally. I believe this repressed trauma is ground zero for addiction.

**HT:** You're not talking about a generalized trauma—say, abusive parents—but rather a specific traumatic event?

**ALDEN:** Both, actually. There is an environment of trauma, and then there is the specific event that occurred within that environment.

**HT:** The repressed trauma?

**ALDEN:** We call it the core trauma. Most often it's associated with guilt: a failure to protect or defend—either oneself or someone else—in a violent and chaotic circumstance. Needless to say, for a young child, there is no possible defense. This creates a sense of helplessness, futility, and fear that becomes a kind of base-level existence moving forward.

**HT:** Identifying this event is the first step in PTAT?

**ALDEN:** Not quite. The first step is a physical cleansing—removing the offending toxins from the bloodstream. We have some of the best doctors in the country overseeing this process. Once the patient is no longer drug- or alcohol-dependent, we can begin to mine the unconscious for that core trauma.

**HT:** And you do this through hypnosis?

**ALDEN:** I wouldn't use that term. What we practice is more of a deep relaxation, a state where the barrier between the unconscious and the conscious mind drops away. There is no longer the id and the ego—or whatever you want to call them. There is only the self. It's impossible to express in words just how powerful this state can be. Sometimes the patient will, without realizing it, physically act out the core traumatic event. Only for them it isn't acting; it's living—they're living the event as if for the first time. It's no longer buried, no longer hidden. It's been brought out into the open, where we can deal with it.

The article cut off there. My instinct was to dismiss the whole enterprise as junk science, but then I remembered what Jerry said: *"They fucked him up, had him*

*seeing shit from when he was a kid."* What "core trauma"
had Alden unleashed? Hadn't Bill's whole life been one
trauma bleeding into the next? Who was it he'd "failed
to protect or defend?" Our mother? Only two people
knew the answer: Alden and my brother.

*Poor Bill,* I thought.

The rain had started to let up. Pedestrians who'd
been sheltering in doorways and under awnings began
to venture back out. I drank down half my americano,
then bit into the pastry I'd almost forgotten was there.
I'd never had a guava turnover before. It would be worth
coming back for someday, with Tom and Aiden in tow.
I started to lose myself in a fantasy outing. I saw the
three of us sitting at this window, wiping crumbs and
glaze from our faces. Afterward, we'd stroll up to Green-
Wood Cemetery, get our fill of historic headstones,
ancient trees, wild parrots. It was a fantasy because suddenly so much would have to go right for it to become
real. Tom would have to recover. I'd have to stay free.

But then who was I kidding? Hiking the grounds
of a majestic old cemetery would bore Aiden to tears.
I could already hear him complaining that the parrots
wouldn't come down from the trees.

CHAPTER

# 11

THE FORTRESS WASN'T lopsided anymore.
My eyes had run right over it when I first came
in. I'd scanned the living room for any major distur-
bance, then gone through the rest of the apartment,
singing a nonsense song and clapping my hands like a
camper warding off bears. Not a stitch out of place. I
told myself I was being paranoid. *Shhh* had been a one-
off. Whoever sent that message was long gone. Besides,
Tom had made our home impregnable.

I went back into the living room, dropped down on
the couch, thought I'd drift off until the hospital called.
That's when it caught my eye. The LEGO walls were an
even height now. The drawbridge was fully operational.
The plastic knights Aiden had dispatched on a scouting
expedition through the dense interior of our shag rug
were back manning the turrets.

*Impossible,* I told myself. Tom must have worked on
it when I wasn't looking. The architect in him couldn't
stay away.

But no, that wasn't possible either. I'd stepped on
one of those knights just this morning, after I got home
from my own failed expedition. It had sent me hopping

and howling. I'd been afraid of waking Aiden. Now I was afraid of something much worse.

For a long minute, I couldn't move, couldn't so much as wiggle a finger or toe. My mind kept spitting out the same question over and over: *What do I do?* A normal person, I thought, would call the police. And say what? Someone broke into my home and renovated my son's toy castle? A B&E mastermind capable of bypassing the best security system money can buy? Apart from which, all of my reasons for not calling the cops still applied.

*You're sure it wasn't Tom?* I asked myself. *Sure it wasn't some other morning your heel came down on that sharp little knight?*

And then I remembered the cameras. There'd be evidence. Video footage of an adult intruder playing LEGOs in my living room. The image seemed ridiculous. *Fear's getting the better of you, Teen.* One way to nip it in the bud. I sprinted to our bedroom, grabbed my own laptop off the dresser and brought it back to the couch. The Foolproof Prevention, Ltd., app took its sweet time loading. Once it was up, I clicked on "Cameras," then "Living Room."

Instantly, I saw myself sitting there, computer open on my knees, hand hovering above the trackpad. I steered over to the archive. The system kept all footage for a minimum of one week. Long enough to fill an epic saga about empty rooms—dust mites by day, then a flurry of activity followed by protracted darkness. I obeyed the directions on the screen, entered the date, then a range of seven AM to three PM.

*You'll see,* I told myself. *A whole lot of nothing.*

And for a while I was right. I fast-forwarded through one hundred and eighty minutes of stationary furniture, confident I'd found the world's dullest way of killing time. But then, at the ten AM mark, the screen went blank. I was about to hit "Refresh," when the living room reappeared. At first, I assumed there'd been a momentary glitch, but then I saw the time stamp: one fifteen PM. The recording had jumped three-plus hours ahead. I rewound just to be sure, and it happened again. I checked the cameras in the hallway and both bedrooms. All blacked out during the same period. Someone had shut the system down. Someone who'd been here and wanted me to know it.

I felt the room tilt and started gulping for air like someone had been holding my head underwater.

*Shit, shit, shit.*

I tried deep breathing. I tried reasoning with myself. Whoever he was, he didn't want to hurt me—he only wanted me to know that he could. He was like a mugger telling his victim not to turn around; as long as I couldn't pick his face out of a lineup, I'd be fine. So far, so good. Even if I were to call the cops, the little I had would be easy enough for them to explain away. They'd see a distraught wife who'd read too much into a power outage and a wrong-number text. In my situation, anyone's imagination would run wild.

*He's just out to scare you, Teen.*

Unless . . .

Maybe renovating Aiden's castle was more than a subtle tell. He could have sent any signal he liked—fixed himself a meal, opened all the windows, changed the time on the clocks—but he chose to tamper with something that belonged to my son. The message: Aiden's mine, any time I want.

*Who the hell are you?*

When I shut my eyes, only one face appeared: Bill's mystery model. I got up, walked on unsteady legs to Tom's study, grabbed the sketchbook from its hiding place. Sitting at the drafting table, I flipped from one portrait to the next.

*Are you Jeff?* I asked again.

And who was Jeff? A mechanic with a habit? Someone my brother met at Hawthorne? In jail? On the street? Was he that third voice Samuel heard? Had Jeff killed Bickert, then hustled north to run over my husband, Bill sitting mutely by his side?

I stared down at that final drawing. Something about the face was familiar, but I couldn't say what. I went feature by feature. Bill had been unsparing. A burst blood vessel spread out in jagged lines above the right pupil; a bloated skin tag hung beneath the chin; jungle-like eyebrows contrasted with a scalp shaved almost to the bone. All that detail got in the way. I was searching for something more fundamental. A shape, maybe. Or an expression. Something that couldn't be grown out or cut away.

I almost had it when my phone started buzzing in my pocket. I checked the number. Desmond: maybe the last person on earth I wanted to hear from just then. I thought about screening, but he was the type who'd just keep calling back.

"Desmond?"

"What the fuck is happening?"

I'd been braced for hysteria, but this sounded more like rage.

"I told you, Tom—"

"You said a *'minor accident.'* Then a cop calls me asking if I might know who'd want to kill my boss. One AM, a block from the Foundation? Christ, Tina. Now they won't tell me anything."

He was talking so fast his words overlapped.

"Take a breath," I said. "Who won't tell you anything?"

"Nurses. Doctors. People in scrubs. They all look the same."

"You're at the hospital?"

"Yeah. Where are you?"

As in, why aren't you by your husband's side? I decided to pull the mother's trump card.

"Aiden," I said, letting him fill in the rest.

There was a pause while he regrouped.

"Sorry," Desmond said. "I'm not thinking straight. Listen, I need the truth. How bad is it? 'Cause if he's going to . . ."

I told him what the nurses had told me: it was too soon to know for sure.

"Go home, Desmond," I said. "You can't do anything there. They won't let anyone but family see him until he's out of ICU. That could be days."

He went quiet again, then let loose with another accusation, this one more measured.

"How are you so calm?"

"Occupational hazard," I said. "I'm trained to talk in monotone."

I was about to end the call, when he asked: "Tom didn't tell you?"

"Tell me what?"

"Who he was going to meet at that hour?"

Something about Desmond's voice made me wonder if Knowles was standing next to him, listening in.

"No," I said. "Did he tell you?"

"Whatever it was, it wasn't business."

I was itching now to get off the phone.

"Listen, Desmond, I'll—"

"Did you say anything about us?"

"Us?"

"To the detective."

That stopped me cold. It was my turn to bark at him.

"There was never any 'us,'" I said. "There was only a punchbowl and a coatroom."

I couldn't tell if he was clearing his throat or sneering.

"I can see why you need to believe that," he said.

And then the line went dead.

# 12

WE WERE SITTING on a bench outside the ICU dou-ble doors: me and Dr. Greene, a spent-looking, sixty-something surgeon, who'd sweated through his scrubs during a daylong battle to save Tom's life. *"A coma,"* he'd told me. The good news: they'd stopped the bleeding, set the broken bones. The next twenty-four hours would be crucial. Nothing for it now but to wait. I could see Tom in a little while, once visiting hours started.

I don't remember thanking him. I don't remember saying anything at all. Probably I just walked away. Straight to the women's room, where I locked myself in a stall until the dry heaving stopped and my sweat turned cold.

* * *

I'd claimed one of the last free seats in the waiting area and had just shut my eyes, when I felt a tug at my sleeve. Detective Knowles, staring down at me, his face all business.

"I've got a few more questions," he said, then nodded toward the exit.

I stood and followed. I thought he'd talk to me in the hall outside, but he kept walking—down an epic corridor, then up a flight of stairs and into the chapel, a long and narrow space crowded with laminate pews, its fluorescent lights fronted by plastic stained glass.

"You mind?" he asked. "There's never anyone here at this hour."

I shook my head, but I doubted it was the quiet that attracted Knowles. Whether or not you believe, church puts the sinner in you on notice. Your better angels start making demands.

We sat a few feet apart in the last pew, Knowles looking up at the cross like he'd forgotten I was there. I cleared my throat. He leaned back, turned to face me.

"It's possible your husband's attack ties in with a missing person," he said.

No preamble, no patter about how I was holding up. I hid my face in the crook of one arm and pretended the stale incense had me fighting off a sneeze.

"Missing person?" I said.

"Missing detective, actually. A private detective. Jake Bickert. Does the name ring any bells?"

I made a show of thinking it over.

"No," I told him. "No bells."

"Your husband didn't say anything about hiring a PI?"

That was one I could answer without lying.

"No."

"Any idea why he might have needed a detective?"

A second question I'd pass on the polygraph.

"No," I said again. Then, a detail borrowed from Paul: "He hired all kinds of people for his foundation."

Knowles shook his head.

"We're not sure what Bickert was working on, but we're confident it wasn't business."

He looked at me like he was waiting for something to sink in. When he saw I wouldn't get there on my own, he said:

"PIs provide a limited number of services, Mrs. Evans. So I have to ask—had there been any trouble in your marriage? Trouble that might lead your husband to—"

"I've never cheated on Tom, Detective. And he wouldn't have any reason to think I had."

It dawned on me then that Knowles knew Tom was in a coma, knew the victim was nowhere near being able to answer these questions himself. Still, no words of support, no suggestion that the little prayer he'd offered was for my husband. *Because I'm a suspect,* I thought. Saying nothing was Knowles's way of making me understand.

"Like I said, I have to ask. Frankly, it's a little early to be treating Bickert as a missing, but he was one of us not so long ago."

"NYPD?"

"Detective with Vice. When he didn't show for a string of meetings this morning, his boss called his old lieutenant. Out of professional courtesy, we rushed a trace on his phone. It turned up at the bottom of a dumpster in East New York."

I managed to keep calm, but the questions were spinning. Had someone moved the body, or just the phone? A squatter would have pawned the latest Samsung, so did that mean Bill had come back to cover his tracks? Or someone acting on Bill's behalf? The face from the sketchbook? Jeff?

Meanwhile, Knowles was staring at me, studying me. All I could think to say was: "What does that have to do with Tom?"

Knowles shrugged. "We haven't had time to do a full forensics on the phone, but we did scroll through the recent calls. There were a half-dozen hang-ups from your husband in a span of fifteen minutes. Starting at around midnight. You really don't have any idea what that was about?"

"How could I when I didn't know he'd hired an investigator?"

It came out overly aggressive.

"Sorry," I said. "My nerves are fried."

His hands shot back up.

"I can only imagine. Just one more question."

"Yes?"

"Why was your husband shushing you at roughly one in the morning?"

If I'd tried to talk, I might have choked on my own tongue.

"Didn't you get the text?" Knowles asked.

I gave him a slow-motion nod.

"The next morning," I lied. "I thought it was a wrong number."

"So, you didn't know about your husband's second line?"

"Second line?"

"One phone, two lines. Which, to be honest, I didn't even know was possible. A personal number and a business number. It seems he was religious about keeping them separate—personal, strictly personal; business, strictly business. Turns out he always called Bickert from his personal number, which is why we're confident he didn't have Bickert working for the Foundation. But then last night he broke his rule: he messaged *you* from the business line. Why would he do that, Mrs. Evans? What was it he wanted you to keep quiet about?"

I pressed back against the pew as though pushing hard enough might open a portal to another world.

"I thought it was a wrong number," I said again.

"Maybe it was," he said. "We'll have to ask your husband. If he wakes up."

That *if* was meant to erase any doubt: I wasn't the sympathetic would-be widow—I was the target of an investigation.

"Tom's going to—"

Knowles held up a finger. His phone was ringing. He turned his back to me and took the call. I heard him say, "Yes, I'm here with her now . . . Yes, all right . . . Okay . . . Fine . . . I'll see you at the station." Then he hung up and spun back around.

"That was a colleague," he said. "He and a team of detectives are at your apartment now, executing a search warrant."

He was gloating—almost like he was proud of himself. I understood why. This little interview was so much subterfuge: Knowles had wanted to make sure I wasn't at home when the detectives arrived. He didn't want me getting in the way. He didn't want me flushing evidence before his "team" could make it up the stairs.

*Steady, Tina. He's trying to rattle you. Don't give the bastard what he wants.*

"A search warrant?" I asked.

"Standard procedure. There's a team at Tom's office too. Someone tried to murder him. We're looking for motive."

"Looking for motive *where*, exactly?"

"Correspondence, day planners, business documents. A diary would be nice. And of course his computer. We'll be poring over every file."

*Thank God Tom's computer is with Paul.*

"It's too bad I'm not there," I said. "I could point them in the right direction."

"Don't worry—I've asked them to be respectful. They shouldn't make too much of a mess."

Housecleaning was the least of my worries. My mind
went straight to Bill's sketchbook. I couldn't say why,
exactly. It hadn't helped me find him. I hadn't identified
the mystery model. Jeff never answered his phone. My
attachment to that little black book went beyond Bill's
disappearance. In the worst-case scenario—the case
where I never saw my brother again—that book would
be what I had to remember him by. He'd never been the
type to write letters. I'd never been the type to take photos. There weren't any mementos from our childhood.
I'd lost the drawings he'd sent me from Stonybrook
when I moved to college. I told myself not to worry: the
detectives wouldn't see any reason to confiscate a collection of doodles. They'd thumb through the pages and
toss it aside. But then what if they didn't? What if they
stuck it in an evidence bag and dumped it in a locker,
never to be seen again? What if they coated his drawings
in fluorescent fingerprint powder? It would be like losing
Bill a second time.

I sprinted home as soon as Knowles was done with
me. By the time I got there, the search party was gone.
I'd expected to find open cabinets, cushions strewn
across the floor, closets emptied—but if anything, the
place seemed tidier than I'd left it. I wondered again
if Tom and I were getting special treatment: Knowles
wouldn't be wrong in thinking that Tom's connections
reached as high as the governor's office.

There was a copy of the warrant lying on the coffee table, along with a receipt listing the items they'd
taken. It was a short list: just my laptop and the contents
of Tom's filing cabinet. No mention of a sketchpad. I
sprinted to Tom's study, stood on tiptoes, and reached
into the safe-shaped hole in the wall. Bill's little black
book was still there. As far as I could tell, it hadn't been
touched.

I went back into the living room, dropped onto the couch, and let my body sink into the fabric. At first I thought I might fall asleep. But as soon as I shut my eyes, I felt wide awake. It was as though all the caffeine I'd consumed in the last forty-eight hours kicked in at once. My knees started bouncing. My hands closed into tight fists. My eyes sprung open. I couldn't sit there another second. I needed to be back at the hospital, close to Tom.

\* \* \*

A nurse stepped into the waiting area, called my name. Laura again. She must have been working a double. Or was it a triple by now? Weeks might have passed since the last time I'd seen her. I stood, lost my balance, and would have toppled onto my neighbor's lap if he hadn't caught me first.

"Sorry," I said.

Laura came bounding forward.

"Blood sugar," I told her. "I'm fine."

"You sure?"

I nodded. She led me back through those ICU doors, into the bowels of the hospital—the part civilians only ever see if their luck has bottomed out. She was talking to me, prepping me, but she might as well have been speaking in tongues. We turned one corner, then another, and then there he was, quarantined in a cloth-screen cubicle. From a distance, the scene looked typical—a body in a hospital bed, limbs plastered and elevated, tubes and monitors everywhere you looked. Then I got closer. His scalp was bandaged. There was a cast over his nose, jagged stitches running down both cheeks. His eyes looked like twin water blisters on the verge of bursting.

This was the after picture. If I'd been on duty, if I'd been called out to the scene, I'd have witnessed the before: skin ripped open, bones jutting out, blood streaming. It wouldn't have been the first time, but this was different. He wasn't a stranger now. He was my husband. We slept side by side, night in and night out. We had a child together. We were the facts of each other's lives.

"You okay?" Laura asked.

Again, I didn't say anything. There was a hard-plastic chair waiting for me beside the bed. I went and sat in it because I knew that was what I was supposed to do. Laura promised she'd be back with something to eat—for my blood sugar. When she was gone, I stood, leaned over Tom, and gave his bandaged forehead the lightest possible kiss.

"Who the hell are you?" I whispered.

# 13

"Long as you need," Paul said. "Aiden's a joy."

Simple as that. No caveats, questions, concerns. I didn't have to explain *why* my son was better off at his place for the time being—or that, depending on how the chips fell, "time being" might stretch out to early adulthood.

"I owe you, Paul," I said. "Big time."

"That's not how the brother–sister thing works."

"Still . . ."

I stepped closer, gave him a long hug.

"I'm just going to peek in on Aiden," I said.

I kicked off my shoes, tiptoed down the hall and opened the door to the spare bedroom a crack. He was asleep, lying on his side, a spaceship-themed blanket tucked up around his neck. I stood watching him, wondering if he had even an inkling of just how wrong things had turned.

"You're going to be all right, kiddo," I whispered. "Whatever happens to your mom and dad."

Back in the living room, Paul had two glasses of wine poured and waiting.

"Thanks," I said, collapsing onto the futon, "but one sip and I'd pass right out."

I didn't have the energy to tell him that the police had searched my home, or that he was in possession of the thing they most wanted.

"Bed's yours if you want it. Half the time I sleep out here anyway."

Paul, four years younger than me and still playing the role of big brother. No different than those rare weekends when I made it home from college. Always looking out for me, offering to do my laundry, type up my papers, fetch me a latte from the café down the street. During the final, ugly throes, it was Paul, age fourteen, who spoon-fed Mr. Davidson and wiped the drool from his chin. Mrs. Davidson had turned all but catatonic. The most I could do was make myself be in the room. Sometimes I think that's why I became a paramedic: to redeem myself for failing the man who gave me a home and a life outside the system. In an odd way, I think Mr. Davidson's illness influenced Paul's choice of profession too: programming became a safe space—a space where he could make alternate worlds appear, then control what happened in them.

"Thanks," I said, "but all my stuff's at home, and I want to be at the hospital by the crack of visiting hours."

I already knew how I'd spend the night: asleep, yes, but on the couch, fully dressed, with our largest kitchen knife lying close by. I'd been there before, when Tom was away and I'd watched the wrong true-crime doc at bedtime.

Paul slid up to the edge of his chair.

"Tom's going to be okay, you know."

Before I could respond, he shook his head.

"Sorry. Dumb thing to say."

"Who knows what to say? There isn't anything to say."

Just to lift the mood, I asked about his evening with Aiden. There'd been a minor skirmish at bath time, but Paul had prevailed. Otherwise, they'd spent most of the night playing a beta version of Paul's latest game—something about searching the solar system for a lost cat named Dr. Living Stone.

"He's learning the constellations," Paul said. "Too bad you can barely see any of them from the city."

Then he said something that caught me by surprise:

"I've got a document to show you. On Tom's computer."

He left the room, then came back moments later with the laptop open and balanced on one palm. He pressed a button, spun it around, handed it to me.

"I thought you'd need days to hack your way in," I told him.

"I'm not all the way in. Tom password-protected his folders—I haven't opened those yet. I found this document in the trash bin."

"What is it?"

"An invoice."

I looked at the screen. Empire Investigation's masthead was a dizzying mix of glitzy colors and calligraphic fonts. The designer must have confused gaudy and professional. The invoice itself began with a few lines of legalese:

*Thomas Evans,* having engaged Empire Investigations in the matter of *REPUTATION PROTECTION AND RETRIEVAL OF STOLEN PROPERTY,* is responsible, pursuant to a contract dated October 1, 2019, for the following expenses, to be paid no later than . . .

"Reputation protection?" I asked.

Paul shrugged.

"A competitor looking to slander him? Some real estate mogul who got tired of being outbid by the philanthropist?"

"Maybe," I said.

But it felt wrong. Tom would have warned me about an imminent smear campaign. Wouldn't he? Twenty-four hours ago, I'd have said yes, no doubt about it. But now? Now there was a menacing text sent from a secret phone line. There was a private investigator who'd been shot to death, most likely by my brother. There was a one AM rendezvous at the Foundation. There was someone out to murder my husband.

I scanned the itemized bill, hoping one of the half-dozen entries might shed some light. But the language was veiled, and there were no reasons given for the *Actions Taken*: a background check on *the subject*; an interview with the subject's parole officer; surveillance of the subject's last known address; travel around and between the five boroughs.

I looked over at Paul.

"This isn't about any developer," I said. "It's about Bill."

"And the robbery."

"What does either have to do with 'reputation protection'?"

Paul took a long swallow of wine.

"Depends on what was in the safe."

I knew what he meant because I'd had the same thought.

"Blackmail?" I said. "That makes no sense."

But it did make sense—at least theoretical sense. It would explain why Tom had waited nearly two months to hire a detective: the burglars had taken that long to unload the contents of the safe. Their buyer was doing the blackmailing.

"What else could 'reputation protection' mean?" Paul asked.

I shook my head.

"If somebody was blackmailing Tom, Bill had nothing to do with it. He doesn't have the attention span. Besides, he's a strictly nonviolent offender."

"Blackmail isn't violent."

"You know what I mean. He wouldn't hurt my family like that. Not if he had the chance to think about it first."

"Maybe he didn't think about it at all."

"Bill's a lot of things, but—"

"That's not what I'm saying. Tom assumed Bill went out and found a buyer, but what if someone approached Bill? Paid him a nice little sum for the codes and the key? No questions asked."

"In which case, blackmail was always the endgame?"

"It's possible."

"But the blackmailer wouldn't have paid Bill that nice sum without knowing what was in the safe. *I* don't even know what Tom keeps in his safe. And then there's the question of timing. Why wait two months?"

"Could be a lot of reasons."

We'd started out with our voices low, but now we were nearing full volume. I had a sudden flash of Aiden with his ear to the door. Lord knows I overheard things when I was his age.

"I really have to go," I said. "Thank you again, Paul. I'm sorry I put you in such an awkward position."

I began to get up, jostled the coffee table, nearly knocked over what was supposed to have been my drink.

"Jesus," I said. "I need some goddamned sleep."

My second attempt at standing didn't go any better than the first. This time I fell backward, hugging the laptop to my chest. The futon gave a little jump under my weight.

"That's it," Paul said, "you aren't going anywhere. I'll throw some fresh sheets on the bed, and you'll—"

I waved him off.

"Here's fine," I said.

I set the laptop on the table, lay on my side, pulled a throw pillow under my head. If Paul put up a fight, I don't remember it.

# 14

MY ALARM WAS going off, but the sound was muffled, almost muted. I reached for it on the nightstand, then realized there was no nightstand. I looked around the room, taking in as much of it as I could make out in the dark. It seemed familiar and foreign at once—like I recognized all the objects but had never seen them arranged in this way. Sitting up, I noticed for the first time that I was fully dressed. My surroundings came into sharper focus: Paul's apartment. His living room. He'd covered me with a duvet, set a glass of water on the coffee table.

My phone kept on buzzing. I remembered now. I'd stuck it under a pillow on the floor, hoping it would wake me without waking Paul and Aiden. I picked it up, switched off the alarm, then checked my voicemail. No hospital, no Bill, no Knowles. Nothing. Not even a 1-800 number. I caught myself breathing in short gasps, gave my face a few quiet slaps and switched on the light.

* * *

I left Paul's without so much as glancing in a mirror, grabbed breakfast out of a deli, and ate while I walked.

"No change," Laura warned me when I entered the ICU.

Still, somehow, when I stroked Tom's arm, I expected those grotesquely swollen eyes to pop open. He had other ideas.

"Fine," I told him. "We'll talk later."

I dropped back down onto that cold metal chair, thinking maybe I'd join Tom in his nap. The idea seemed sweet—like I'd be adding my rest to his, speeding his recovery along. But it takes either serious trauma or heavy narcotics to fall asleep in an ICU, so I just sat there with one hand resting lightly on his chest. The anger and recriminations could wait until he was conscious, until the bandages were removed and the swelling was gone, until his hair had grown in and he could walk again. Then I'd have plenty of questions. He might even wish himself back in a coma.

Right now, I couldn't feel anything but a fearful kind of love.

*　*　*

When the bell sounded on visiting hours, I headed straight for the local garage where Tom housed his father's baby-blue, two-door 1995 BMW. Twenty-four years into its existence and still fewer than thirty thousand miles on the speedometer. Sometimes I forgot we even had a car.

Unless Bill called before I hit the street, I was driving up to Hawthorne. I'd phoned ahead, made sure Dr. Alden would be there. The woman I spoke with sounded evasive until I told her I was scouting the place for my son and would pay extra to get him a bed by the end of the month. Then Dr. Alden had a half hour free, starting at eleven fifteen. The lie made me queasy—especially given that I'd have to cop to it in just a few hours—but

I doubted Alden would be eager to speak with the sister of a deserter.

Then there was the question of whether or not she'd betray Bill's confidence. I kept coming back to something Jerry said: *"They fucked with his head . . . had him seeing shit from when he was a kid."* Only Dr. Alden could bring me up to speed on the shit my brother had seen—his "hidden trauma." Something told me it was the key to finding him now. And, of course, part of me was wondering if I'd seen the same shit.

A few hours later, I exited the highway, made a few sharp turns, and then there was the mansion from the website, looming above, polished and shiny, like someone had just given it a waxing. Or maybe like it was made of wax, because the closer I got, the phonier it looked—a four-story log cabin built with laminate logs and synthetic chinking. A movie-set facade from the days before green screens and computer-generated imagery.

The view, on the other hand, was real. As I crested the hill and pulled into the small lot out front, I was treated to a long stretch of river with only the odd structure on its banks and a skinny bridge in the distance—a glimpse of the Hudson as it must have looked hundreds of years ago, before there was a United States or a New York. I got out, rolled my neck, walked around to the back of the mansion, and scanned the grounds: a gazebo on the river, a flower garden flanked by rose trellises, even a small apple orchard. It didn't hurt that it was fall, the trees half bare, half bursts of color.

I could see it now—how this might be a good place to get clean. It was like stepping into a different life. No crowded sidewalks, no blaring horns. No constant grinding pressure to move faster and do more despite the epic lines and stalled subways. Hard to believe this kind of calm sat just two hours up the Parkway.

And yet I knew in a heartbeat that it was all wrong for Bill. The smallest sign of wealth made him angry and self-conscious; nature only reminded him of the woods behind Stony Brook Academy, where he first learned to cook heroin. He'd have done better in a church basement in Queens, swapping stories with addicts whose rock bottom wasn't cushioned by a trust fund. What had Tom been thinking? If it really was Tom who'd sentenced Bill to this place. Tom, whose wealth made Bill extra angry and extra self-conscious.

I looked at my watch. It was ten to twelve. The stop for an early lunch had killed just enough time. I rang the bell and waited outside the cathedral doors for someone to answer. Instead, a buzzer sounded, and I pushed my own way in. If the exterior was ersatz pioneer, then the interior was Italian Palazzo on a budget: what should have been marble flooring looked more like high-end linoleum; the classical columns were about as convincing as Aiden's LEGO ramparts; the imitation cast-iron hearth looked like it would melt if it got anywhere near a real flame. Build it big and build it cheap. Made sense. Why invest in top-shelf materials when even your long-term guests wouldn't stick around for more than a month or two?

What unnerved me was the quiet. No voices, no footsteps, no hint of a living being. It was as though I'd wandered into the model house for a new luxury development. I sat on a black vinyl love seat, expecting a receptionist to come and offer me tea while I waited, but then, just a few minutes later, it was Alden herself who appeared, looking a little older and a little less goth in person. She crossed straight to me, smiled, extended a hand.

"Hello, Mrs. Evans," she said. "I'm so glad to meet Bill's sister."

# 15

"I DIDN'T GIVE YOU my maiden name," I said.

"No, but you gave me your husband's name. And then there's the family resemblance."

We sat on opposite sides of her desk in an office that was cozier and more human than anything I'd seen at Hawthorne so far. Muted floor lamps, soft-blue walls, floor and furniture made of real wood. Like any good shrink, she'd hung up her diplomas, but she'd hung up other, more decorative things too: a dream catcher, a hand-woven rug, a black-and-white photo of Jupiter and its rings. Behind me there was a plush couch and a leather recliner. I pictured Bill lying in the recliner, Alden dangling a gold watch. I saw him get up and lope around the room as he performed his *core traumatic event*.

"You think I look like Bill?"

She smiled.

"Maybe a little healthier."

Based on her thumbnail and that one interview, I'd expected a type A stick figure, the kind who never said anything out loud that could be used against her and ate no more than the allotted number of calories per day.

Face-to-face, the impression didn't hold; her cheeks were too rosy, and from the neck down she was borderline plump. If I'd met her before I'd read the interview, I might have heard the words differently.

"I imagine you're concerned about your brother," she said.

I nodded. I'd spent the ride up here debating what and how much to tell her, and decided I'd hew close to the truth but withhold liberally.

"I'm afraid something's happened to him," I said.

"But you don't know for sure?"

"He's disappeared. No one can tell me where he is."

"And that's new behavior?"

Translation: Bill's on an extended bender.

"No," I said. "But this is different."

"How so?"

"He called me. He said he was in trouble, but when I got there, he was gone. I haven't heard from him since."

"I'm sorry," she said. "That must be very stressful."

"I need to find him."

"And how is it you think I can help?"

*"How is it you think . . ."* A downshift into therapy mode, as though my coming to her was evidence of some psychological defect. Or maybe it was only *more* evidence: whatever she knew about Bill's early years had to be true for me too. Same junkie parents, same bedroom in the same shitty apartment.

"I read about PTAT," I said, "and I talked to one of Bill's friends. I know he got as far as his core trauma."

"And you think whatever trouble he's in has something to do with that trauma?"

"Yes."

"You may be right."

"But . . .?"

"It isn't for me to say. You'll have to ask your brother."

"I told you, I can't find him. That's why I'm here."

She took off her glasses, rubbed at the lenses with a cloth.

"Who would come to me for treatment if they thought I was going to share their most vulnerable moment with their closest relative?"

"Bill's in danger."

"Have you called the police?"

"No."

"Why not?"

"Because I don't know what *kind* of danger he's in."

It was as much of a hint as I'd give her.

"That's the real issue, isn't it? *You* don't know. You don't know because Bill didn't tell you, just like your husband didn't tell you he was paying for your brother's treatment."

I stared down at my knees, thinking, *No wonder Bill fled*.

"So I'm right," she continued. "Secrets are a big red flag in any family. Now you're trying to find Bill by violating his confidence. And you want me to help you, though you're clearly not willing to give me the whole story. Do you recognize the pattern?"

She was reminding me of the social worker I'd been forced to keep seeing after the Davidsons took me in. I'd tell her I wanted to deal with one thing, and she'd tell me that I had it all wrong, that I was only distracting myself from the real problem. But then she wouldn't tell me what the real problem was. She wanted me to work it out for myself.

"Sitting in your office doesn't make me your patient," I said. "I'm trying to save my brother's life."

My voice started to break over those last words. I bit my lip. No way I'd let myself start bawling in front of this clinical fuckwad.

Alden squared up in her chair, leaned her forearms on the desk.

"I can't discuss Bill's session," she said. "And when I say I can't, I mean legally: I'd be putting Hawthorne in all kinds of jeopardy. But there is someone you should talk to."

"Who?"

I felt my gut drop like I knew already.

"Your father," she said.

\*   \*   \*

Alden walked me outside, handed me her card.

"PTAT was designed to treat addiction," she said, "but it can help anyone who's suffered trauma—anyone who sometimes finds their mind stuck, unwilling to let go."

"That isn't me," I told her.

The way she patted my arm implied a connection between us that I didn't feel.

"Think about it," she said.

I waited until the doors shut behind her, then climbed into Tom's ancient BMW and beat the shit out of its steering wheel with both fists.

# 16

For a long, two-lane stretch, I wound up trapped behind twin semis, one driver having pulled out to pass the other, then lost his nerve. More than once, I had to stop myself from leaning on the horn. A forty-five-mph crawl with Alden's voice looping in my head: *Your father, your father, your father . . .*

Before the state split us up, Bill and I made a pact: our old man died with our mother. No prison visits, no phone calls, no cards at Christmas. Mail from Sing Sing would go unopened. If we stumbled on a photo, we'd burn it. If we dreamed about him, we'd do our best to erase the dream. We'd never so much as say his name. Not to each other and not to anyone else.

It was a pact I broke exactly one time. On the morning of my twelfth birthday, I sat down and wrote a two-line letter in bloodred crayon: *I hope prison is worse than hell. I hope you never get out and never die.* I didn't sign it because I couldn't stomach the thought of him reading my name.

The last time either of us saw our father, he was being led away in cuffs while we watched from the back seat of a social worker's station wagon. Our mother was lying dead upstairs. I'd been playing with a friend who lived two buildings over, but Bill was home, most likely in our room, drawing, headphones cranked high. I don't know for sure because he wouldn't say a word about it. Not then, not now. Not to me and not to Mr. Davidson, who tried more than once to get him talking—both for Bill's own sake and for mine.

* * *

I had the car back in the garage by two fifteen. Four hours until I could see Tom again. Meanwhile, no news from Bill, Knowles, or Laura. Aiden was in school. Paul would be working. Nowhere to go but home—suddenly the least safe space on earth. What if my tormentor had tired of kids' games and was waiting there to slit my throat? I thought about checking into a hotel, crashing with Paul, bunking at the station—each unappealing in its own way.

*He's only out to scare you—if he even exists.* For the umpteenth time, I told myself the lost footage was nothing but a technical snafu—it was Aiden's dad who'd fortified the castle. Still, I stopped at an Army Navy store and bought my first ever can of mace. A clerk in a camouflage jumpsuit photocopied my driver's license, made me sign a registry. My name on record. If felt like one more bit of evidence for Knowles to use against me: *You must have thought someone was after you, Mrs. Evans. Mind telling me who?*

I shouldn't have bothered—the only thing waiting for me at home was a gift basket from my crew at the station. They'd made it themselves. The "basket" was a lunch-pail-style first-aid kit piled high with my favorites: Dark Godiva bonbons, airplane-sized bottles of Baileys, a jar of anchovy-stuffed olives. For Aiden: a toy ambulance with a siren that lit up when you pushed on the wheels. There was a card, but no flowers—that would have seemed maudlin. No cash envelope either, out of respect for Tom's income bracket.

I carried the kit upstairs, set it on the dining room table, and downed a fistful of bonbons. I couldn't bring myself to open the card, wasn't ready for all the *"If you need anything"* inscriptions. *Later,* I thought. *When the ground feels more solid.* Meanwhile, I curled up on the couch and shut my eyes.

I might have slept long and soundly if it weren't for a driver outside laying on his horn. I sat up, shook off the cobwebs, went to the kitchen, and poured myself a glass of water. Standing by the window, watching a fight develop between two double-parked cabbies, something clicked, or at least was on the verge of clicking. Something to do with a dream the honking had interrupted. I went into Tom's study, pulled the sketchbook from the wall, and sat back down at the drafting table. Alden claimed I looked like Bill. Would she also see the resemblance here, in the portraits he'd drawn? You only had to imagine Bill twenty years older, the junk out of his system.

Memories started coming back. At first, they seemed like false memories, lifted from some other family's scrapbook. Fishing off a pier at Jamaica Bay. Barbecuing on the roof of our building. Playing hide-and-seek in a tire park. The stuff people reminisce about at funerals. But they weren't false—just incomplete. Snapshots of the calm before the storm. Click the viewfinder one more time and you'd catch the sudden backhand. You'd see two muddy kids emerge from a tire castle, wondering where their father had gone. Always disappearing, leaving us with strangers. Always bruised and bandaged. Daylong benders and nights in the drunk tank. Lame excuses. Back then, I thought it was all normal. I thought that was how everyone lived.

I stared down at that painstakingly rendered mug-shot and wondered how I'd missed it until now. Our father, middle-aged. Bill had been to see him. He'd made the trip to Sing Sing without telling me.

*I guess you really do keep secrets, Bill Morgan,* I thought.

# 17

I TRIED TALKING TO Tom this time. I pulled the chair in close, whispered:

"It was you who fixed up Aiden's castle, wasn't it?"

I told him things I didn't know for sure were true. I told him we'd be okay and that I was ready to listen if he was ready to talk.

"Nice try with Bill," I said, "but you can't throw money at every problem."

I replayed my trip to Hawthorne, my conversation with Dr. Alden.

"She wants me to talk to my father," I said. "Apparently, Bill's already been to see him. You'd think he might have invited me along. At the very least, he should have talked to me about it first. The two of you have that in common."

Tom's eyelids didn't so much as flutter. I leaned in until my lips were brushing his ear.

"You can't hide forever," I said.

*  *  *

I stopped at Paul's again on my way home. I'd already put Aiden to bed via FaceTime, nodded and made encouraging noises while he recapped his day: construction paper collages at school, mac and cheese with Uncle Paul. He asked about my "special mission," wanted to know why phones were banned wherever his father had disappeared to. He didn't accept my answers so much as work with them: *"And nobody but you in the world can do it, right? . . . Dad will take me with him when I'm bigger, won't he?"*

Paul came to the door looking like a man half dead.

"Aiden does that to people," I said.

"Don't know what you're talking about," Paul grinned.

He waved me in. A small army of figurines had migrated from the shelves to the floor. I stepped over and around them and took my place on the futon.

"We were playing Troll Wars," Paul said.

"Who won?"

"Hard to tell—the rules kept changing."

"You're a saint."

"The kid has more ideas than he knows what to do with. I'd like to think I was the same at his age."

I started to nod, then realized I had no idea. Paul was already in the second grade by the time I'd joined up with the Davidsons. Bill, on the other hand, I remembered. His energy was quieter than Aiden's, but he'd had the same bottomless imagination. My first picture books were written and illustrated by *B. MORGAN*. The one I remember best involved gibbons tunneling their way out of the Bronx Zoo and into a subterranean city. I wish I knew what had happened to it. My best guess: a building manager hawked it in the trash after the police tape came down.

Paul went into the kitchen, pulled a bottle of white from the fridge. This time I gave him the thumbs-up.

He came back carrying two glasses, Tom's laptop tucked under one arm.

"I've unlocked all the folders," he said. "You'll be able to access everything on the hard drive now. His email too. I changed the password to Aiden2013."

Paul was sounding like a big brother again. A disapproving big brother.

"But, Tina, I have to ask: Are you sure you don't want to give this to the police? If someone was blackmailing Tom, the cops need to know about it. Tom's life—"

"I will," I said. "I just have to know what I'm giving them first."

"Have you talked to Bill?"

I shook my head.

"Why not?"

"I can't find him."

"And you don't think that's—"

"I don't know what to think."

It came out sharp and clipped. Paul held up his free hand, signaled he was backing off.

"I'm sorry," I said. "I should be thanking you. You've been—"

"I get it. Really, I do."

Paul always did get it. There were times when Mr. Davidson, woozy with pills and pain, would lash out, say the kinds of things I might have expected from my birth father. But Paul, young as he was, never flinched, never quit his patient's side. He pushed away his own needs then, just like he was pushing them away now.

He raised his glass, then couldn't find anything to toast.

"We'll be celebrating Tom's recovery soon enough," I said.

"Cheers."

We sat for a while talking about other things—Paul's latest and most lucrative contract with the Texas public school system, the funny/tragic time I'd given CPR to a man who'd meant to jump off a Brooklyn high-rise but fainted a few yards shy of the ledge. Then I noticed Paul fighting to keep his eyes open. I set my glass on the table, stood, and kissed his forehead.

"Sweet dreams," I said.

*　*　*

No new renovations to the castle, no subtle alterations anywhere in the apartment.

*Of course not,* I told myself.

It was Tom who'd fixed up Aiden's fortress. Bill didn't get all the imagination in the family: with my back to the wall, I was more than capable of churning out a crackpot fantasy. The *Phantom LEGOs Killer* was just my mind taking a break from the real threats. Aiden would have been perfectly safe at home, though it was still better that he crash with Paul. I might get a middle-of-the-night summons from the hospital. Knowles might come knocking. I didn't want Aiden to see Mommy in hysterics . . . or in cuffs. I didn't want the starring role in my son's core trauma.

I changed into my pajamas, filled a water glass with pinot grigio, and carried the glass and Tom's laptop into our bedroom. *Like curling up with a movie,* I told myself—a white lie to slow my heartbeat. It didn't work. I flipped open the screen, sat with my back pressed flat against the headboard. The picture of Aiden was still there, but the box prompting me for a password had been replaced by a slew of blue folders: "Ancient Greece," "Anatomy," "Opera," "Irish Theater" . . . Tom's little projects. One day he was going to memorize world history, the next he was going to master French. Boundless curiosity, zero staying power. Sometimes his roving mind scared me: Did I have enough going on to hold his interest *"till death do us part"*?

At first glance, there weren't any obvious clues. No folder labeled "Bickert" or "Bill" or "Blackmail." But one title did catch my eye: "Honeymoon." Not exactly what I was looking for, but a minor detour couldn't hurt. Two clicks later, there Tom and I were, a decade younger, arm in arm in front of Notre Dame, the fountains at Versailles, the scaffolding-like facade of Le Centre Pompidou. I remembered posing for the photo on *Pont Neuf* because I recalled the man who took it: beard down to his knees, acoustic guitar strapped to his back, pet rat pacing on one shoulder. I couldn't believe Tom had handed his camera over. The fact that he'd gotten it back unscathed seemed like a blessing on our marriage.

Tom had taken pictures of our hotel room and of the view from our hotel room and of the café across from our hotel, where we ate chocolate croissants for breakfast every morning. He'd photographed street signs and metro signs and storefronts and flowers and dogs and bicycles and houseboats along the Seine. Everything was something he never wanted to forget. Never wanted us to forget.

*Don't worry,* I told him. *This is only the beginning.*

The album ended with a shot of the awning outside Au Pied de Cochon, the restaurant where we ate on our last night. I was surprised he'd kept that one: we fought from the appetizers through to the digestif—the only blemish on an otherwise postcard-perfect week. The fight began with him saying something like: *"You can stop being a paramedic now."* When I asked him why on earth I'd want to quit doing the thing I loved, he said, *"There are easier ways to get an adrenaline high."* I started to laugh, then realized he was serious. The diners on either side of us were within elbow-rubbing distance. I bit my tongue, gave Tom's shin a hard kick under the table. The bastard didn't even have the courtesy to yelp.

"You wouldn't be here if it wasn't for this paramedic," I said.

"They'd have sent someone else."

I stared across at him like I recognized the features, but not the man. Part of me was afraid of making a scene; the louder, more persuasive part of me thought, *You'll never see any of these people again.*

"Shove your silver spoon up your ass, you fucking prick," I said.

I stood to leave. He grabbed my wrist. I started to pull away. Cutlery and glassware rattled. There was a chorus of French gasps.

"I didn't mean it," Tom said. "I'm sorry."

I sat back down. But then, moments later, it was as though he just couldn't help himself: he said now that we were married, I should refuse my salary. We'd had a kir each and split a bottle of wine before we even got to the restaurant. Was I just now discovering that I'd married a nasty drunk? I glared my way through the rest of the meal, then got my own cab back to the hotel.

Next morning, Tom was himself again. He didn't seem to remember. In the hustle and bustle of making our flight, I decided to let it drop. That meanness never resurfaced, but now I wondered if it was just one more thing he'd learned to keep from me.

# 18

F OR SOMEONE WHO liked his physical space unclut-
tered, Tom was a top-notch digital hoarder. I found
years-old film reviews, a decade's worth of motivational
speeches, maps to cities around the globe. He'd downloaded scores of funk, blues, and jazz albums (he told me
once that jazz "worked his last nerve"), dedicated multiple folders to health-food recipes and exercise routines
(he could barely operate the microwave, went jogging
maybe twice a year). Strangest of all for a man who considered himself unsentimental was the trove of human-
interest articles: "Couple Rescues Neighbor's Seeing
Eye Dog from Forest Fire"; "WWI Love Letters Wash
Ashore on Okinawa Beach"; "Woman, 102, Reunites
with Estranged Daughter, 80."

Had he studied all those maps and photos, listened to all those albums, read all those articles? If so,
when did he find the time? According to Desmond,
the Foundation was only able to keep overhead low
because Tom wore so many hats: CEO, CFO, chief
architect, accountant, public relations guru . . . Was he
one of those left-brain types who thrived on almost no
sleep? Had he already been up for hours, glued to this

screen, by the time I staggered into the kitchen, usually around six AM?

What I didn't see anywhere on his hard drive was even a hint of Foundation-related material. What Knowles had said about the phone lines held true: personal strictly personal, business strictly business. Tom must have saved any work he did from home directly to the Foundation's server. No point asking Desmond to give me a password—Tom wouldn't leave his dirtiest laundry dangling on a public network.

I told myself to call it quits. Paul must have been right: Tom shredded everything to and from Bickert. That invoice in the trash bin was a rare oversight. Still, I couldn't make myself stop. An hour went by. Then two. I switched over to the internet, opened his Gmail account. Tom was a hoarder here too—more than ten thousand messages, a quarter of them unread. His "Social" and "Promotions" boxes were jammed with overly optimistic (*Stop aging now!*) and politely threatening (*Hurry! Only 24 hrs left!*) subject lines. Besides the odd message from Paul or Desmond or a doctor's office, the primary inbox looked like a catalog of our exchanges . . . years and years' worth.

I reversed the sort order, clicked on our oldest chain. Reading it now made me blush: five years into our marriage, we were still randy, still signing off with declarations and innuendos. Now and again, I came across an extended, raunchy fantasy—role-play, mostly: teacher and pupil, nurse and patient. More explicit than original. Aiden would have been learning to walk right around then. How had we found the energy? Or the time? I must have taken advantage of my extended breaks at the station—for a while I worked graveyard in order to spend days with Aiden. Tom and I saw each other for childcare handoffs and the occasional late dinner (my breakfast).

I navigated back to our most recent thread, found nothing more than a Q&A in broken shorthand:

*R U taking Aiden to Fri. bday party?*
*Can't. Meeting with city planner.*

The kind of back-and-forth we'd have carried out by text if Tom weren't anti–cell phones in the workplace. How had so much changed in five short years? We'd become parents first, lovers last, with very little in between. For my part, the desire was still there—it just wasn't automatic anymore. It took the right gesture, the right look, the right setting. Was that true for Tom as well? Or did he think of us as roommates with a kid?

I moved on from his email, guided the cursor up to "Bookmarks." Most of the pages he'd favorited looked like source material for the folders on his desktop: sites on international news, language learning, museums, history, antiques. Some were mainstream (BBC, Duolingo, the History Channel), others more obscure (Paris's Museum of Hunting and Nature, the Brass Armadillo Antique Mall). There was only a handful whose purpose wasn't right there in the title: interiorcab.com; stationallparts.com; beamertalk.com. I clicked on the first, afraid I'd find myself gawking at a hardcore web version of *Taxicab Confessions*.

The link opened up a video of a man and a woman standing or sitting shoulder to shoulder, the camera just inches away. No homepage to explain who they were or why anyone would want to watch them. One of the two stared straight ahead while the other sipped from a Styrofoam cup. If the insignia on their jackets had been visible, I would have recognized them right away: Mara and Barry, fellow EMTs from the late-night squad. They took over our bus when Dan and I clocked out.

Mara was driving, Barry in the passenger seat. Their faces moved in and out of shadow cast by the street-lights. Neither of them spoke, but Barry's head was cocked as though he was listening to something impor-tant. I turned up the volume, heard a voice obscured by static announcing an accident and a location. I looked for a rewind icon, but there wasn't one. The footage was streaming live.

A webcam? It had to be some kind of trick or joke. Why would Tom . . . *How* would Tom have put a camera in the cab of my bus? I watched Barry take up the hand-set, heard him say "Responding" before his voice was drowned out by the siren. *I'll leave you to it,* I muttered. Nothing to see here that I hadn't seen a thousand times before in person.

I went back to "Bookmarks" and tried beamer.com. In the periphery of the garage lights, I could make out the interior of the car I'd just driven up to Hawthorne. I knew now what stationallparts.com would give me, but I clicked on it anyway. Four equal-sized boxes appeared: apparatus bay, dorm room, day room, gym. I selected the blinkering image of the day room. Chief Vetrano must have been pulling a double, or maybe his wife had kicked him out again, and he was bunking at the station. He and Joy, the night squad's lone female fire-fighter, were playing backgammon. A teapot sat on one side of the board, two plastic mugs on the other. I had the paranoid notion that maybe they were talking about me, but no, she was telling a joke she'd overheard on the subway. I quit Safari before she got to the punchline.

Car, bus, stationhouse—the places you'd be most likely to find me when I wasn't at home, with home already surveilled by Foolproof Prevention. Tom as stalker? Did he think I was having an affair after all? Was he searching for evidence? Plotting our divorce?

And then it hit me. The idea that felt right. Tom insisted it was Bill who'd robbed him, Bill who'd bro-kered the contents of his safe. Either Tom believed I was hiding my brother away somewhere, or he figured Bill would come crawling back to me the second he found himself in a fresh jam. He might turn up at my work. I might drive him to some far-flung safehouse. So, Tom had Bickert install the cameras. Or maybe it was Bick-ert's idea. Which one of them, I wondered, had done the monitoring? And how long ago had it started? After the robbery? After Bill fled Hawthorne?

I tossed the laptop onto Tom's side of the bed and pressed one palm against a sudden knifelike pain in my gut. Nothing was what I'd thought it was. Nobody was who they were supposed to be. Bill the killer. Tom the voyeur. Who did that make me? Can you call yourself a wife when you don't know your husband? A sister when you've been lying to yourself for as long as you can remember, insisting your brother is nothing like your murderous old man? I felt empty, like the slightest breeze would knock me over.

I got out of bed, went into the bathroom, opened the cabinet above the sink, and pulled a bottle of Ambien from the top shelf. Knockout pills weren't a habit—I kept them in reserve for those rare nights when I couldn't stop replaying the day's traumas. A suicide who died in our bus, a child beaten to within an inch of her life. The kinds of traumas that weren't accidents but never should have happened. The kind I felt closing in on me now.

CHAPTER

19

I WOKE UP WITH a gravel tongue and a head full of fog.
Cold water helped bring me around. Coffee helped
some more. I carried a cup into the living room, switched
on the TV, and sank down into the couch. A meteorolo-
gist on NY1 was giving the forecast. Scattered rain showers with wind gusts followed by possible late-afternoon
sunshine. The kind of day that seems like a mash-up of
other days, with none of the parts making a whole.

Bill's SOS call; his sketchpad left behind in a
bleached attic room; Dumb Jake, hired by my husband,
lying dead in my brother's backyard; a sergeant telling
me Tom had been run over—a detective telling me it
was attempted murder; Bill's core trauma; the father–son
reunion; Tom as blackmail victim, then voyeur. I couldn't
make sense of the pieces, let alone the big picture.

I stood and started pacing the perimeter of the coffee table, made a wide turn and nearly tripped over that
goddamn castle. Looking down at it now, I felt somehow certain that I hadn't been paranoid: I'd gouged my
foot on a stray LEGO the morning I'd returned from
the squat. The renovations had happened afterward,
when Tom was already in the ER. Then I remembered

something I couldn't believe I'd forgotten until now: it was Desmond who'd recommended Foolproof Prevention. The owner, a childhood friend, handled the installation himself. Had Desmond convinced him to share the codes? The URL? The password?

*"Did you say anything about us?"* Desmond had asked.

As though something more than a rebuffed kiss had transpired in that cloakroom. As though I were complicit in said kiss.

Was I?

Desmond had always been background noise to me. He was well-meaning but dull verging on lifeless. I'd always suspected a touch of charity on Tom's part, both in their friendship and in their working relationship. Had I followed my husband's lead? Been a little too attentive? A little too kind? Did Desmond believe that I'd led him on only to scorn him in the end?

I shook the idea off. Desmond made a good second-in-command because he ate up work and had no ideas of his own. He wasn't Iago to Tom's Othello—he wasn't out there masterminding a plot to unseat his rival while simultaneously terrorizing the object of his unrequited love. If Desmond wanted vengeance, he wouldn't be subtle about it. He wouldn't play around with LEGOs and surveillance cameras. And he definitely wouldn't come at me through my brother. Desmond's a germaphobe. Bill's world, with its squalor and needles and abscesses, would have all the bile in Desmond's body running for the exits.

Everything kept cycling back to Bill. He was the linchpin, the link between Bickert and Tom, between Tom and his would-be killer. Bill was the reason we'd all been at that squat. I had a sudden gut-drop premonition that my brother was dead. I reached out with one hand, braced myself against the back of the couch. *"Nah, Teen,*

"I heard Bill say, *"they're not done with me yet."* He was probably right. But then who were "they?" *And where are you, Bill?*

I quit pacing, dropped back onto the couch. I knew three things about my brother that I hadn't known just two days ago: Tom had forced him into rehab; he'd remembered something big about his childhood; and he'd been to see our father.

But what if I had the order wrong? I'd been assuming Bill made his first visit to Sing Sing *after* Alden dug up his core trauma. But there weren't any dates in Bill's sketchbook. What if the father–son reunion came first?

*Our father,* I thought.

Our father who'd spent the last twenty years in the company of felons. Killers like him. Armed robbers. Dealers. Rapists. Maybe even a few blackmailers. Again, like most addicts, Bill was easy to manipulate. He wanted to be loved. He wanted to be forgiven. He wanted dope. Promise him all three, and you just might get him to extort the son-in-law you've never met.

I picked my phone up off the coffee table, opened Google, and typed in *Sing Sing: How to visit an inmate.* I stopped when I heard a voice I recognized. I'd forgotten the TV was on. I looked over, saw Desmond standing at the entrance to Brooklyn Methodist, a half-dozen microphones in his face. My first thought: *Tom's dead.* I pounded my chest with the heel of one palm, got my heart back up and running. According to the text at the bottom of the screen, Tom was still critical but stable. Desmond had other news to deliver.

"Police have determined this was no accident," he said, pausing to let the words sink in. "That's why the Foundation—Tom's foundation—is offering a one-hundred-thousand-dollar reward for information leading to the driver's arrest."

Desmond didn't look like himself. Stray tufts of his normally sculpted hair blew around in the breeze. His cheeks were flushed, his eyes bloodshot. I half expected spit to fly from his lips.

"Do *you* have any idea who might have wanted to hurt Mr. Evans?" a reporter asked.

"None. Tom was—is—the most generous person I've ever known. Generous with his time, his ideas, his money. Whoever did this needs to be put away."

Then he was gone, replaced by a talking head at a desk. Almost instantly, my phone started ringing. A number I didn't recognize. Then another. And another. Journalists. The bastard had given them my info. I figured I had maybe fifteen minutes before they started filling up the street outside. This was Desmond punishing me for not being at the hospital. Or maybe for something else.

# 20

I SAT STARING OUT the window of a Metro-North train to Ossining. *Ossining . . . Sing Sing.* It was like a little kid trying to say the name of the town. A maximum-security nursery rhyme. Welcome to *Sing Sing*: nothing very bad ever happens here.

Arranging the visit had been surprisingly easy; an early-morning call got me same-day service. One caveat: the inmate had to approve the visitor. Wouldn't that be a kicker—*my father* turning *me* away? I thought again of my Crayola hate letter. *He had it coming, Teen.* Still, there was a little voice inside me saying, *You left him to rot for twenty years.* He had that coming too.

The prison popped up on the horizon sooner than I'd expected. It wasn't anything like the bleak abattoir I'd been imagining. The generic TV stuff was all there—the barbed wire, the sniper tower, the boxlike buildings—but strip it away and you'd be looking at a riverfront property backed by rolling, wooded hills. A developer's dream. Tom would have a field day.

The train doors made a gasping sound, and I stepped out onto the platform. Crazy to think he'd been just an hour away this whole time. Closer than Stony Brook. A lot closer than Hawthorne. I lingered for a minute, taking in the vista—town, prison, water stacked in a downhill trajectory. Lampposts festooned with crepe paper reminded me that Halloween was around the corner. It would be Paul taking Aiden this year. Maybe they could dress up as twin heroes from one of Paul's video games.

I let a band of fellow passengers lead me to the prison gates.

*  *  *

"Name of inmate?" a very beige-looking CO asked.

"Rick Morgan," I told him.

"Relation?"

It felt like a foreign word caught at the back of my throat:

"Father."

There was a metal detector, an ion scanner, a minimally invasive pat down. They confiscated my keys, phone, wallet. Then came the epic wait in a windowless room brimming with loved ones and public defenders, all of them looking saggy and bored, like they couldn't believe they had nowhere better to be. I sat glaring at the exit, thinking, *On your mark, get set . . .*

Time passed. I stopped seeing the people around me, stopped noticing the musty, cologne-and-sweat smell that dominates rooms where odors start to break down but never quite die. I was in my head now, chasing all kinds of stray thoughts. What was I doing here? I had an objective, but no strategy—something I wanted, but nothing to offer in return. That was how I thought of it: I wasn't a daughter—more like a journalist interviewing the latest psycho-bogeyman. I'd play nice until I got the information I'd come for. Afterward, my father could go lie back down in his coffin and wait for the first shovelful of dirt.

*"They tortured him up there,"* Jerry had said. *"Had him seeing shit from when he was a kid."*

Sitting in Sing Sing's dank antechamber, I realized I hadn't tried very hard to guess what that *shit* might be. Maybe I'd been too caught up in other crises; maybe I figured I already knew. Bill hadn't been in our room with his headphones on. He'd been right there, just out of reach of the blood spatter. He watched the blade swing an arc into her neck. He watched her stagger, knock the dishrack to the floor, grab at the handles on the cabinets, the faucet in the sink. He watched her fall, then writhe. He wanted to help but couldn't make his legs move. Maybe that was one of the details he mimed for Adler. He'd been thirteen years old, but that wouldn't matter; in his mind, he'd always be looking back at the coward who stood by while his father killed his mother. In Bill's mind, he'd always be that coward.

*Shit.* I was crying. The faces around me looked bloated and blurry. Good thing I hadn't bothered with mascara. *I'll find another way,* I thought. I cleared my eyes with the heels of both palms, stood, and started for the exit.

"Tina Evans?" a CO with a drill-sergeant voice said.

I didn't think, just spun around and raised my hand: *Present and accounted for, sir!* I felt eyes on me as I crossed the room, though I doubt anyone was looking—it's easy to imagine yourself in the spotlight when all you want is to disappear.

The CO, for his part, barely glanced in my direction. I followed him down a dim corridor and took my seat in front of a thick pane of glass. More waiting, more time to think. I caught myself ripping pills from my sweater, mouth-breathing hard. And then, just like that, there he was, a few feet away, wearing shackles and a jumpsuit. If I'd thought the glass would shatter, I would have lunged right then.

My father sat down, leaned forward, squinted me into focus through the smudges and cracks. I squinted back, trying to synch up the man I was looking at with the wiry, almost gaunt thirty-year-old I remembered. I wondered again how I'd managed to miss it in Bill's drawings. Same sloping forehead, same shallow dimples. The big difference: middle-aged Rick Morgan had been making good use of that daily hour in the rec room. Barrel chest, anvil arms—only a slight prison-diet potbelly. He looked like he could snap his former self over one knee.

We reached for our handsets at the same time.

"Hello, little girl," he said. "What's it been? Eighteen years?"

"More like twenty."

He whistled.

"I guess time don't stop just 'cause you're inside. It sure didn't stop for you. You're all grown up."

For a while we just stared at each other, heads cocked, like we were suspicious of the state. Like maybe they'd sat the wrong daughter in front of the wrong father.

"I hear Bill's been to see you," I said.

"He mentioned our visits?"

*Visits*, plural.

"He showed me a portrait he'd drawn of you."

"And you had to come and see for yourself?"

"Something like that."

He grinned.

"Kid always had talent. Don't know where he got it from. Not me, that's for damned sure."

*No,* I thought. *He got something else from you.*

"Sounds like you landed well," he said.

"Yeah?"

"Swank apartment, Fortune 500 husband. Plus, I'm grandad to a whip-smart little boy. Not that I feel old enough. Like I said, time keeps on marching."

"That must be hard."

Four words flooded with venom. *Rein it in, Teen.*

"I know it," he said. "I'm right where I'm supposed to be."

His look said he wanted to steer the conversation in another direction but didn't know how. I gave him space, thought maybe he'd take us where I wanted to go on his own.

"I answered your letter," he said. "And then I sent more letters after that. Found out later the social worker used them for confetti."

Was he making an apology? Or fishing for one?

"What did your letters say?"

"Same thing I'll say now. I'm sorry. For all of it. Every last bit. It doesn't change what happened, but that was the dope. I'm a different man now."

*What happened . . .* It was as close as either of us would get to naming her out loud.

"Is that what you told Bill?" I asked.

"Along those lines."

"And what did Bill tell you?"

"I don't know. We talked about a lot of stuff."

"Maybe, but he didn't just come see you out of the blue after twenty years. He must have had a reason."

His expression hollowed out—a total blank, like an automaton straight off the assembly line.

"You're thinking that way because *you* have a reason," he said. "Want to share?"

"I want you to share. Bill quit rehab, then disappeared. His shrink told me he remembered something while he was there. Something from when we were kids. I want to know what it was."

My father's voice dropped to a decibel I could barely hear.

"That's not for me to say. You'll have to ask your brother."

I felt sure then. He knew where Bill was holed up. He was working too hard at giving nothing away.

"Where is he?" I asked.

"Bill?"

I didn't bother to answer.

"You mean right this minute?" he asked.

"You know what I mean."

"I don't."

"He's gone missing," I said. "First time in my life I can't get a hold of my brother, and the only thing that's changed is he's been talking to you."

My father held up his shackled hands, as if to say, *"You've come to the wrong man."* I had an idea about who the right man might be.

"Is he with Jeff?" I asked.

He shifted his weight around, like even after all this time he found the added bulk uncomfortable.

"Bill told you about Jeff?"

I nodded.

"Everyone called him J. R. in here."

"Called?"

"He's out now."

Of course he was: How else would he be whispering in Bill's ear?

"The two of you were close?"

"Had to be. We shared an eight-by-ten cell for fifteen years. Cellies don't generally last. Guys get done for snoring too loud in here. J. R. was one of the good ones."

"What does the 'R' stand for?"

"Right cross—his was so fast you couldn't see it. Fought one of the Mayweather brothers at Madison Square Garden back in the day. As a last-minute replacement, but still. Stayed standing for the full twelve. He was training me. Not for any real fighting—just to keep sane and sound."

"You mean clean?"

"That was part of it."

"And what keeps you sane now?"

"Knowing I'm almost free."

It took me a second to believe I'd heard him right.

"What are you talking about?"

He grinned.

"Got my first parole hearing in forty-nine short days."

I'd driven that ugly little clause from my mind: *With the possibility of . . .* For so long, it had seemed like a day that would never come, a day he'd never live to see. Now I felt like I was standing on a narrow highway median, struggling to hold my balance while cars blurred by on either side. I shut my eyes, just for a second. A guard's voice brought me back.

"You've got five minutes, people."

I leaned forward so my nose was nearly touching the glass.

"Bill's with J. R, isn't he?"

"I really couldn't say."

"But you put them in touch?"

"J. R. got me sober. That's no small feat in here. I thought maybe he could help Bill too."

"Bullshit."

"What's bullshit?"

"Your pal J. R.'s hiding Bill away until it all blows over."

"All what blows over?"

"Where's Bill?"

"I don't know what you're talking about."

"I'm talking about murder and blackmail. I'm talking about a felon who just learned he has a 'Fortune 500' son-in-law."

The guard's voice again: time to say our goodbyes.

My old man was talking, but I barely heard him. I was back in our Lower East Side kitchen, watching the blade swing its arc, watching our mother's blood fill gaps in the linoleum.

"You remember what I said in my letter?" I asked.

He looked at me like I'd cut him off in the middle of an acceptance speech.

"Yeah, I remember."

"Well, is it?"

"Is it what?"

"Worse than hell?"

"I wouldn't know. I've never been to hell."

"Don't worry, you'll get the chance to compare. Meanwhile, I'll be testifying at your hearing. For Bill. For our mother. I'll have my Fortune 500 husband spring for the best legal team in the city. They'll make sure I get the phrasing just right. And in case that's not enough, they'll grease all the right palms. Like Bill told you, money's no object. Seven weeks from now is just about Thanksgiving. The members of the parole board will have a lot to be thankful for. A brand-new Lexus in the driveway. Or maybe a few million in an offshore account. Whatever it takes. So, you can quit making those chalk marks in your cell. You're never getting out. Not if you live another fifty years. There's no salvation for you. No hope. Just time and walls."

He started to say something, but my handset was already hanging from its cradle.

CHAPTER

21

I T WAS AN odd hour of the afternoon, but still the
train back to Grand Central was bustling—at least
one body per two-seater, with clumps of passengers opt-
ing to stand rather than share. I walked the length of
one car, then turned back and claimed an aisle seat next
to a middle-aged man in a battle-worn beige suit. He
held a bruised-looking briefcase balanced on his lap,
like a tray table, and sat staring out the window while
chewing on the inside of one cheek. A public defender,
maybe? Someone whose visit hadn't gone much better
than mine. He didn't seem like the type to strike up a
conversation, but just to be sure, I folded my arms and
shut my eyes.

   *Stupid, stupid, stupid,* I told myself.

   I'd undone twenty years of silence, broken the seal
on an ancient wound, and for what? I wasn't any closer
to Bill's core trauma, still didn't know for sure what he
had or hadn't done, still had no idea where he'd vanished to. I'd told myself to play nice, then signed off by
doubling down on my adolescent bloodlust. I'd turned
into the maniac who went around brandishing lighter
fluid and a match. Out of control. No sense of a bigger

picture. Willing to blow everything up if she couldn't have justice right then and there.

I shut my eyes tighter, tried to picture his expression as my parting words hit home: *"No salvation for you. Just time and walls."* At first, all I saw was the glare of fluorescent lights reflecting off the glass between us. Then, little by little, the light cleared, and he was sitting there in front of me. Not the Rick Morgan I'd visited, but the one from Bill's drawings. I could make out every line, every shadow. Those portraits struck me now as the saddest things I'd ever seen. Bill hadn't drawn the man he'd visited—he'd drawn the father he wanted. A man whose face was full of compassion, grief, love. A man who was haunted, but also hopeful. A man who knew all the questions but didn't pretend to have the answers. A man who'd sit with you for hours and hold your hand . . . if it weren't for the fact that he didn't exist.

\* \* \*

The public defender got off at Dobbs Ferry. I slid over into the window seat, squinted at the Hudson as the train stutter-stepped out of the station. I waited to make sure that no one new sat down next to me, and then I pulled my phone from my pocket. I hadn't pressed my old man for J. R.'s info because knowing they'd been cellmates gave me all I needed to find him on my own. Dan, my partner at the station, had an uncle who'd started out directing traffic and worked his way up to a corner office at Police Plaza. Dan wasn't very fond of this uncle, but I figured he was fond enough of me to tip the scale.

I ignored the long stream of missed-call alerts, tapped on "Contacts," and scrolled down to Dan's photo. With any luck, I'd catch him on a break.

"This is Dan."

It sounded like the opening of a voicemail message, but that was just how he answered the phone. For a millennial, he had old-fashioned notions about caller ID: screening—deciding who was worth talking to and who wasn't—struck him as the kind of thing rich people did in order to make sure they didn't rub noses with the poor. The fact that I'd married into money had weighed heavily against me until he'd heard my backstory: one junkie parent murdering the other trumps a little disposable income.

"It's me, dumbass," I said.

"Holy shit, Tina! I've been wanting to call, but I thought, like, you'd have family around, and maybe it was too soon, and I just—"

"It's all right, Dan. Really."

Like me, emotion isn't his thing; he'd take blood and guts over weeping and wailing any day.

"Man, we miss you like crazy around here," he said. "Anything I can do, just ask."

"Actually, there is something . . ."

I kept it simple, told him I needed the full name and current whereabouts of my father's long-time bunkmate. I didn't say why.

"And I wouldn't mind knowing what he was in for," I added.

"Shit, really? You want me to talk to my uncle? Last time I saw him, he asked me how I hoped to save enough for my own funeral on an EMT's salary. My mother was sitting right there."

"You said 'anything.'"

"Yeah, I know. I just didn't see that one coming. When you need it by?"

"As close to now as possible."

"I'll try. This have anything to do with what I heard on the news?"

"It might."

"Then again it might not?"

"For now. I'll tell you all about it when we're back in the cab."

*And I've disabled the webcam.*

"Hope that's soon," Dan said. "And I hope they catch the son of a bitch."

I ended the call, swiped over to my mailbox, started deleting messages from any number I didn't recognize while keeping an eye out for the usual suspects: the hospital, Bill, Knowles. The one I least wanted to hear from came up first. The time stamp read eleven thirty AM. My phone had been sitting in a Sing Sing locker. Had the detective somehow known? Did the irony appeal to him— me visiting the institution he was eager to make my home?

I hesitated, then pressed "Play." Knowles was his usual gruff self. He had to talk to me pronto. It was about my kid.

*Aiden?*

I told myself it was just a ploy to make sure I got in touch. Still, I couldn't hit the call-back icon fast enough. I inched up against the window, scanned the surrounding seats as though someone might be listening in. He picked up on the fourth ring.

"Detective Knowles speaking."

"This is . . ."

I hesitated, not sure what to call myself. I didn't want to be *Tina* to him, but then I didn't want to be *Mrs. Evans* either. In the end, he didn't call me anything.

"Thanks for getting back to me," he said.

"It's about my son?"

"Hold on for a sec."

I heard him whispering like he was answering someone's question, but I couldn't hear the other person. When he came back, he skipped right over Aiden.

"You said you were asleep when your husband left the house on the night of the incident?"

"That's right."

"And you didn't hear him take a call before he left?"

"No."

"The phone didn't wake you?"

"No."

"You have any idea who your husband might have been talking to at a little after midnight?"

There was a purposefulness to the way he kept saying *your husband*, like he wanted to emphasize the bond he believed I'd broken.

"None," I told him.

"Then I'll have to interview your son."

I felt my gut churning. My mind started flipping through distant images of the cops and social workers I'd talked to in the days after Bill and I became orphans. They were all professionalism and fake smiles. Their jobs had turned them cold. Just thinking of them now left a metallic taste in my mouth.

"You need my permission for that," I said.

"With all due respect, Mrs. Evans, that's TV bunk. I'm doing you a courtesy. If I wanted to, I could march right down to his school and have the principal pull him from class."

"On what grounds?"

"Your husband received a call that night from an untraceable number. Judging by the time line, we think he must have taken it just prior to leaving the house. It lasted a little over five minutes. Since you didn't overhear anything, we're hoping your son did."

Was it too late to make something up? *Oh, yeah, that call . . .*

"He's a city kid," I said. "He'd sleep through Armageddon."

"All the same. I'd like you to bring him to the station. We have a child psychologist who specializes in talking with kids as young as your son. She puts them right at ease. She's very good."

"Is that necessary? Isn't it a yes-or-no question? Either he heard something, or he didn't."

"Well, we might have a few other questions for him too. Trust me, it's better this way."

I checked the time: two PM. The train was inching into Manhattan. I'd make it to Aiden's school just before the closing bell.

"I could have him there by three thirty," I said.

"No sooner?"

"I'm not in Brooklyn."

"Three thirty, then."

I stuck the phone back in my pocket, spun my head, and glared out the window. It didn't matter that Aiden was six—a police-station shrink grilling him about his AWOL father would make for the kind of memory that didn't fade. Any chance of him going unscathed was in tatters.

And wasn't that what I wanted most for my son? For him to one day leave the nest with a feeling that everything would be okay because it always had been. No dark spots he couldn't account for later. No flashing back to nights spent on a neighbor's couch because mommy and daddy hadn't come home. No images of mommy nodding off on a park bench. Of daddy shoved up against a wall with a knife to his throat because he'd slipped a dealer some *funny money* (*"Just a game, princess,"* he'd said afterward. *"Just a game"*). Jesus, was that why I'd married Tom in the first place? Because he'd seemed like the antidote to all the dope-fiend-drama Bill and I couldn't stop reliving?

The train was passing through Marble Hill. I caught glimpses of streets and avenues between the buildings.

Coming back to the city always gave me a sense of calm, like a soothing voice slowing my heartbeat. It's supposed to be the other way around: stressed-out urbanites fleeing in search of trees and waterfalls. Not me. Not Bill. Without nonstop movement all around us, our brains start creating movement of their own. And the cities in our minds are dangerous places. We get lost in them. We start to feel like we'll never find our way out.

CHAPTER

## 22

I STOPPED AT A kiosk in Grand Central and bought a burner phone. I needed a number the journalists didn't have, one I could give to the hospital, Paul, Knowles, Dan—everyone but Desmond. Scanning the models, comparing the features, I felt like I was channeling Bill; if I were Tom, I'd just add a second line to my existing phone. I called Paul first, told him I'd be picking Aiden up from school. Then I grabbed a sandwich and a coffee and headed down into the subway.

I arrived in time to hear the three o'clock bell sounding. I thought Aiden would be disappointed to find me instead of his uncle, the purveyor of chocolate-chip waffles and video games, but when I bent down to greet him, he jumped right into my arms. Which made what was about to happen feel all the more like a betrayal.

\* \* \*

The shrink met us outside Knowles's cubicle. Even in flat-soled shoes, she stood a half-head taller than Knowles, a full head taller than me. She was lean and angular, dressed in black, with permed salt-and-pepper hair. It would have been easy enough for any child to cast her as a witch.

"I'm Dr. Menendez," she said. "It's so nice to meet you both."

She shook my hand, then touched Aiden's shoulder.

"Likewise," I said, my spine as stiff as I could make it.

Aiden was busy taking inventory of Knowles's trophies and pennants and bobbleheads, hoping, maybe, that the adults would let something slip if they believed he wasn't listening, something like the truth about why he was here. I'd done a lousy job of prepping him, told him the police were helping Daddy with his work and wanted to ask us a few questions.

*"Why don't they just ask Daddy?"*

*"Because he's very, very busy,"* I'd said.

The look Aiden gave me felt like a preview of the teenage years, but for once he didn't press.

Knowles led us through the squad room and up a flight of stairs to a daycare-style office painted in bright pastels and furnished with a child-sized armchair and an overstuffed couch. Between the couch and armchair was a knee-high table, and beside the table were two plastic baskets, one pink and one blue, the first full of imitation Barbie dolls and stuffed animals; the second, toy cars and action figures. Three of the four walls were crowded with children's artwork and colorful maps. The fourth wall featured a long, narrow mirror.

With no instruction from Menendez, Aiden made a beeline for the blue basket, fished out a Tonka dump truck, and plunked himself down on the armchair.

"I guess we'll leave you to it," Knowles said.

I started to follow Menendez into the room, but Knowles tugged me back.

"Goes a lot quicker one on one," he said.

I started to argue, but Menendez was already closing the door in my face.

"I'll be right here," I called, "talking with the detective."

Aiden looked at me over his shoulder. He seemed remarkably nonplussed.

"She's very good," Knowles reminded me. "Gentle. Kids usually leave feeling better."

As though I'd brought my son in for a real session with a real child psychologist. As though Menendez would be using her training and experience to help Aiden rather than interrogate him.

"There's a snack room right over here," Knowles said, pointing to an open doorway. "It's even got an espresso machine. We can sip while we wait."

I was too frazzled to come up with an objection. Knowles, for his part, was a different man in his native habitat. All smiles and hospitality, as though in the absence of a partner he was sometimes forced to play good cop. I was confident I knew which role came closer to the real thing.

He sat me down at a Formica table, then turned his back and started working the espresso machine. The room was small and oddly cheerful. The posters on the walls had nothing to do with policing. One was titled *Brooklyn Reads* and showed a sea otter in glasses, reading *Charlotte's Web* to a giraffe. Another read *Brooklyn Children's Museum* and featured a green robot wearing a hat made out of flowers.

"I didn't know the precinct had a kid's wing," I said.

"Most criminals are parents," he said.

He could have just as easily said *"most victims."* He knew about my old man. He wanted me to know that he knew. Even the good cop had a mean streak.

He set an Americano and a little pitcher of cream on the table, then poured himself a cup of regular and joined me.

"I can get you something from the vending machine if you're hungry," he said.

"I'm fine, thanks."

We had the room to ourselves, which made me wonder if it wasn't really an interrogation room in disguise—a place that conjured up childhood innocence so that you'd drop your guard, let your guilt come leaking through. Maybe the interview was a sham. Maybe Aiden and Menendez were playing rounds of Connect Four.

"I spent the morning interviewing some of Bickert's old squad," Knowles said.

He let it hang there like he wanted me to pry, but I didn't see the point: he'd steer the conversation where he wanted it to go, with or without my help. Instead, I took a sip of my Americano, found it leagues better than anything I might have expected from a cop shop.

"Turns out Bickert had a reputation," Knowles continued, "and not a good one. There were even some hints he might've been forced out. It takes a lot for cops to point a finger at other cops. Whatever they say he did, he probably did ten times worse."

Now I was supposed to ask: *And what do they say he did, Detective Knowles?* Like I couldn't already see where this was headed: Tom bungling some criminal endeavor, calling on Bickert to bail him out. Meanwhile, all I wanted was to grab hold of Aiden and sprint back to safety.

"How long will they be in there?" I asked.

"Depends," Knowles said. "Shouldn't be too long."

"No, it shouldn't."

He ignored me, went right on impugning his ex-colleague.

"Bickert worked undercover," he said. "White-collar crimes. Corruption, fraud, money laundering. Now and again, high-end prostitution. He hunted Wall Street types. People like your husband."

"Tom's about as far away from Wall Street as it gets."

"People with money, then."

I was only half listening, my mind running on a different track. Menendez was a shrink turned child inquisitor. If Alden could get adults to relive decades-old, repressed memories, then what could Menendez do with a first-grader? Was she hypnotizing him now? Drawing out the source of his future core trauma?

"Anyway, people in the department suspected Bickert of tipping off his targets. He'd go through the steps, dig up all the dirt he could find, and then—for a fee only folks like your husband could afford to pay—he'd make that dirt disappear. Burn the paper trail, destroy key evidence, tamper with the right witnesses. Not every time. He made some big cases. Otherwise, he wouldn't have lasted as long as he did."

Knowles was sounding less like the good cop, more like a car salesman reeling in a potential buyer. Smug, sure he had the upper hand. As if I were the trophy wife Tom picked out of a lineup at the country club. Tell her a scary story about a bad man, and she'll fold. And yet I was sure Knowles had done his homework. He knew where my father was and why. He knew the silver spoon came late.

"In a nutshell, Bickert made himself into a kind of fixer. Extortion with a twist—pay me, and no one will ever know that you bought yourself that yacht with Cancer Kids donations. Don't pay me, and the paparazzi will be snapping pictures of you on your way down the river."

I'd had a thought I couldn't shake.

"There's a mirror in that room where she has Aiden," I said. "It's got to be a two-way, right? So why aren't we on the other side? Why can't I know what she's doing with my son?"

Knowles smiled.

"Sometimes a mirror is just a mirror," he said.

Maybe, but I was starting to believe he'd fed me a line. I could have refused to let him anywhere near Aiden. He'd dazed me with an image of cops hauling my baby away while his classmates pointed and laughed. No mother would let that happen.

"Thing is," he went on, "Bickert's reputation hasn't improved in the private sector. Word is, he hires ex-cons like day laborers. People he put away for minor offenses when he knew they'd committed major crimes. You see what I'm saying? Bickert traffics in information. He collects people based on what he can use against them."

Knowles pushed aside his mug, leaned out over the table, and lined his eyes up with mine.

"Mrs. Evans," he said, "I'm going to ask you point blank. Why did your husband need a fixer with a bent reputation? And how was your brother involved?"

# 23

KNOWLES HAD MY attention now. I reached down with both hands and gripped either side of my chair.

"Bill and Tom have almost nothing to do with each other," I said.

"Must be a lot of wiggle room in that 'almost.'"

"Wiggle room?"

He pivoted without standing, pulled a manila folder from the cabinet beneath the sink, and dropped it on the table between us. No doubt now: this trip to the snack room had been scripted in advance. I wondered again if interviewing Aiden was just a piece of the script.

"We found these pictures in Bickert's office," he said.

I slid the folder toward me, found it weighed down by a thick bulge in the center.

"Go on," he said. "Have a look."

He smiled, reached across, flipped the file open.

I let my eyes drift down, ordered my face to remain blank.

The top photo showed Bill sitting on a park bench, drawing in his sketchbook and chatting with an addict who looked to be nearing the end of his run: jaundiced skin, scabs dotting the jawline, thin enough to blow over with a paper fan. Another, more substantial man sat beside him, caught here running a comb through his hair. He was in his early forties, give or take, with model-worthy cheekbones and deep smile lines. Dress him up nice and you could plop him down in a boardroom without anyone sneaking a second look. So, the photo seemed to ask, why was he spending a sunny afternoon shooting the breeze with a pair of smackheads?

Next up, a shot I might have liked under different circumstances—Bill sharing a smoke with a gray-haired priest in front of a sagging brick building. The priest held his cigarette in his mouth while gesturing with both hands; Bill, head cocked to one side, seemed to be listening intently, giving the priest's words serious consideration, as though the priest were describing a path to redemption, and Bill was thinking that he might just take it.

I kept turning through the pile. Nothing but candid after candid of my brother. Bill on a subway platform, slapping hands with a man in a parka and a neon sun visor; Bill seated at a cafeteria table, hunched over his tray, spoon raised, surrounded by men who seemed to be laughing at something he'd said; Bill in an alley, making an exchange, his face lost in shadow though the dealer was framed perfectly, a zitty teenager with a concave chest, the spitting image of Bill, aged sixteen. I wanted to slip into the frame and scare the kid off, tell him exactly what the next sixteen years had in store. Not that he'd listen. School counselors, social workers, Mr. Davidson, me—plenty of people had warned Bill.

I quit halfway through the stack. No need to see anymore: I knew what Bickert was up to. These weren't photos of Bill so much as photos of the company he kept. In particular, the male company. Bickert had been searching for those fake moving men, snapping pics of Bill's entourage, then comparing them to stills from the surveillance footage. Not that I'd share this insight with Knowles.

"How did you know he was my brother?" I asked.

"We found a steno pad full of field notes. Bickert wrote to himself in a personal shorthand, but it wasn't all that hard to decipher. What is hard is establishing that your husband hired Bickert in the first place. We combed through Bickert's office from top to bottom. The techs have gone through his computer. We've subpoenaed his banking records. Nothing with the name Tom Evans on it anywhere. Nothing but these photos and the calls from your husband's phone. Now, does that sound aboveboard to you, Mrs. Evans?"

He locked eyes with me, hoping I'd squirm. I kept thinking, *Aiden, Aiden, Aiden . . .*

"Look, Bickert's missing, and your husband's in a coma. Time to tell me what you know, Mrs. Evans. Why was Bickert trailing your brother? What was your husband hoping to find? He must have told you something."

Another chance to speak the truth without fear of reprisal.

"Tom didn't tell me anything."

Knowles sucked in his bottom lip, held it there for a beat, then set it free with a loud popping sound.

"In that case," he said, "maybe I've got it all wrong. Maybe your husband didn't hire Bickert. Maybe *you* hired him. After all, it's your brother in the photos. Maybe your husband made those late-night calls because he'd just found out. Maybe he—"

"Are you saying I should have a lawyer present?"

"I'm saying you need to share what you know. What was Bickert working on? We'll get there the hard way if we have to. We'll turn over everything Tom ever touched, and you'll be the one cleaning up after us. Or, you could just bite the bullet and say it out loud right now. Don't let things spiral out of control, Mrs. Evans. Don't do that to your son."

*My son.* The child who was being held hostage two doors down. For the second time that day, I wanted to assault the man sitting in front of me. I saw myself air-mailing his espresso back in his face. I imagined diving over the table, gouging his eyes with my thumbs. Everything that had been building in me was clawing hard for the surface. Lies told, truths withheld, accusations hurled. By Knowles, Tom, Bill, Desmond, my old man. And now my son was being used against me. He was being harmed because of me. I bit my tongue and bit my tongue and bit my tongue, and then it started to come out. Not all at once. Just short bursts of steam escaping before I could shut the valve.

"You're a fucking hypocrite," I said. "And I want to see Aiden. Now."

"Easy, Mrs. Evans. They'll be done any minute."

"What is she doing to my son?"

"She isn't doing anything to him. They're talking."

"This is going on too long. He's only six."

"Young minds see and hear things they don't under-stand. It takes time to get at the information."

"Well, times up. I'm taking Aiden home."

I stood. Knowles stood with me, stepped in front of the door. I thought: *Lighter fluid and a match.*

"Get out of my way."

"Just another minute, Mrs. Evans."

"You can't treat people like this. I want to talk to your superior."

"My superior? Grab anyone passing by in the hall—they'll probably outrank me."

I stepped to him so our toes were touching.

"You better be sure that what you're doing is strictly legal," I said, "because if not, I can guarantee it'll come back to bite you in the ass."

"Best lawyers money can buy—right, Mrs. Evans?"

He winked, then moved aside. But now there was someone new blocking the exit.

"All done," Menendez said, beaming like she'd just given Aiden a tour of the Chocolate Factory.

"Where is he?" I asked.

"He's just there in the room. My assistant is keeping an eye on him."

I backed her out into the hall.

"Your assistant?"

"She's helping him put the toys away. He has quite an imagination."

*I wouldn't know,* I thought. *I'm not a doctor.*

"How'd he do?" Knowles asked.

He'd crept up behind me, almost like he feared I might hurl myself at his colleague.

"Aiden did great."

"Did he catch any of that phone call?"

I saw Menendez hesitate, sensed Knowles nodding for her to go ahead. He wanted me to hear. It was like he knew what was coming.

"Aiden heard his father say, 'This will kill her. You know it will kill her.'"

So many questions, so many accusations of my own. But there wasn't time. A chubby little blond woman emerged from an open doorway, leading Aiden by the hand. He was smiling and looking up at her. It was the happiest I'd seen him since I'd gotten Bill's call.

# 24

**"How about a** cheeseburger?" I asked once we were standing a safe distance from the precinct house. "And maybe a float after, if we have room."

"Mint chocolate chip?" Aiden asked.

"Of course."

"I'll have room. Is Uncle Paul coming?"

"No," I said. "We'll see him later."

I guided us to his favorite diner, a grease pit he'd discovered through a classmate's birthday party. Aiden loved it because every dish tasted like butter, and every table came with a box of crayons and a white paper tablecloth. Now we dangled the place as a reward for soldiering through tough times—flu shots, badly scraped knees, epic car rides. This trip was more of a reward for mommy: Aiden's hour with Dr. Menendez might not have been tough on him, but it had been brutal on me. I wanted a little fun time with my kid.

At five o'clock we had our pick of booths. Aiden chose the one closest to the window, not for the view, but because it put us directly beneath a display of colorful piñata farm animals, all handcrafted by local high school students. He thought if he was lucky, one of the animals might spontaneously burst and shower him with candy. Meanwhile, his hands went straight for the crayons.

On the walk over, Aiden had been pure stream of consciousness, riffing off whatever happened to cross our path: a labradoodle made him speculate about other possible combinations—a Chihuahua and a Great Dane, or maybe a clam and a hamster; a Chanel billboard had him asking how old you had to be before you were allowed to wear perfume; a window display left him wondering why you so rarely saw child mannequins; a long traffic light inspired him to found a company that mass-produced pedestrian bridges. Now that we were settled, I hoped for some focus.

"So, kiddo," I said, "how are things?"

I wasn't angling for specifics—I just wanted to hear him say that he was okay. And maybe that he missed me. Missed home. Even if he was having a blast with Paul.

"Things are good," he said.

"How good?"

He spread his arms out to the sides in a gesture that reminded me of the priest in that photo of Bill.

"You've got plenty of energy today," I said.

"I took a nap."

"At school?'

"After. At the police station."

"When you were with Dr. Menendez?"

"She said to call her Angie."

I was about to ask what he thought of Angie, when the server arrived to take our order. He wore a handlebar mustache and addressed Aiden as *sir*. Aiden wasn't shy about staring. When we were alone again, I had to tug on his ear to get him to turn back around and face me.

"Did you nap the whole time you were with Dr. Menendez?" I asked.

He shook his head.

"First, she asked me to draw something for her. Then I took a nap. Then she let me play with her son's firetrucks."

"Her son's?"

"He's too old for them now."

"What did you draw for Dr. Menendez?"

"It's better if I show you."

He put the crayons he'd already selected back in the box, searched out the necessary colors—green and brown—and got to work.

"Where did you take your nap?" I asked.

"She has a chair you can lie down in. It's *really* comfortable. Nobody can stay awake in it."

"Is that what she told you?"

He nodded.

"Did you have nice dreams?"

"I didn't have dreams."

"No?"

"It's different than regular sleeping."

"Different how?"

"I don't know. It felt like a bath."

Like he was weightless, cocooned, protected. Maybe she'd played a recording of a waterfall. Maybe a soothing voice was enough. Alden hadn't wanted to call it hypnosis; she preferred *deep relaxation*. The state Aiden was describing now. Had he gotten up from Menendez's "*really* comfortable" chair, acted out his father's half of that late-night phone call?

"Do you remember Angie talking during your nap? Asking you questions, maybe?"

Aiden shook his head, his attention now devoted to his reconstruction of the picture he'd drawn for Dr. Menendez. So much so that our mustachioed server had to leave his burger off to the side.

"Come on, Aiden," I said. "Time to eat now."

"I'm almost done."

"You can finish after, while we have our shake."

"Just one second."

"Now, Aiden. Before it gets cold."

He put the crayon down. I slid his plate over.

"Did Dr. Menendez say why she wanted to see you?"

"To help Daddy," he said, squeezing the words out around a mouthful of fries. This wasn't the time for a lecture on table manners.

"Help him how?"

"He's lost."

"Daddy's lost?"

"Not lost like he can't find his way back to where we live. He's lost like he can't find what he's looking for."

"What do you think he's looking for?"

"A lady. She's the one who's really lost. That's why Daddy can't find her. He doesn't know where she is because *she* doesn't know where she is. But if he doesn't find her, she'll die."

*"This will kill her. You know it will kill her."*

He held his burger in one hand, pushed his plate back toward the edge of the table.

"See," he said.

He'd drawn a forest of stick trees with a square hole in the middle. I pointed to the hole.

"That's where daddy is?"

"Yes. I didn't get to draw him yet."

"And where's the lady?"

"She's hiding in one of the trees. But look how many of them there are. How is he ever supposed to find her?"

A story to fill the vacuum. The adults wouldn't level with him, so he'd worked something out on his own. His own way of understanding. For now, it was better than anything I had to offer. Had he arrived in Menendez's

office with the lady-in-the-trees story ready and waiting,
or had she helped him along?

"Daddy's very clever," I said.

"Yeah, but that's *a lot* of trees."

"It sure is."

I waited until the shake arrived before I tried him
with another question. I kept my tone light, made it
sound like I was indulging a mild curiosity.

"Did you and Daddy work more on the LEGOs castle before he left?"

Aiden quit sucking on his straw, gave me a very serious scowl.

"I had to make it by myself," he said. "Those are the
rules. Daddy was going to make his own, so we could
have battles."

"But you had to finish yours first?"

Aiden nodded, stuck the straw back in his mouth.
His account was entirely credible. Play was never just
play for my husband: it was an opportunity to develop
independence, discipline, a work ethic. Fun was hollow
and fleeting unless you'd earned it.

"You did a great job," I told him.

For a six-year-old. The fortress sitting in our living
room was beyond what a six-year-old could do. Someone
had been in our home. The evidence wouldn't hold up in
a court of law, but it felt conclusive to me.

\* \* \*

We were back at Paul's by seven PM. Time enough for a
bath and a bedtime story. Aiden treated bathing like a
watersport; I expended more energy wiping down Paul's
blue slate tiling than I did wiping down my son. It wasn't
until he was dry and wearing pajamas that the protests
began.

"But I'm not sleepy."

"That's why we're going to read a story first."

"I don't want a story. I want to see *Babes in Toyland*."

Paul stifled a laugh.

"You're raising an old soul."

For me, it was a sad kind of funny: Aiden's love for Ollie Dee and Stannie Dum came straight from Tom. *March of the Wooden Soldiers* was a year-round regular on their watch list.

"Tell you what," I said. "If it's okay with Uncle Paul, you can watch half tonight, half tomorrow night."

A deal I made knowing Aiden would last fifteen minutes, tops.

But what a sublime fifteen minutes they were. Paul made popcorn. Aiden sat between us, his warm little body sloping into mine. Laughter and applause followed by a faint snoring. He woke for a second when I picked him up, then dropped back asleep in my arms. I kissed his forehead, lingered before turning out the light.

It was a gentle end to a harsh and shitty day.

If only it really had been the end.

# 25

A STROKE OF MERCY: no flashbulbs or LED video lights blinding me as I turned the corner onto our street. The reporters must have called it quits for the night, decided wherever I'd gone to, I wasn't coming back: *Mrs. Evans could not be reached for comment.* They'd start fresh tomorrow, wanting to know all the same things I wanted to know: who and why and what were Tom's chances? At least they hadn't stumbled onto the Bickert angle: a connection between my high-society husband and heroin-addict brother would have had them pitching tents up and down the block.

I'd made it as far as the top landing before I noticed our door was ajar. My automatic thought: *Tom's home.* Then reality kicked in. No way I'd forgotten to turn the dead bolt and set the alarm, not given the current threat level. *About face, Teen. Nice and slow.* I had one hand on the banister when I heard someone singing behind me. A voice I recognized. A voice that only sang when it was drunk. I spun back around, pushed the door open with my foot, stepped inside, and flicked on the overhead.

Desmond was sitting on the island separating the kitchen and living room, feet swinging, heels scuffing the drywall. He must have left the lights off in case the reporters came back—drunk or sober, image-obsessed Desmond wouldn't want to make a scene. A mostly empty bottle of top-shelf tequila stood beside him on the island. Someone had given it to Tom for his birthday— someone who didn't know him very well: Tom's allergic to agave.

"Were you already shitfaced when you got here?" I asked.

Desmond didn't say anything, just stared straight ahead, eyes glazed, like he hadn't noticed the switch from dark to light. After all the time spent with Knowles and my old man, it felt good to have a low-risk target in my sites.

"Get the fuck out," I said.

He turned toward me in cartoon-level slow-mo.

"I was worried," he said.

"Worried?"

"You weren't at the hospital. You weren't answering your phone. I thought maybe something had happened."

"So you broke in?"

He wagged an unsteady finger in my direction.

"Tom gave me the codes," he said.

"Not so you could sit in the dark, drinking his liquor."

"I was waiting for you."

Despite the slurring, he sounded proud of himself. He had the trust of an important man. I pointed to Aiden's fortress.

"Your handiwork?"

The question didn't register. It occurred to me that I hoped it was Desmond. The castle, the hit-and-run, the dead PI. All of it. Even now, I couldn't think of anyone I feared less.

"Shut the door," he said.

"Once you're gone."

Desmond didn't budge. I pulled out my phone.

"What are you doing?"

"Calling the cops."

He slid off the counter and closed the distance between us with remarkable agility for someone whose liver was stewing. Then he grabbed the phone out of my hand and tossed it onto the couch.

"Listen to me, Tina. I just want—"

"Leave."

"I've seen the way you look at me."

"That's called disgust."

"Don't deny your feelings. I've never denied mine."

His cheeks were crimson, and his sweat stunk of liquor. I backed away, slipped one hand into my pocket, feeling for the mace.

"I left Maria because of you," he said. "Because I couldn't stop thinking about you."

Maria: his lone relationship in the decade I'd known him. They'd been a good pair—both dishwater bland, with the kind of faces you couldn't picture unless they were sitting right in front of you. All I remembered about her was that she'd hated New York—the crowds, the noise, the heat and the cold. She even hated the trees outside her bedroom window. *"They reek like sperm,"* she'd told me. One morning she packed up all her things, along with a fair number of Desmond's, and split, never to be heard from again.

"Maria walked out on you," I said. "She took your iPad and—"

"Just shut the fuck up and listen. You're making this hard. It shouldn't have to be hard."

He was shouting and trying not to shout at the same time. The last man I'd seen this far gone was my father. I'd seen him that way so many times they all blended together. Usually it was my mother standing toe to toe with him, giving nearly as good as she got. Now and again it was Bill on the receiving end. Less often, it was me. More than once, there was a belt involved. More than once, Bill had to skip school until the swelling in his face subsided.

"Okay, Desmond," I said. "I'm listening."

I inched back, hand wrapped around the canister of mace, thumb resting on the trigger.

"It wasn't just me kissing you that night. Don't tell me it was."

I wondered about the neighbors in the duplex below—Dr. and Dr. Griffin, husband and wife micro-biologists. Were they calling the cops? Summoning the courage to intervene themselves? They had to know it wasn't Tom doing the yelling. Tom's voice shrunk to a sub-whisper when he was mad. Then I remembered: the Griffins were at a conference in Montpellier. I was sup-posed to be watering their plants.

"You're right," I said. "I did. I kissed you back."

He was sober enough to sense I was stalling, drunk enough to hope it was something more. Hope was win-ning for now, but the anger was still right there, just below the surface. That had been what terrified me most about my old man. He'd go from rage to something else—laughter, tears, a coughing fit—then ricochet straight back to rage. You were never on solid ground until he'd passed out.

"We should talk," I said. "How about another drink?"

He followed me into the kitchen. Now that his guard was at half-mast, it would have been easy enough to cut his little home invasion short. There was the mace. There was a frying pan out on the stove. But part of me was thinking I'd been too quick to dismiss him. Enough of the pieces fit. Maybe he'd recommended Foolproof so that he could spy on us at will; maybe he'd set up the robbery so that he'd have a reason to make the recommendation. The impromptu press conference was a way of deflecting suspicion. Aiden's castle was a pointed clue: Desmond fancied himself an architect on par with Tom.

But then there were pieces that didn't fit too. Bill, Bickert, Tom's text warning me to keep quiet, the webcams on Tom's computer. I poured what was left of the tequila into a single shot glass and pulled the pinot grigio from the fridge. I had questions. A tanked Desmond might let the answers slip.

"Why don't we sit?" I said, heading back into the living room.

He claimed the middle cushion on the sofa. I opted for the recliner.

"What do you know about my brother?" I said it casually, like it was the prelude to a story I thought he'd enjoy.

"Paul?"

I shook my head. No surprise he'd think of Paul first: Desmond knew him through Tom. Once in a blue moon, Desmond joined them for pub night.

"Bill," I said. "My biological brother."

"Biological brother?"

Desmond didn't like having the sofa to himself. He knocked back his drink, then looked down at his empty glass like he was already tired of holding it.

"Tom never mentioned Bill?"

"No."

Of course he hadn't. Bill was a stain—something you buried under a couch cover or a throw rug.

"Or my father?"

The blank stare was back. I took a generous swallow of wine, then unleashed my whole, sad story—daddy killing mommy over a dime bag, losing Bill to Stony Brook, losing him to drugs. I wasn't telling Desmond so much as spiting his boss: *Take that, Tom. Now the world will know.* An army of Bickerts wouldn't be able to stuff this genie back in the bottle. So long as Desmond remembered come morning.

"That's horrible," he said.

He said it again and again, his face practically melting with compassion. I'd broken through to a new level of drunkenness. Desmond was ready to absorb all the world's troubles, take on the whole human condition. Big, crocodile tears. If he had anything to confess, it would come spilling out with the slightest push. I went ahead and gave him a nice, fat shove.

"You must really hate Tom," I said.

"What?"

"My husband. You must hate his guts."

It was as though I'd slapped him.

"Tom's my savior. I owe him everything."

"You want to fuck your savior's wife?"

His finger started wagging again.

"One's got nothing to do with the other."

"The heart wants what the heart wants. Is that it?"

"You and Tom are wrong for each other."

"Meaning you and I are right for each other?"

"We are."

His voice was rising again, the pendulum swinging back toward rage.

"What did you say to get him out of the house?" I asked.

"Out of the house?"

"That night, there was a call just before Tom left. Tom said something like, 'This will kill her.' The *her* was me, right? What was it you told him?"

"I don't know what you're talking about."

"You never do. Maybe we aren't right for each other after all."

I could have stopped then. There was nothing more I needed to know. Desmond was a mess of a human being, but he hadn't hurt Tom. If anything, he wanted to be Tom. I was just part of the package.

"You're mean," he said—a child scolding the playground bully.

"Me? You're the one who ran over Saint Tom."

"You think I—"

"I know you did."

He was so weak, and I was so worn down. The rawest part of me had taken over. I wanted Desmond to suffer. I wanted it to be me making him suffer.

"Why would I—"

"So you could be with me. You said it yourself."

"I didn't mean . . . not like that. I—"

"You must be praying Tom doesn't wake up. Too bad the ICU is so strict about visitors or else you could slip in and give it another try. Maybe you wouldn't fuck it up this time. But then that's kind of your MO, isn't it? You're the guy who fucks things up. That's why you needed a savior in the first place. That's why the idea of you and me together is such a joke."

Desmond stood, gathered himself like a gored bull, then looked down at Aiden's fortress and gave it a flying kick. There was an explosion of LEGOs against the far wall. Desmond, meanwhile, fell flat on his back. I pointed and laughed.

"Look at yourself. Did you really think I'd leave someone like Tom for someone like you?"

He made it back to his feet. For a second he seemed almost sober.

"I feel sick," he said.

He was talking to himself, as if I weren't there anymore. Because for him I wasn't. I'd punctured the spell. As soon as I stopped being nice to him, the whole fantasy fell apart. I stood, set my glass on the windowsill and pulled the mace from my pocket. I didn't aim it at him, but I made sure he saw it.

"Get out, Desmond," I said. "Now."

He called me a tramp and a bitch and a whore. He called me worse. Then he ran out the door and down the stairs. I watched from the window as he collided with a parked car; fell; pushed himself up; and instead of going around the car, crawled over the hood and tumbled onto the street. Then he got back up and kept running.

# 26

I SWEPT THE LEGOs into a pile, then poured myself another glass of wine. Hard to believe it was just ten thirty. Somehow, the battles with my old man, Knowles, and Desmond had taken less than a full day. And yet I didn't feel the least bit tired.

I carried my glass into the bathroom, downed another pill, and changed into a T-shirt and sweatpants. When I was done washing up, I fetched the bottle of wine and set it next to my glass on the nightstand before turning off the lights. I climbed into bed, Tom's laptop balanced on my stomach. I wanted a little company as I drifted off. A little glimpse of what life had been like just a few short days ago.

The ambulance was parked in the bay, the cab dark and empty. At least someone was having a quiet night. I clicked over to the day room. Mara, Barry, and Vetrano again, sitting around the table, deep into a game of gin rummy—the only card game Vetrano knew how to play. The fire crew was either out on a call or up in their bunks. Mara and Barry had their backs to the camera. Vetrano looked like the bonus night shifts were wearing on him. His silver hair peaked in a cowlick, and he kept taking off his glasses, rubbing the bridge of his nose.

Mara was talking about a case from the night before, a woman who'd lost an eye when a can of whipped cream blew up in her hand. That reminded Barry of a chef who needed skin grafts after his cooking spray exploded above a gas flame. Vetrano countered with a carpenter who forgot to step out of the circle he was cutting in the floor and broke his tailbone on a marble countertop one flight down.

It went on like that for a while, the three of them trying to best each other. I shut my eyes, dipped in and out of the conversation, same as if I'd been there. Vetrano paused the game to go make himself another cup of tea.

"You hiding a spare bladder someplace, Chief?" Mara asked.

There was a lull during Vetrano's absence. My brain filled it by spinning the day's ugliest moments on a loop. *My* ugliest moments. *"Time and walls . . . I can guarantee it'll come back to bite you in the ass . . . You're the guy who fucks things up. That's why you needed a savior in the first place."* All said in the heat of action, but would I take any of it back now? Probably not. It was like Bill and I had split our old man down the middle: Bill got the dope, I got the venom.

Vetrano returned with his mug. Barry started talking. It sounded like he was picking up on an earlier thread.

"Not to be crude, but like, how rich is rich?"

"Once you get past a certain figure," Vetrano said, "it stops mattering."

"And you think he's past that figure?"

"Way past. I remember reading about it when his old man died. If you added up all the floors of all the buildings he owned, you'd have a two-thousand-six-hundred-story skyscraper."

I felt my back stiffen against the headboard. Vetrano was calm as could be, stirring his latest herbal blend with an old-school swivel straw. The card game seemed forgotten.

"That's what? Twenty-six Empire State Buildings?" Mara asked.

"Got to be worth billions," Barry said.

"Got to be bullshit," Mara said.

Vetrano blew into his mug.

"Whatever it is, it's a lot. And Tom liquidated. Every last square foot. Used the proceeds to start his foundation."

Mara snorted.

"I'm guessing there's plenty left over," she said. "The Foundation's an ego trip and a tax write-off. Those guys all have foundations."

"Not like Tom's," Vetrano said. "Listen, I'm as cynical as they come, but I've known Tina a long time—there's no yacht, no mansion in the Hamptons, no five-star hotel rooms on the Riviera. They've got a nice place, but it's nothing my cardiologist couldn't afford. Tom's the real deal."

*Daniel, Vetrano, Paul . . .* People I could trust. A dwindling list.

"Then why'd someone try to snuff him?" Mara asked.

Like me, Vetrano didn't have an answer beyond "Tom's a good guy."

Another lull. I thought maybe they'd move on, but then Barry piped back up.

"You think she gets it all? I mean if Tom doesn't make it?"

I'd have given anything to be able to see all three faces.

"Who else?" Vetrano asked.

He was starting to sound pissed. Mara and Barry let it drop. The talk turned to sports—something about

Barclay's Center outclassing Madison Square Garden. I slammed the laptop shut. Barry and Mara had given me a taste of what was in store now that Desmond had put the word out. Rubbernecking. Armchair doctors slating Tom for the morgue. Armchair detectives sending me to the gallows. Wasn't that what Barry meant when he'd asked, *"You think she gets it all?"* No better motive. With Tom gone, I could quit slumming it in a cardiologist's apartment and buy myself that trilevel brownstone. It was what the real detective thought too.

It would be easy enough to shut off the television and radio and avert my eyes when I walked past a news-stand, but I wouldn't be able to drown out those deliberately loud whispers, ignore those extra-long glances. How much of it would filter down to Aiden? How much of it would stick to him? And for how long?

And why wouldn't those fucking pills kick in?

The computer screen's blue glow seemed to linger in the room even after I'd shut the lid. I thought maybe a cop car was idling outside with its siren off and lights on. Knowles and friends creeping up on me. Just then, I felt ready to surrender. But no, the shades were drawn. The light was coming from inside the room. I sat up straighter, looked around and finally found the source: the surveillance camera above our bed was projecting onto the opposite wall. I set Tom's laptop aside, swung my legs over the edge of the bed, stopped when I saw an image begin to take shape against the exposed brick. Little by little, it came into focus. The image was me. I was kneeling over a blue tarp, leaning my weight against an anvil-shaped brick.

*Breathe, breathe, breathe . . .*

The me on the wall started to move. I watched myself topple one of the bricks, pull back the tarp. I saw myself rummaging through Bickert's pockets, digging out his keys, wallet, phone, money clip, vape pen. I watched myself lift the dead man's arm, press his thumb to the phone.

*Who the fuck are you?*

Not Desmond. No way he'd sobered up in time to pull this off.

The scene on the wall vanished, and a single line of thick, highlighter-yellow text took its place: *I'll be in touch* . . . Then darkness.

I hurled myself out of bed, ran from one end of the apartment to the other, throwing on lights, yanking camera plugs from the walls. I stopped at the front door, double- and triple-checked the dead bolt, then spun around and collapsed onto the floor, with my knees drawn to my chest.

I didn't move again for a very long time.

# 27

WHEN THE PILLS finally kicked in, they took no prisoners. I woke on the couch, one leg dangling off the side, my tongue Velcroed to the roof of my mouth. Last night's twin terrors came rushing back—Desmond lying in wait, the private late-night screening. It took me a minute to convince myself the second one was real. *I'll be in touch* . . . Who would be in touch? And for what? Was I dealing with a single stalker? A duo? A whole cabal?

I made a connection I should have seen earlier. According to Knowles, Bickert *"hired ex-cons like day laborers."* According to Samuel, there'd been someone else in the room with Bill and Bickert: *"a third guy who split before Billy called me over."* I'd been assuming that the third man belonged to Bill—that he was either Jeff or a half-baked fiend who'd bolted when things turned bad. But what if Bickert had brought along backup? An ex-con with razor-thin loyalty. Someone who wouldn't want to be found standing over a gut-shot ex-cop, or else figured Bill was about to turn the gun on him. Maybe the third guy had wound up crouching behind an abandoned appliance in that junk-ridden backyard. If he'd

been working with Bickert, he'd have known me by
sight. Maybe he sensed an opportunity when I turned
up—something he could use to bleed Tom dry. Only
you can't extort a man while he's in a coma. So Bickert's
lackey waited a day or two, then made up his mind to
come straight at me.

It wasn't an airtight theory, but the essence felt true:
my tormentor was someone from Bickert's camp. The
question was how to find out which cons Bickert hired.
It wasn't like he'd have kept records—the whole point
was to avoid a paper trail. I couldn't have Daniel go back
to his uncle: it was one thing to ask for the name of
a parole officer, another thing altogether to ask for the
arrest reports of a former cop. Knowles, however, would
have them at his fingertips. If I was right, if the witness to Bickert's shooting was his own henchman, then
it wouldn't take Knowles long to track him down. That
video of me would become leverage: *"I've got enough to
charge you right now, so why not earn a little goodwill?
Give us your version of what happened that night."*

I told myself it could have been anyone in that room
with Bill and Bickert. It could have been no one at all—
Samuel projecting one of his own voices out into the
world. Either way, I couldn't do a thing about it. How
did that AA prayer go? Something about accepting what
we can and can't change . . . and being wise enough to
know the difference. In other words, first things first. Jeff
was a known entity. He might lead me to my brother.
My brother would know who had or hadn't witnessed
Bickert's murder.

I went into the kitchen and drank from the tap
until my tongue turned mobile. The microwave clock
said a quarter to nine. I'd slept through the hospital's
AM visiting hours. I wasn't sure I'd have gone anyway—
all the wrong people would think to look for me there.

Speaking of which . . . I parted the blinds and peered out at the street. No lurking journalists that I could see. Tom's fifteen minutes were up, at least for now. I put on a pot of coffee while I called the hospital. *"No change."* They might as well have made a recording.

There was a message from Daniel on the burner phone. No opening salutation, just, *"Here's what I know."* He knew Jeff's last name was Henriksen, that he'd given his parole officer, Toni Gilberts, an address in Howard Beach, not far from JFK—the same address listed for work and home. He knew that Jeff was required to attend sobriety counseling and couldn't leave the city without his officer's consent. Daniel also knew the charge had been manslaughter.

*Finally,* I thought. *A little something I can use.*

I showered, dressed, then pulled our largest suitcase from under the bed and filled it with whatever clothes and toiletries were at hand. Two additional things I made sure to pack: Tom's computer and Bill's sketchbook. I wasn't sure yet where I'd be staying or for how long, only that no one could know I was there. No more surprises. I needed a stable patch of ground, a home base I could keep coming back to until the horror movie was over. Assuming I was one of the characters who made it to the end.

I was locking the door behind me when I remembered the nanny cam in our car. Its two most likely viewers were either dead or in a coma, but there might be others. I went back into the kitchen and grabbed three different kinds of screwdrivers from the toolbox under the sink. I'd been wrong about the journalists: a small gaggle seemed to materialize out of the asphalt the second my foot hit the stoop. I pushed past them without saying a word; meanwhile, they snapped all the pictures they could ever want of Tom Evans's distraught wife making her break for an undisclosed location.

In the end, I didn't need any of the three screwdrivers, though by then I'd already popped out the air vents and disassembled the horn. I should have noticed right away: the entire rearview mirror had been replaced. There was a slight difference in the width, a barely perceptible sheen to the metallic rim. When you pushed on a small depression in the backing, the mirror sprung open like an eyeglasses case. The nickel-sized camera was sitting inside, locked in position by a magnetic base. I pulled it free, then set it down under one of the car's rear tires.

*   *   *

It was a perfect fall day, cloudless and crisp. I tried not to dwell on the fact that the man I was traveling to see might be the same man who'd robbed us, then blackmailed Tom and tried to kill him. Jeff might be Mr. *Shhh*. Mr. *I'll be in touch*. He might be all of the above, but what mattered most was that he might also be the man who was holding or harboring Bill. At the very least, I felt certain he knew where Bill was hiding.

Traffic was unusually calm. Part of me wanted to blow past my exit and keep on driving. I saw myself hitting the brakes in some dustbowl town, dyeing my hair bloodred, getting a job as a waitress, flirting with truckers to bolster my tips. It's what women on the lam did in films and pulp novels. But then, someone always found them—usually a hunky detective who promised silence in exchange for a few answers. Later, when they were done talking, the heroine would watch him walk away, knowing her future was finally her own. A fresh start didn't sound so bad. If it weren't for Aiden, maybe I really would have kept driving. Knowles didn't qualify as hunky, but I'd have loved to see the back of him once and for all.

My GPS led me into the thick of the neighborhood via the kind of short and crooked blocks that most maps omit. There wasn't any house at the address, just an A-frame garage with a top-floor apartment sitting beside a large dirt lot covered in weeds and dotted with cars that appeared abandoned but were probably customers waiting their turn. The garage door was rolled open. Inside, a man in overalls stood hunched over the engine of a vintage white-and-tan pickup. The overalls surprised me: I would have imagined they'd feel too much like a jumpsuit. A placard on the sidewalk out front read "Jeff's Automotive."

I kept coasting down the street, past a scattering of windblown, slapdash houses, the roofs looking like they might slide right off. One yard featured a plaster statue of the Virgin Mary, another an assortment of rotting boat parts. But it was quiet here. Almost soundless. As far as I could tell, Jeff Henriksen was the only soul stirring.

I circled back around, parked near the corner, three doors down from the garage. I didn't want Jeff getting a close look at my car. For a while, I just stood across the street, watching him. It was nice being the lurker for a change. He had his back to me, his head buried under the hood of that pickup. A tinny radio was tuned to a classic rock station, the DJ promising an uninterrupted block of '60s hits on the other side of a short commercial break. I kept one eye on the upstairs window, half expecting Bill's face to materialize. If I were him, I'd feel safe enough up there, looking out on this rustic-seeming back alley. It felt as hidden away as any dustbowl town.

I could have called Jeff's name from where I was standing, but figured it would be better to come at him through the side office. A bell sounded when I opened the glass door. It wasn't much of an office—more like a plywood cubicle fitted with a badly dented metal desk and a couple of folding chairs. The air stunk of gasoline. The desk was clear except for a stack of business cards and a bowl of chocolates shaped like old Model Ts.

The man I assumed was Jeff peered at me through a second glass door and signaled that he'd need a minute. I turned to the laminated article hanging on the wall behind the desk. It was a human-interest piece from a local paper. The human of interest was Jeff—an ex-con getting his life together, plying the trade he'd learned inside, and giving back to the community. For him, giving back meant coaching baby boxers at a youth club and delivering the occasional scared-straight speech at public junior highs.

The article seemed to suggest that Mr. Henriksen never should have been arrested in the first place. He'd been goaded into a bar fight by a local thug looking to prove himself. If the single punch he'd thrown had landed a centimeter to the left or right, the thug would have lived. The cops might not even have been called. But according to the judge, an up-and-coming pro boxer should have known better than to lose his temper with a civilian. So Jeff spent what was left of his twenties and all of his thirties locked in a cell with my old man.

"Sorry, wasn't at a place where I could stop straight away."

I turned, got my first up-close look at the newly minted ex-con.

"What can I do for you?" he asked.

He was a decade younger than my father, his wavy hair not quite shoulder length but longer than Sing Sing regulation. There were a few gray strands mixed in with the blond. He was shorter than I'd pictured—a featherweight who kept himself slim and sleek long after his glory years were gone. And he was handsome, with high cheekbones and deep smile lines. I'd seen him before in one of Bickert's surveillance photos. He'd been the guy sitting on a park bench with Bill and another smackhead.

"Wasn't sure you were open for business," I said.

"What else would I be open for?"

His smile was eager, almost childlike.

"I tried calling," I said. "Couldn't get through."

"You must have the old number. That was—what's the word?—provisional. I've got my forever line now."

He pointed to an old-fashioned wall-mounted phone hanging beside the interior door.

"I guess I'll shell out for a mobile one someday," he said. "For now, I don't trust any device that knows more about you than you know about it."

He lifted a business card off the stack and passed it to me.

"Take a chocolate too," he said. "Handmade by a friend of mine. A gift to help me launch my shop."

"Thanks, J. R.," I said.

That earned me a second look. I gestured to the article.

"Seems like you're proud of being an ex-con."

"I'm not hiding from it. Want to tell me who you are?"

His look was hard, but not hardened. If I'd had to guess, I'd have said that the article on the wall hewed close to the truth. Jeff wasn't a natural-born criminal—just a fighter with lousy judgment outside the ring.

"What I want is to see my brother."

"Your brother?"

I decided to bluff.

"My old man told me he's with you."

"And who's your old man?"

"Come on, J. R. Fifteen years in an eight-by-ten cell? I may not want to admit it, but there's a resemblance."

"Yeah, I see it. Tina, right? Hell, I feel like I'm your damn uncle."

My expression told him he wasn't.

"You saw your dad?"

"I had to," I said. "Bill's missing."

"Bill's your brother, right? Your dad had some of his drawings hanging in the cell."

Every *dad* stung like a landed jab. I was pretty sure he meant them to.

"Cut the shit," I said. "Is he upstairs?"

"Who?"

"Stop asking questions you know the answer to."

"There's nobody upstairs."

"But you know where Bill is."

"I didn't say that."

"No, my old man did."

"Yeah, huh?"

His grin reminded me of Knowles. It said we were playing a game—a kind of exhibition game where the result was worked out in advance, and not to my favor.

"Bill's in trouble," I said. "My father sent him to you."

"I'm out six months. You think I'm going anywhere near trouble?"

A line that might have been convincing if the delivery weren't so weak.

"I didn't say what kind of trouble."

"Doesn't matter. Acting on your dad's behalf would violate my parole. Right now, my one and only aim in life is to stay free."

All of which was strictly true, but it was truth covering for a lie.

"That's why you've convinced Bill not to talk to me. Not to talk to anyone."

"Look, I've had enough of people's accusations. I don't know why you think your brother's here, but—"

"Is he clean? At least tell me that much."

"I don't—"

"He must be. No way you'd risk your parole otherwise. And if you hadn't taken him in, he'd have come straight to me. How long's it been since his last fix?"

"I don't know what you're talking about. And I've got work to get back to."

*Fuck me.* I was getting emotional. I missed Bill. Not the drama. Not the heartache. Just Bill. My brother.

"Did he tell you what he'd remembered?" I asked. "About his childhood? The thing that sent him to our old man in the first place."

He let his head drop. He was going for exasperated, but it looked more like he was keeping something to himself.

"Break's done," he said.

Once his back was turned, I grabbed two fistfuls of chocolates and stuffed them in my jacket pockets. I had a feeling I'd be hunkered down in my car for a while. My first ever stakeout.

# CHAPTER

# 28

From my vantage point, I could just make out the curve of Jeff's backside as he stood huddled over the pickup's engine. The garage's interior was cut off from view, but if I parked any closer, he'd spot me the second he turned around. I kept one eye trained on the upstairs window. So far, not so much as a passing shadow.

*Come on, Bill. Take a peek. You must be bored to tears up there.*

Hours went by. If nothing else, Jeff was a nose-to-the-grindstone worker. He'd moved the pickup onto the grass lot, replaced it with a rust-colored coupe, then replaced the coupe with a circa 1970s minivan. As far as I could tell, he didn't even stop for potty breaks. Meanwhile, my passenger seat was littered with chocolate wrappers. I'd promised myself I'd save a few for Aiden, but then I discovered Jeff's buddy had ruined them with almonds. Aiden told me once that nuts were made of wood. *"It's why they taste like pencils,"* he'd said.

I entertained myself by exploring New York City's FM dial, the volume set slightly above audible. Wherever I landed, I tried to imagine who else might be listening in the middle of the day. Classical: an old woman shuffling around her vintage 1950s kitchen, cutting up a sandwich and tossing bits of cucumber to her corgi. Country: a teenager working retail, cursing his middle-aged boss for playing hillbilly music all shift long. News: taxicab drivers and business types in waiting rooms.

I tuned into Jeff's classic rock station, thinking it might help me meditate on the man. He'd stuck by our father for all those years. Maybe even straightened him out. Was Jeff helping my brother now? Somehow, I couldn't see Jeff as anything but a villain. Maybe I resented him for fixing my old man when I couldn't. I'd been a kid, but that didn't matter: my brain wouldn't let me off the hook. Now, possibly, he was fixing Bill. Something I hadn't been able to do at any age.

For roughly ten minutes, it rained so hard that I couldn't hear the radio. Then the sun broke through, and the clouds were gone. A crow celebrated by screaming its lungs out from a perch atop Jeff's garage. Maybe it was trying to tell me something: *He whom you seek lies within.* Maybe it was warning Bill against me.

\* \* \*

The chocolates did a surprisingly good job of staving off hunger, but eventually my bladder got the better of me. I drove to a diner on Cross Bay Boulevard, used the facilities, then ordered a meatball hero and a side of onion rings. I took a half booth in the back by the coatracks and checked the burner phone for messages. Nothing. I made another fruitless call to the hospital, then had a quick chat with Paul. He put Aiden on the phone.

"Mommy, you'll never guess . . ."

My plate was clear by the time he'd finished filling me in. I told him I loved him, but the line was already dead: he'd said what he had to say.

I came up with a new plan. I'd head back to the garage in a few hours. According to Jeff's business card, his shop was open until seven PM. I hoped he might step out after work, either alone or with my brother in tow. If they were together, I'd run straight for Bill and drag him away by the ear. If Jeff left alone, I'd wait until he was out of sight, then ring the bell, kick the door, throw rocks at the window. I'd call in a wellness check if I had to. Whatever it took to get my brother out of there. If Jeff stayed in for the evening, then I wasn't sure what I'd do. I'd have to take it a step at a time, see how the mood struck me.

I had ninety minutes left to kill. I cruised around, filled the tank, checked into a motel near JFK—the blandest, most block-like one I could find. The fact that it had indoor parking was a bonus. Just to be extra safe, I paid cash up front and gave my foster name— Tina Davidson—the one people were least likely to know. The name turned out to fit nicely: the hotel's flower-themed wallpaper and liberal use of lavender Febreze reminded me of the motels we stayed in during the only extended road trip I'd ever taken with the Davidsons, a three-day excursion to Niagara Falls. We spent most of it in the car, though Mr. Davidson and I did go for one morning hike, just the two of us. I remember lying on a dry and shady outcropping and listening to a nearby waterfall. Mr. Davidson said something like *"Don't you find it peaceful here?"* But he was really asking, *"Does this help? Is it quieter now inside your head?"* I didn't know how to answer, so I just said yes.

I tucked Tom's laptop and Bill's sketchbook into the extra towels stacked on a shelf outside the bathroom, then headed back down to the car. Jeff's Auto was only a mile away. I stopped at a convenience store to stock up

on energy bars and bottles of iced coffee—bladder be
damned.

*   *   *

I got there just in time to see Jeff fumbling with his keys
outside the office door. He was calling it a night fifteen
minutes early—privilege of being your own boss. I drove
past, head turned to the side, and made a slow tour of
the surrounding blocks. By the time I got back, the place
was locked down tight. I took the same spot I'd had
before, cut the engine, and resumed waiting.

The neighborhood didn't get any livelier after dark.
There were lights on in some of the cockeyed houses,
but no activity on the street. Jeff had blacked out the
front-facing window above the garage with what looked
like the kind of blanket movers use. The window hadn't
been covered before. I tried not to make too much of it:
given where he'd spent the last fifteen years, he had every
right to be wary of prying eyes. At night, with the tiny
apartment lit up, he'd feel like he was back on display.
He'd imagine COs patrolling the street below, aiming
their flashlights into his living room.

Then again, maybe he had something to hide.

*   *   *

I didn't have long to wait—just long enough for Jeff
to down a bowl of ramen noodles and run some gel
through his hair. He appeared from behind the far side
of the garage, wearing a faded bomber jacket, blue jeans,
and high-top Converse All-Stars. It might have been
the same outfit he wore to high school in the nineties.
I expected him to take one of the cars from the lot, but
when he reached the pavement, he turned so his back
was to me, and kept walking, away from the boulevard
with all the shops and public transportation.

Apart from the odd bodega and laundromat, I couldn't imagine the rest of the neighborhood being anything but residential. The article on his office wall suggested Jeff was native to the area. Maybe he was going to visit a friend or a family member. Somehow, I hadn't imagined him having a family before. Maybe Mama Henriksen lived around the corner. Maybe she had a little room in her basement that was just perfect for Bill. She might not even know she had a lodger. I hadn't thought of that before either—the possibility that Jeff might be stashing Bill off campus.

I decided to follow him. Not on foot—he might have turned around and spotted me. Instead, I let him get a full block ahead, then coasted to the corner when he crossed the street. It was easy enough to lag behind in this semi-abandoned enclave of the borough—no drivers laying on their horns in back of me, plenty of spaces to pull into if Jeff seemed to feel my presence.

As it turned out, he wasn't going far. He made a right followed by a left and another right. For a second I thought I'd lost him, but then I saw where he must have gone; there were only four buildings on the block, one of them a pub. The remaining storefronts were all shuttered behind metal grates.

I pulled over, waited a beat, then got out and took a leisurely stroll past the window. Peering between the neon beer signs, I saw maybe a half-dozen patrons, all male, sitting a stool or two apart around the bar. Locals with a capital L. The type who made a nightly ritual of the short stumble home. Spider-veined noses and S-shaped spines. Pants that quit above the ankle, stretched-out sweatshirts in bargain-bin colors. Jeff was Cary Grant by comparison. He'd only been there a minute, but already he was holding court, laughing and gesturing and looking everyone in the eye. Jeff Henriksen had fought at Madison Square Garden. He had those glory days to look back on, even if now this was the only adoring crowd he could muster. Even if the venue was small and dank and mostly empty. Even if he was violating his parole by frequenting an establishment that served alcohol. The kind of place where he'd once killed a man. Maybe the same place.

While all heads were pointed his way, I took out my phone, pressed it against the glass, and snapped a flurry of photos. A little leverage, just in case.

CHAPTER

# 29

I DROVE BACK TO Jeff's garage. For a while, I just sat in the car out front, frozen by a simple fear: *What if Bill really was up there?* What was I hoping for, exactly? An explanation? An apology? I hadn't so much as prepared an opening line. I couldn't seem to come up with one now that wasn't knee-jerk and full of rage. *Thanks for the pending accessory charge. So glad you and Pop are besties. Ghosting me was a nice touch. By the way, was it you who put my husband in a coma? And what was it that Alden made you remember?*

So many questions, no idea what I'd do with the answers. Suppose Bill had become our old man's puppet? Suppose it was his foot on the gas? No more convincing myself that, beneath all the damage, Bill was a good and gentle soul. Goodness and gentleness wouldn't matter anymore. It wouldn't be a question of forgiving or condemning—it would just be the end. No way forward. My brother existing out there in the world, but not for me.

I stood on the curb, staring up at the attic window, willing Bill to pull back that blanket and give a little wave. Nothing. Not even a shimmer.

I walked around to the side of the garage Jeff had emerged from earlier. There wasn't any asphalt path here—just an ankle-high trail through the weeds. A bank of unwieldy shrubs separated the garage from the fenced-off lot. Luxury real estate for rats. The splintering side door wouldn't do much to keep them out once the weather turned cold. I wondered who'd put this work–home setup together. Parents? Siblings? The gang at the bar? Maybe Jeff had money left over from his prize fights. Maybe he planned to build his forever home on the adjacent lot. And a family to go with it.

At least the bell was new, installed by or for Jeff. I rang it four times: long, short, long, long. It was a code Bill and I had used my senior year of college, when he spent a week on the futon in my off-campus apartment. Another story with a dismal end: my roommate's ten-speed racing bike went missing the day he left. Bill swore it wasn't him. My roommate wasn't convinced. Neither was I. The replacement sucked up all my funds and cost me a summer trip to Rome.

No answer. I rang again. Then I tried the knob. It rattled but wouldn't turn. I stepped back, started to call Bill's name, stopped when I saw there was no window on this side of the garage. I gave the door a few aggressive knocks.

"Come on, Bill," I said. "I know you're in there."

Except I didn't know. And Alden was right: I wasn't built for not knowing. I pictured Bill standing on the opposite side of the door, praying I'd slink away. Maybe for good. That image coupled with the sweep of the last forty-eight hours pushed me right up to the edge. I kept hearing all the little things people had said along the way—the earworms I couldn't erase. *Your husband's been in an accident . . .* *Attempted homicide, for now . . .* *He's rich as fuck, and he knows people . . .* *Secrets are a big red flag in any family . . ." "Got my first parole hearing in forty-nine short days . . ." "This will kill her . . ." "She's hiding in one of the trees . . ." "It wasn't just me kissing you . . ." "You think she gets it all?"*

*"SHUT THE FUCK UP!"*

I didn't realize until afterward that I'd yelled it out loud. Anyone watching would have thought the voices were ganging up on me. I launched a series of running kicks at the door. Shoddy as it looked, it wouldn't give. I backed away, stood with my hands on my knees, storing up energy to go at it again. That was when I spotted them—a pair of white, high-top sneakers sticking out from under the bushes, framed by the light from a nearby streetlamp.

*Please, God, not Bill.*

I whipped around. The sneakers were moving now. The man was on his feet.

He lowered a shoulder, propelled himself forward, sent me ricocheting off that immoveable door. I landed on my hands and knees, turned my head in time to catch a quick glimpse before he disappeared around the back corner.

For the second time in two days, I had the mace out and ready. I pushed myself up, started after him, felt my right knee buckle. Cursing, I reached out and palmed the wall. For a while I just stood there, frozen. Then I leaned down, rubbed my knee. It wasn't shattered—just locked and bruising. It didn't occur to me until later that the locking may have saved my life.

I pulled out my phone, swiped on the flashlight, and hobbled over to the shrubs. I spotted it right away—a green, logo-less baseball cap speared on an overgrown branch. Same make and model as the ones the fake movers who robbed us wore. No such thing as coincidence. My mind went straight to degrees of separation. One of the thieves for hire had business with Jeff; Jeff knew my old man; my old man learned of his daughter's Fortune 500 husband through Bill.

Any doubt I'd had about my father pulling the strings was gone. Robbing us hadn't been enough for him—he wanted to blackmail us into bankruptcy. He wanted to destroy the daughter who'd abandoned him. But the blackmail scheme had gone terribly wrong. An ex-cop had been shot and killed, and their target was in a coma. So why was one of the robbers lying in wait outside Jeff's garage? Had the grunt workers been stiffed? Were they coming around now to collect?

A ball cap was nice, but a driver's license or a library card would have been better. No way I'd be able to ID him on my own. He'd blurred by so fast, he might as well have been wearing a mask. But he was tall. I'd caught that much. A good half foot taller than Bill.

*So what's next, Nancy Drew?*

I wasn't in any mood for a soak in the motel bathtub. I got back in the car, my knee throbbing but functional, made a sharp three-point turn, then headed back to that shitty little bar.

\* \* \*

Jeff wasn't there, but that didn't stop me from making a scene. It would have been impossible not to. Any entrance by a female would have landed as an event. The crowd was down to four cirrhotic men and the bartender. The place was tiny, bare bones. No music. Not even a muted TV.

"Is Jeff here?" I asked.

It was a simple enough question, but they glanced around at one another as though they were hopelessly lost. I stood waiting for them to reach a consensus. It wasn't a pleasant wait. The air hovered around ninety percent humidity, most of it beer. I had a feeling that whatever I touched, my hand would come away sticky.

"You his girlfriend?"

This from a man in a purple sweatshirt fronted by a glitter-encrusted stag's head. I ignored him, spoke to the bartender as though his flock didn't exist.

"Is he here?" I asked.

The bartender opened his arms wide in a gesture that meant, *What you see is what you get.*

"We're just his first stop on the tour, hon."

I let the *hon* pass.

"What's his second stop?"

"Couldn't say. He doesn't give me his itinerary."

I left to a chorus of invitations: to stay a while, to have a drink on the house, to come back soon, to set out for a midnight sail across Flushing Bay—provided I had a boat. Jeff kept world-class company. A roomful of wasters and my old man.

*             *             *

I wasn't about to search out every bar within walking distance. Easier to plant myself where I knew he'd end up eventually. I made another pit stop at the diner and grabbed a cheese Danish to go on my way out. My diet of late left a lot to be desired—namely, nutrients.

This time I parked right in front of the garage. Still no lights on upstairs. I got out, leaned on the bell hard enough and long enough to feel confident no one was home. I wasn't worried about my old man's lackey hiding in the bushes—I figured he'd stay away for a while on the off chance I'd called the cops.

I got back in the car, washed down the Danish with eight ounces of lukewarm ice coffee while half listening to an episode of *This American Life*. It had to do with identical twins, one a morbidly obese chain smoker, the other a pro athlete. The pro athlete contracted cancer and died at the age of fifty-eight. Two decades later, the morbidly obese brother was still smoking, still going strong. The irony might have been compelling if it weren't for my mind flitting all over the map. The question I kept coming back to: What the hell was I doing sitting outside Jeff's Auto in the dead of night? It wasn't like Jeff posed a flight risk. I knew where he'd be tomorrow morning, and the morning after that. So what was it that couldn't wait? Did I think he'd return home with my brother in tow? Did I think a liquored-up Jeff would be more likely to spill his guts? Turn on my old man?

Maybe, but there was more to it than that. Somehow, being here, I felt close to Bill. Driving away would be like letting go, and I was determined to cling tight for as long as my grip would hold.

*   *   *

Jeff turned up at a little after midnight, braying and slobbering. His words weren't words—just long, guttural syllables. If it weren't for a well-placed lamppost, he'd have found himself crawling the last half-block to his door. Desmond had been pleasantly buzzed by comparison.

It was good of Jeff to hand me this kind of leverage. The photo from the bar might have earned him a slap on the wrist, but this display of public drunkenness could land him back inside. I stepped out onto the sidewalk and got a solid two minutes of footage before he'd advanced a yard. He had no idea I was there. I moved closer, waited for him to pass under the next streetlight. I wanted a clear shot of his face.

I wasn't more than five feet away when he finally spotted me, or at least spotted someone—someone he couldn't quite squint into focus.

"Hey there, Jeff," I called. "Thanks for being in my movie."

He jabbed a finger in my direction like he thought he might make contact. Then he collapsed onto all fours and started vomiting. I climbed back into the car and drove off. I'd pay him another visit in the morning, armed with the name and number of his parole officer. I'd be the icing on his hangover.

# CHAPTER

# 30

I CRANKED UP THE AC just for white noise, crawled under the blankets from both beds, sandwiched my head between two fat pillows, and shut my eyes. "No one knows you're here," I whispered. It helped. I drifted off in no time and didn't wake again until the alarm on my phone started ringing. Six uninterrupted hours felt like a month's R&R.

Two things hit me when I stepped out of bed: the ice-box air and a solid block of pain where my right knee should have been. I hopped over to the AC—bracing myself against the nightstand, the second bed, the fake-oak dresser—and switched it off. A few slow laps around the room, and the pain started to subside, the knee to bend. Before long, I was down to a barely perceptible limp. I took that as a promising omen for the day.

I wasn't in any rush. Officially, Jeff's Auto didn't open until ten, and given the shape he'd been in last night, anything earlier than noon seemed optimistic. I ate the last of the energy bars while the tub filled, then settled in for a long soak. Submerged up to my neck, I realized it wasn't just my knee that had stiffened. From head to toe, I was a collection of knots, pulls, and dull aches. When I rolled my neck, the crack was loud enough to startle me. I discovered a knob of bone at the base of my spine that I felt pretty sure hadn't been there before. Even the soles of my feet were radiating pain. I shut my eyes, concentrated on letting all that tension ooze out into the water, imagined it swirling down into the New York City sewer system as soon as I yanked the plug.

*    *    *

Still only nine AM. I fueled up at a Starbucks, took a small table by the window, and considered how I'd make my final run at Jeff. I could go fire and brimstone—walk in without saying a word, shove my phone in his face, and press "Play," then pull it back and mouth the words *Parole Officer Gilberts.* Or I could hold the threat in reserve, show up with twenty ounces of coffee and a bottle of Motrin, give him a hug, and call him Uncle Jeff. Maybe it was the solid sleep followed by a warm bath, but option two had the greater appeal. It also seemed the most likely to work: Jeff had spent the last fifteen years staring down threats, but when was the last time someone other than my old man had shown him a little kindness? I went back to the counter, ordered a titan-sized dark roast and a side of cream.

On the quick drive over, I felt my penchant to play good cop wavering. If our old man was the mastermind, then Jeff was his eyes and ears on the ground—more project manager than Bill's guardian angel. Part of Jeff's job was to double down on my old man's lies. *"It's your sister who doesn't give a shit about you. She's got that kind of money, and you're bunking in a squat? But then it's always been that way—you in juvie, her living the suburban dream. You're only taking what you're owed."* Followed by promises to plug up all the long-standing holes in Bill's life. *"It'll be you and your old man once he's back on the outside."*

*"You're writing another script, Teen."*

It was a line Mr. Davidson used whenever my imagination got the worst of me, whenever I couldn't find my way out of a doomsday scenario. *"But none of that's happened, Tina,"* he'd say. *"You're writing another script."*

My impulse to guess the tragic ending was the reason I'd never make it as a real detective. Real detectives wait for the facts to emerge. As a paramedic, everything you need to know is laid out by the time you show up. No thinking—straight to action or someone's life tanks. Maybe that's what Tom meant when he said there were easier ways to chase an adrenaline high: I shouldn't need the equivalent of a five-car pileup to pull me out of my own head. Of course, there was more to it than that. The drive to be there for other people was genuine. So was the camaraderie at the station, no matter what Barry and Mara said. But there was something else too. An escape from the ghosts—from all the little core traumas my own brain might churn up if I gave it the room.

Pulling onto Jeff's block, it took me a second to remember that I wasn't on call. The street had been cordoned off. The other side of the cordon looked like a showroom for emergency vehicles—fire trucks of varying sizes, twin ambulances, multiple squad cars. The last spark had been put out. The firefighters were making final inspections, storing away their gear. The paramedics lingered in case one of the firefighters tripped and hurt themselves or else came down with delayed onset smoke inhalation. The cops in uniform were handing off to the cops in plainclothes. No need for crowd control in this neck of the woods—if there'd been any onlookers, they'd given up by now.

It was hard to see what the detectives hoped to investigate. All that remained of Jeff's Auto was a charred garage and the blackened frame of an SUV. A single concrete beam still reached as high as the second story, but the apartment itself had collapsed onto the main floor.

What were the chances Jeff, seeing double and tripping over his own feet, had made it out alive? Unless maybe someone had been there to help him.

I jumped out of the car, fumbled through my wallet, pulled out my ID, and sprinted up to the police tape. This wasn't my beat. There weren't any faces I recognized, no one I could call out to by name. I waved my arms at the nearest firefighter. He came lumbering toward me. The soot must have added five pounds to his uniform. I told him who I was, where I worked.

"Jeff Henriksen is my father's oldest friend," I said. "I drove out from Brooklyn when I heard. Do you know if Jeff was hurt? My father's losing his mind."

He shrugged.

"Can't say for sure. Don't have names yet."

"Names?"

"Two bodies. Both DOA."

I put his lack of sugarcoating down to respect for my profession. And exhaustion.

"Beyond recognition?"

He nodded. I watched him amble back toward his truck. Two bodies. It didn't hit me until I was locked in my car with the windows shut tight. Still, heads turned. A decibel that would have shattered concrete. I peeled away before anyone could come save me.

The driving seemed to happen by itself. Then, suddenly, I was back in the hotel parking garage, slumped forward, steering wheel digging into my stomach, sobs echoing like a car alarm.

"I'm sorry, Bill. I'm so sorry."

I said it over and over, like breathing. Like being sorry was the only way for me to stay alive.

# 31

THE NEXT TWENTY-FOUR hours are mostly a blank. I know I thought about going home. *Let him come for me like he came for Bill,* I told myself. *Whoever he is.* Maybe he was already there, waiting. The only thing that stopped me was inertia. Rolling from my side onto my stomach was the most I could manage.

I'm not sure what made me answer the call. I'm not sure why I felt a quick jolt of hope when I heard the burner phone ring. A cruel hope, it turned out: it was Knowles on the other end. *All right,* I thought. *Let* him *come for me.* I sat up a little, looked around the room at my final taste of freedom. With the shades drawn and the lights out, I couldn't see much. There was a sour smell I knew came from my own breathing. Maybe the transition to a cell wouldn't be so hard.

"Where are you?" Knowles asked.

Meaning he knew where I wasn't. Meaning he'd been to the apartment.

"Queens," I said.

It was the first syllable I'd spoken in a day.

"Now there's a coincidence," he said.

"Coincidence?"

"Maybe you heard about a fire out in Howard Beach? Arson. Two people dead."

His tone was flat, affectless. Cold, even for him. Did he think I'd struck the match? Could I blame him if he did?

"Yes," I told him. "I heard."

"Small world, isn't it? Your father's long-time cell-mate and one of Bickert's felons."

*One of Bickert's felons.* I chased the phrase around my mind, trying to make sense of it. I repeated it back to him as a question.

"A man named Jacob Lowry. Charged with deal-ing and armed robbery, but never convicted. Bickert arrested Lowry almost twenty years ago, back when he was still working a regular beat with Vice. Evidence went missing. The case didn't make it to trial. Bickert's MO."

I'd been so certain. The possibility of the second DOA being anyone but Bill hadn't so much as flitted across my consciousness. All my faculties came rushing back. I was suddenly very hungry. Very awake. I stood up. The aching in my leg felt like something other than pain. I went to the window, slid the curtain open. The sun sent my head spinning.

"I guess it really is a small world," I said.

"Yeah, but it's still a confusing one. I need you to come in and answer a few questions."

Bill was alive. I'd been handed a new lease. Every-thing seemed possible again.

"I can't answer them by phone?"

"The phone works for little questions. The questions I have aren't little. Bickert connects to your husband and brother. Lowry connects to Bickert. I get that much. But your father's recently sprung cellmate? Now I'm out of my depth."

"I don't know anything about Lowry. I barely know anything about Bickert or Henriksen. Have you talked to my father?"

"I'm driving back from Sing Sing now. I can't say he was very helpful."

"Did you think he would be?"

"No, but for different reasons. He didn't know Jeff was dead before I told him. He lived with the man day and night for fifteen years. That's like a marriage. Two marriages, in my case. I'm as cynical as they come, but your old man wasn't faking. He did everything but claw his eyes out."

*Maybe he'll have calmed down by the time I get there.* My mind was back on Bill's sketchbook—on the only phone number he'd bothered to record. Jeff could have told me where to find my brother. And if Jeff could have told me, then I had no doubt he'd told my old man.

"Where are you?" Knowles asked. "I can come to you."

The truth—*In a hotel room, a mile from the latest crime scene*—would have sounded very bad. But Knowles didn't suspect the truth. He suspected something else.

"You think I'm with Bill. You think Bill killed Jeff and this Lowry."

"Why would I think that, Mrs. Evans?"

*Because you asked for my location twice. Because your voice gave you away just now. You don't want me to come in—you want to know where I've got Bill stashed. And it won't be you who shows up—it'll be a swarm of patrol cars looking to pen my brother in.* The NYPD tech geeks must have been having trouble tracing the call. Or else they'd already traced it, and Knowles was hoping to catch me in a lie.

"You're dead wrong," I said. "Until you told me about Lowry, I'd assumed Bill was the second victim in that fire."

"That isn't what I meant," Knowles said. "I'm asking if—"

"It's time to make our relationship official, Detective. I'll come in with my lawyer. As long as she thinks it's a good idea."

"Mrs. Ev—"

I ended the call and switched off my phone. I didn't know if I had a legal leg to stand on, but I didn't care as long as I'd bought some time.

The bigger picture was coming into focus. Lowry was the link—the piece that connected Bickert and my old man. The fact that Lowry, who worked for Bickert, and Jeff died side by side was a final bit of proof. With Bickert gone and Tom out of commission, the blackmail scheme crumbled. But the hired guns in the green baseball caps still wanted their cut. Maybe they'd been promised a percentage of the payday that never came. They couldn't get it out of Jeff or Lowry, and there was no point going after Rick Morgan while he was still inside. That left Bill. The question that scared me most: Had Jeff, in a last-ditch effort to save his own life, told *them* where to find my brother?

The whole tortured plan had spun out of my old man's control. He might want to hurt me, but never Jeff. Knowles was right about that much. I doubted my old man would want to hurt Bill either. My father saw Bill as an extension of himself—the tragic soul he might have been if his life as a civilian had gone unchecked.

My old man would know now that Bill was in danger. Real danger. And with Jeff dead, my so-called father would need a fresh helper. Someone who could protect his son without locking him away. As far as I knew, I was the only volunteer.

\* \* \*

I parked at the Metro-North station and walked from there. Circumstances aside, I couldn't help but think again that Ossining would be a nice enough place to live. Wide, tree-lined streets, Victorian storefronts, a backdrop of rolling hills, glimpses of the river. There were rumors the prison might close. Maybe I really could get Tom to put in a bid. I imagined him converting the grounds to some kind of educational paradise for disaffected youth—like Stony Brook, but gentler, and without the stigma. We'd finish raising Aiden on a riverfront acre just a few miles outside town. That is, if Tom was ever Tom again. If we were ever us again.

The prison gates put an end to any daydreams. It was hard to believe I'd been standing in this same spot just forty-eight hours ago. So much had happened since. My six-year-old son had been interrogated by a cop shrink. I'd been treated to a private screening in my bedroom. My husband's lackey had broken into my home and propositioned me. A fake mover had sent me barreling into a wall. Two other men had been murdered. It made me wonder what the next forty-eight had in store.

\* \* \*

It was the same slow slog through security. The same epic wait in the same musty antechamber, surrounded by what might have been the same bored faces. A different CO led me to the visitation area. This time, my old man was there ahead of me. His skin was blotchy, the whites of his eyes mostly red. Nothing like twenty years ago. There hadn't been any tears when he looked over at me from the back of that squad car.

"I'm sorry," I said.

"For what? Hating my guts?"

"I'm sorry about Jeff."

"You make the trip out here to console me?"

"I know you didn't mean for it to happen."

He cocked his head, leaned as far forward as the glass would allow.

"Maybe you should tell me what I did mean to happen."

He was right—after my last visit, there wasn't much point in playing nice. But there wasn't any point in bombing him with accusations either. Best to keep it simple, get what I came for and get out.

"Where's Bill?" I asked.

He raised his manacled hands.

"You think I know?"

"Yes."

"Why?"

"Because Jeff knew. And it got him killed."

"His death had nothing—"

"Bill was supposed to burn in that fire too."

He shook his head.

"You're pulling shit out of thin air."

"Am I? Jeff was one of the good ones, remember? He kept you sane and sound. Your words. He was doing the same for Bill, and now he's dead."

I didn't doubt the tears were real, but squinting at him through that fluorescent glare, all I saw was Bickert's corpse, Tom in a coma, the ruins of Jeff's Automotive.

"You're hard," he said. "Not like your brother. Not like him at all."

"That's why he needs me."

"All I wanted was for J. R. to turn my son around, get him ready for me on the outside."

"Well it didn't work. There are people hunting for your son right now."

"Yeah, I know it."

"So tell me where he is."

He gave the cuffs a rattle, made a show of looking around.

"Bill's not built for this place. He wouldn't last."

*You're the prodigal dad who sent his son on a felony spree.*

"That's not what I want," I said.

"But can you stop it?"

"I can try. I've got resources."

"A brand-new Lexus in the judge's driveway?"

"Whatever it takes."

He dropped his chin to his chest. When he lifted it back up, he looked more like the face from Bill's drawings: haunted but also hopeful.

"J. R. never gave me an address," he said, "but there's a fishing cabin on a lake not far from Bear Mountain. He used to train up there before fights. The cabin's been sitting empty since his old man died. The perfect safehouse, J. R. said. As long as Bill could keep his shit together. The days get long when you're on your own with no way to score."

"I'm sure they do," I told him.

# 32

Tom and I had gone hiking once in Bear Mountain. I remembered it being near West Point but had no idea where West Point was in relation to Ossining. I sat in the car at the train station and pulled up Google Maps on my phone. The mountain itself was just twenty-five minutes away. But then I wasn't looking for the mountain—I was looking for a lakeside cabin somewhere near the mountain.

It had been a while since I'd consumed anything more than a pastry and a chocolate bar. I took an external battery from the glove compartment and started out in search of a place to eat. I found one on Main Street, a living-room-sized café with black-and-white photos of the prison hanging on the walls, including a portrait of Old Sparky, an early twentieth-century electric chair responsible, according to a glossy plaque, for more than six hundred executions. I wondered who the local color was meant to attract: river and hills aside, Sing Sing seemed like a grim tourist destination, even for a day trip.

I bought a focaccia sandwich and a double espresso and took a seat at the back of the room, afraid that if

I sat by the window, I might somehow look up to find Knowles staring in at me. I brushed crumbs from the table, tapped *Jeff Henriksen* into Google. It seemed odd that I hadn't searched for him before, but then there hadn't been any need to while he was alive. No shortage of Jeff Henriksens in the world. There were LinkedIn profiles, Facebook profiles, Twitter accounts, YouTube videos. None of them seemed to belong to anyone over the age of twenty-five.

I tried *Jeff Henriksen, boxer.* The first few entries went to a Jeff Henriksen who bred boxer dogs in the UK. Then came something a little more promising: a win–loss record in a database that tracked fighters going back to the 1930s. Only one loss—the Mayweather bout at Madison Square Garden—and even that was a split decision. A footnote said that Jeff, like his father, had been a Golden Gloves featherweight champion; unlike his father, he'd taken the national prize—not just once, but twice: 1998 and 1999.

Beneath the footnote was a link to an article. I clicked on it and found myself in the archives of the Orange County Library system. The paper the article appeared in—*The Orange Chronicles*—was ten years defunct, the article itself scanned from an apparently damaged hard copy, the print puckered as though someone had dropped the paper in a puddle, then set it on top of a radiator to dry. An accompanying photo showed a wiry, late-teen Jeff, in shorts and gloves, standing beside a proud papa who must have been about as old then as Jeff was when he died. The photo was posed: they were standing in a clearing, woods on either side, a timber frame cabin behind them. You could almost hear the stream running in the distance.

The article touched down on all the old chestnuts. Dedication, desire, hard knocks. A father's tough love.

*"Though I never have to get too tough with Jeff,"*
*Henriksen Sr. said. "He's tough enough on himself."*

It was hard to square all that discipline and grit with a man dead in a bar fight. Jeff's father certainly hadn't seen it coming. But then the bottom's never as far from the top as it appears.

I went back to the win–loss database and clicked on a second link in the footnotes. It was a bingo of sorts. Another article from *The Orange Chronicles*, this one with a photo of Jeff jogging along a lakefront, his father lagging a step behind. The caption read: *"Part-time local celebs out for morning run around Ferril Lake."*

I opened a new window, typed *Ferril Lake New York property owners* into a search engine. It wasn't as big a long shot as I'd thought. The first hit belonged to a site called Ownership Confidential. I clicked on it. *Confidential* was a misnomer. The page listed all the residences on Ferril Lake Road. It gave the estimated value of each home, the years each had been built, and the annual taxes paid. It also gave the last name and first initial of the owner, as well as his or her age. The phone numbers and email addresses were partial; to get the full digits, you had to subscribe. Maybe that was the confidential part—your privacy protected against anyone who couldn't afford the fourteen-dollar-and-forty-four-cent fee.

I scrolled down. There were so many entries that at first I thought Ferril Lake had to be the size of a small city. Then I realized I was looking at a history of ownership for each property. Some of the homes had changed hands more than a dozen times. Some were well past their centennial. The property at 8055 Ferril Lake Road had been purchased by an R. Henriksen in 1952 for the sum of ten thousand dollars. It now belonged to J.

Henriksen and was valued at just over eighty thousand dollars. A nice eightfold return, until you noticed that the properties on either side were worth upward of a million. That small detail felt to me like confirmation that I had the right place: during the years Jeff spent on ice, his neighbors razed and rebuilt. The five-hundred-square-foot summer cabin was now the embarrassment of the block. I imagined holes in the roof, cobwebs you could see from the road. The country home counterpart of that garage in Queens.

I saved the address, unplugged my phone from the external battery, and stuffed both in my purse. Privacy might be a thing of the past, but the Information Age has its upside: I'd found what I was looking for in the time it took to eat half a focaccia sandwich.

*     *     *

Ossining was barely gone from my rearview mirror when the burner phone started vibrating. I had a sudden premonition as I dug it out of my pocket. I saw Tom with his eyes open, speaking in slow, deliberate sentences. Deliberate, but also confused. *"Where am I? Why am I so thirsty?"* Then, as objects came into focus: *"Where's Tina?"*

*Out fixing your fuckups, dear.*

But it wasn't the hospital calling—it was Paul calling from the hospital. I heard a distinct tremor in his voice.

"What is it?" I asked.

For a second, I thought the connection went dead.

"Paul?"

"It's Aiden," he said. "Something's wrong with Aiden."

# 33

I VEERED ONTO THE grass median, skidded through an about-face.

"Vomiting," Paul said. "Almost nonstop since he left school."

They were at the children's wing of Brooklyn Methodist.

*A goddamn family reunion,* I thought.

Pushing the speed limit, steering clear of the Brooklyn–Queens Expressway, I made it in just over an hour. The sun was nearly down. The twilit air seemed extra cold. Running from the parking garage to the hospital, I had the uncanny sense that I might wink out mid-stride. No winding down. No grinding to a halt. A sudden and total collapse, as though someone had snuck up behind me and flipped a switch.

But then I saw Aiden and knew right away that it wasn't so bad. He was sitting up. There was sweat on his brow and an IV in his arm, but he didn't look weak or pale. He was playing a handheld videogame—one of Paul's creations.

"They've hydrated him," Paul said. "Nothing more serious than that. Whatever it was seems to have passed."

Aiden lifted his eyes from the small screen.

"Mommy!"

He dropped the game, tried to hug me from across the room.

"Whoa, buddy," Paul said, putting a hand on his chest. "Don't forget you're plugged in here."

Aiden looked down at his arm, seemingly unimpressed.

"Can I go home now?"

I wondered which home he meant: ours or Paul's?

"I'm not sure, champ," I said. "I need to talk to a doctor first."

"But I'm fit as a fiddle."

Paul and I swapped glances—no telling where he'd gotten that one from.

"I'll be right back, okay?" I said.

"You promise?" Aiden asked.

I nodded. Paul followed me into the hall.

"I'm so sorry," he said.

"What happened?"

He shrugged.

"It had to be food poisoning. We stopped at the diner after school. He was begging me for a milkshake. It's not like he asks for one every day, so I figured why not. He threw up right there at the table, then again on the street outside. Then I got him home, and he just kept vomiting. I didn't know what to do, so I brought him here."

"I'm glad you did," I said. "Has he been sick again since you called me?"

"Just some dry heaving. Nothing in the last half hour."

"All right. Let me see if I can get him discharged."

I could, but it involved another hour of waiting. There was a second child in Aiden's room, lying on the other side of a thick, green curtain. We could hear him whimpering between low, steady moans. His mother countered by cooing to him. It made for a sad duet. We tried to distract Aiden with knock-knock jokes and childhood stories about a haunted house across the street from the Davidsons. After a while, we got on his nerves.

"Can I just play my game?" he asked.

We left the hospital with instructions to feed him tap water and Jell-O. On the way down in the elevator, Paul asked if the lobby was clear of reporters. I'd been so preoccupied with Aiden that I hadn't thought to look.

"If there were any, they didn't stop me," I said.

"They've probably moved on to the next headline."

"It's a busy city."

Which meant my reasons for avoiding Tom's bedside were growing thin. Desmond wouldn't dare show his face. Knowles didn't need to stalk the ICU waiting area anymore—he had my burner number on speed dial. And chances were good that my actual stalker—Lowry, Bickert's sidekick—had died with Jeff in the fire.

Still, I couldn't see myself back in Tom's dismal corner of the ICU, stroking his arm and pretending he could feel my touch. Hawthorne, hiring Bickert, the webcams—the fact he hadn't bothered to inform me, let alone include me, in his decision to send Bill away. All I could think was, *You did this to yourself.* And to Aiden. And to me.

\* \* \*

We went to Paul's.

"Consistency," I said. "Home will just make Aiden wonder about his dad."

That was only a partial truth. The full story: I didn't feel ready to confront whatever message Lowry might have left behind. And just in case I was wrong—in case someone other than Lowry had fixed up the castle and screened that film on my bedroom wall—I didn't want Aiden anywhere near the place.

"Still no word about Tom?" Paul asked.

"Two words: no change."

Paul's *goddamn it* was heartfelt.

"I wish I could be with him," he said.

Coming from anyone but Paul, I might have taken that as a dig at me.

We had *Babes in Toyland* cued up and ready to go, but Aiden's eyes quit fighting before the MGM lion let out its first roar. I kissed the top of his head and lifted him in my arms. He didn't feel feverish—just warm, the way only a child's body can feel warm.

"Wish I could drop off like that," I said to Paul.

"Kid's had a rough day."

He meant the food poisoning, but I wondered if there was more to the story than a bad milkshake. Was this Aiden putting me on notice? *Hey, Mom, you're fucking me up.* By the time he was old enough to say it in words, it would be too late—he'd already be sitting in front of a Menendez or an Alden, learning how to cope with whatever it was that couldn't be undone.

I tucked him in, hovered for a beat, then padded back out to the living room.

"Any beverages on offer?" I asked.

There was music playing—piano and cello, so soft I hadn't noticed at first.

"White okay?" Paul asked.

"Perfect. As long as I can crash on your futon again."

I had a thought for the motel room in Queens, but I wanted to be close by in case Aiden had a relapse, in case he woke up scared.

"I'd rather you took my room," Paul said.

"I can hear him better from out here."

"Suit yourself."

He crossed into the kitchen, came back with a bottle and two glasses. For a while, neither of us said anything. I thought we were enjoying a rare quiet moment, meditating to the music and allowing the wine to take hold. It turned out Paul was working up his nerve.

"Can I ask you something?" he said.

I nodded.

"What went wrong between you and Mom?"

Again, it took me a second to realize that he meant Mrs. Davidson.

"Nothing I can point to," I said. "She just chose cactuses over her grandson."

"Come on, Tina. That isn't fair."

"Fair has nothing to do with it. She made a decision."

"To move on with her life after her husband died?"

"That's not what I mean."

His look said, *"I'm listening . . ."*

"She never accepted me, Paul. I was always an unwelcome guest in her home."

It was worse than that. She resented me. She thought of me as the pet couples adopt so they can pay even less attention to each other.

"That's not true."

"It is."

"She took you in."

"Your father took me in."

"*Your* father?"

*Shit.* My mind flooded with all the diplomatic things I might have said: *I'll call her tomorrow. It's not that I forgot . . . life's just been such a whirlwind lately.* Too late now—the only direction left for me to dig in was deeper.

"I'm sorry," I said. "He's a hero to me. He saved me. But I think of him as Mr. Davidson. Maybe if I'd been younger—"

"Then I'm not really your brother?"

"You're family, Paul. You're—"

"Meaning I'm *like* a brother to you? You know, Dad wasn't so selfless. He was trying to give you the childhood nobody gave him. That was as much for his sake as yours."

"You mean I was his do-over?"

"No, that's not—"

"He cared. It doesn't matter why. He looked out for me. He tried to help Bill. It's not his fault that—"

I cut myself short. My God, even now, all these years later, part of me still believed that I had caused Mr. Davidson's cancer—that nothing, nobody good could ever stick to me. Tom would die, not because someone ran him over, but because I was his wife. What was in store for Aiden? I thought I'd escaped into a fairy tale. Mrs. Davidson knew better. She was right to keep clear of me.

"Teen, are you okay?"

He reached across and touched my shoulder. I wiped my eyes with the heels of my palms.

"I'm sorry," I said again. "You're one of the most important people in my life. There's you, Tom, Aiden, and Bill. That's it. No one else. No one who will still be there when my wardrobe's down to muumuus and Depends."

He tried to smile, but it came out more like he was willing himself to smile.

"I'm the one who should be apologizing," he said. "About Aiden. I should have—"

"Kids come down with things, Paul. They're like feral cats that way. There's no one I'd rather have watching over my son right now."

"You mean it?"

"Of course."

Paul stood and stretched his arms. The epic yawn was clearly intended as cover—his way of saying, *"There's more to this than we can resolve in a night."* It was unfamiliar terrain for me and Paul.

"I'm going to turn in," he said. "Let me know if you need anything."

"You too, Paul."

I watched him tiptoe down the hall, past Aiden's room. For a while I just sat there, wondering what kind of granddad Mr. Davidson would have made. Not so long ago, I was sure he'd have seen Aiden as his crowning victory—his love for me carried into a new generation. A cycle broken. Proof that misery isn't always in the genes. Now, I wasn't sure of anything.

# 34

Aiden was desperate to go to school. It hadn't even occurred to him that he might stay home.

"You're sure you feel okay?" I asked.

"We're having a treasure hunt," he said. "I can't miss our first fun day in forever."

"All right, then. You know the drill. Let's get moving."

He sprinted into the bathroom. The doctor had said it would be all right to send him so long as he didn't have another incident during the night—whatever he'd contracted, it wasn't contagious. The possibility of a fresh episode in the middle of his treasure hunt made me nervous, but routine and consistency were still my guideposts. A weekday at home would give his mind room to wonder, to come up with questions I hoped to keep at bay a while longer.

I could hear Paul working on breakfast. I decided to straighten up the guest room—even by little-kid standards, Aiden wasn't exactly orderly. And then, I wasn't anxious to be alone with Paul. We'd ended the night in a decent place, but I worried about belated recriminations, or else awkward small talk suggesting that something major had gone unsaid. I'd wait until my six-year-old buffer was done brushing his teeth.

I gathered a small library of children's books up off the floor and set them in a stack atop the waist-high dresser. I put crayons back in their box. I pulled crumpled papers from Aiden's Spiderman backpack and made a sad attempt to smooth them out with the heel of one palm. Penmanship exercises, addition exercises, an assortment of farm-related drawings. I started thinking again about how I'd make this all up to him—the poorly explained decampment, the fact that I wasn't there to help him with his homework, the fact that his father wasn't there at all. Soon, it would be time to say it out loud: *Daddy's been in an accident.* Not now, but soon. Over mint-chip ice cream with a slice of fudge at the bottom. And maybe a little mommy water for me.

I started reloading his backpack, felt some loose items rattling around at the bottom. Aiden never remembered to zip up his pencil case. I reached in, groped blindly, came away with a cap-less Crayola marker, a pair of blunt-tip scissors, a black-cat eraser the school must have given him in anticipation of Halloween . . . and something else. Something that made time stop for a beat while I tried to place it. Though I didn't have to try very hard. Not long ago, I'd stuffed my pockets with nearly identical objects. Tiny vintage cars wrapped in hand-painted foil. Chocolates, with almonds on the inside.

The nuts explained why this one had been sampled but not devoured. There was a sizeable bite missing, large enough to take out both front tires and a portion of the hood. He'd tried to rewrap the foil, then realized too late that there was no hiding what he'd done. Knowing Aiden, he'd spent a painful chunk of time failing to convince himself that the damage was barely noticeable.

I racked my brain, trying to think where I might have dropped one of those chocolates. Someplace where Aiden and I had overlapped since his discharge from the hospital. There was the short drive home, but I'd cleaned the car out, gotten on my hands and knees and searched to make sure there was no trace left of my daylong surveillance. Was it possible one had worked its way down into the recesses of the passenger seat? I didn't think so—and besides, Aiden sat in the back, cuddled up against his uncle Paul. Maybe he'd fished one out of my coat pocket while I was carrying him? Again, it seemed unlikely. I'd been hungry and jittery waiting there outside Jeff's garage. I'd eaten every last crumb, then looked around for more. I must have double-checked my pockets a dozen times.

Aiden trotted back into the room, caught me kneeling over his backpack and staring at the mangled chocolate resting in my cupped hand.

"Where did you get this?" I asked.

It came out like an accusation. Zero-to-sixty, Aiden started bawling.

"I'm sorry," he said.

"Oh, sweetie, it's okay. It's just a question. I promise."

"I did it," he said.

"You did it?"

"I'm sorry."

"What did you do?"

"I stole it."

"You stole this chocolate?"

The tears redoubled. Snot bubbled from his nose.

"I wanted to put it back, but I'd already bitten it, and then I couldn't make it look like it did before. I don't even like nuts."

"Put it back where, Aiden?"

"Does uncle Paul know?"

I looked at the open door, lowered my voice.

"You took this chocolate from Uncle Paul?"

He nodded.

"While he was in the shower. I took it off the desk where he works. I thought it was a toy."

"It's okay," I said. "You didn't do anything so terrible. Everybody gets curious."

"I'll say sorry."

He turned, started to pull away from me, heading for the kitchen.

"No, no, sweetie," I said, tugging him back. "I'll get Uncle Paul a new chocolate. This'll be our little secret."

"But you and Daddy always say—"

"I know, but this is different. Uncle Paul won't want to see you feeling bad. It will just make *him* feel bad. He probably meant to give you the chocolate anyway."

Aiden seemed to take some comfort in the idea.

"Okay," he said. "But you should get him two chocolates."

"Two?"

"One to replace the bitten one and one to say sorry."

"It's a deal," I said.

I kissed the top of his head and wiped his cheeks dry with my thumbs.

"One more question, Aiden."

"Yes?"

"When did you find this chocolate?"

"When Uncle Paul was in the shower."

"Yes, I know. But when was that? When does Uncle Paul take his showers?"

"In the morning. Before school."

"Did you find the chocolate yesterday morning?"

He furrowed his brow like he was determined to provide good intel.

"Yes."

"Okay, kiddo," I said, "go put some food in your belly. You must be starving."

"Are you coming?"

"I'll be there in a second."

I watched him trot off, then sat on the edge of his bed, my head in my hands. I had a chain of custody to work out. Was it possible I'd left that chocolate someplace where Paul might have found it? I must have, and yet I hadn't seen him since my brief interview with Jeff. Not until last night's trip to the hospital. Aiden was certain he'd committed his theft yesterday morning, before school. Which meant there was no way that chocolate came from me.

I played it as cool as I could manage during breakfast, cast the occasional quick glance at Paul, my intrepid adoptive brother, serving my recently ill son a very lightly buttered batch of cinnamon toast. I felt as though some bitchy teenage girl had passed me a note in gym class: *Don't buy the act—he gets off on broken hearts.*

*No way,* I told myself. Not Paul. Just about anyone else, but not Paul.

\* \* \*

I dropped Aiden off at school, patted his tummy and asked for the umpteenth time if he was sure he felt okay. He gave me another "Fit as a fiddle." Handing him over to school personnel felt somehow final—as though this were the last I'd see of my son for a long while. I told myself it was only a feeling. A sense that things were coming to a head, coupled with a fear that this particular end wouldn't open up any new beginnings.

I needed to pause and think before I went speeding up to Ferril Lake. Another café—this one right outside a subway stop on Fulton Street. The interior was the size of a camper van, but the few seats were generally available because people treated it like a grab-and-go place. I

took a stool at the window-front counter and waited for
the espresso to kick in while I watched the tail end of
rush hour come charging out of the station.

*No such thing as coincidence,* I reminded myself.
No way Paul stumbled into a random shop and picked
up a little chocolate car identical to the ones in Jeff's
office. All the more impossible given that Jeff said they
were made specially for his garage—a gift to celebrate
the grand opening. I could go on inventing ways that a
chocolate might have traveled from Jeff's desk to Paul's
study, but my gut told me not to bother—Paul made
the trip to Queens. But then how in the world had Jeff
appeared on his radar in the first place?

*Radar* . . . Technology. The webcams I found on
Tom's computer. A computer Paul had only just handed
back to me. Maybe those cameras belonged to him.
Maybe he'd planted the links on Tom's computer for me
to discover.

*Crazy,* I told myself. *You sound like a crazy person.*

Why would Paul be stalking me? Why would he
want to frame Tom? And could I really believe that he'd
burned Jeff's Automotive to the ground with Jeff and
Lowry inside?

One thing seemed certain: even if he hadn't par-
ticipated in the looting of our home, the arsonist was a
member of the original cast, part of whatever connected
Bill, Bickert, Tom, Jeff, Lowry, and my old man. But
then didn't that take Paul out of contention? Because
what did he know about any of it before I handed him
Tom's computer? And even then, all he found was a single inconclusive invoice.

Unless he'd found more. More than he'd shared.
Documents he'd downloaded, then deleted. Detailed
progress reports. Evidence concerning the burglary. The
blackmail. Evidence incriminating *him.*

*This is Paul you're talking about.*

I was jumping to conclusions. More than jumping. I was plunging headlong. A chocolate from Jeff's shop didn't make Paul an evil genius. It didn't make him a killer. Jeff, Bickert, Lowry, my old man, the phony movers in the green baseball caps—they were the thieves and murderers. They were the ones with motive. Paul, on the other hand, was as principled as they come. Never the slightest hesitation when someone he loved was in need. Never a hint of instability. If anything, he was so damn stable that it became easy to overlook him. So why was he in my crosshairs now? Because a chocolate linked him to three dead men and a missing person. A chocolate I'd never have discovered if it weren't for the fact that my son hated nuts.

I hit on the only explanation that felt right, or at least possible: Paul had been protecting me. He hadn't been involved in making the mess, but he couldn't resist cleaning it up. That much, at least, would be in character. Maybe he'd scoured Tom's hard drive in an effort to shelter me. Shield me from the ransom notes, death threats, compromising photos, proof of whatever secret Tom wanted kept. And then Paul stumbled on a message from Bickert to Tom: Bickert was headed out to Bill's squat in order to shut the whole operation down. It was the last anyone heard from Bickert, and now Knowles was asking questions. Paul had put two and two together: Bill killed Bickert. He knew seeing Bill in prison beside my old man would destroy me.

Had Paul figured out that someone was threatening me? Had he somehow seen the video that sent me scampering to a motel by the airport, and assumed that either Jeff or Lowry was behind it? Even if Paul had seen the video, the thought of him killing two men and burning their bodies was ludicrous. There had to be another answer to the riddle. He must have gone out to Queens earlier—earlier than I did—to confront Jeff. I remembered something Jeff said: *I've had enough of people's accusations.* "People's," not "your." Meaning someone else had been making accusations too. Paul. It had to be. He was no murderer. No firebug. He'd been defending his family. The chocolate on his desk and the arson were unrelated.

So I told myself, but I must not have been convinced. If I had been, I would have picked up the phone, called Paul's number, told him in no uncertain terms that we needed to talk. Instead, I stayed put, pushed my mind back over everything Paul had said and done since the night Bickert was shot to death and Tom wound up in a coma. In the *done* category, Paul had taken over the raising of my child, and wasn't that the most you could ask of anyone? In the *said* category, he'd pushed me to come clean, go to the police.

On the other hand, he'd steered me straight toward Bill—as the orchestrator of the robbery and the potential blackmail. I remembered how exhausted and almost sickly he'd looked that first morning. I'd chalked it up to his concern for Tom, but maybe his night had been as busy as mine.

I needed proof. I'd have to go home, face whatever was waiting for me, fetch Paul's spare key. Then I'd have to find a way to get him out of his apartment.

*The betrayals keep stacking up.*

I was becoming an expert. I didn't even feel guilty anymore.

# 35

THIS WAS RAGE, not robbery. Far worse than the emptied drawers and overturned furniture we'd come home to after our weekend in the Poconos. This was someone doing to my property what they hadn't yet been able to do to me. Couch disemboweled, television shattered, cabinet doors ripped from their hinges. And now I was alone. No six foot four husband by my side. No small child counting on me to be brave.

I toured the damage, mace in hand. I started with the kitchen. The refrigerator and freezer had been emptied of their containers, which were in turn emptied onto the floor, making a swamp of half-and-half, sauerkraut, salmon filets, cherry ice cream. If I knew enough about forensics, I could have judged by the smell how long ago the intruder had been here. Instead, I bent down and poked one of the fish filets with my finger. Thawed, but still colder than room temperature. Six hours, maybe? Give or take. Long enough to feel sure I was alone in the apartment.

I started down the hall. Tom's study had been decimated, his stack of blueprints converted to confetti and spread everywhere. The safe-shaped hole in the wall had become a repository for dog feces, most likely collected fresh at the park up the block. I covered my nose with one hand, turned, saw the painting of Tom's father knifed to ribbons, the frame fractured into dozens of long, jagged splinters.

I stepped back into the hallway, felt glass crunching under my shoes and noticed for the first time that the cameras had been torn from the ceiling, then pulverized with some kind of blunt object—a hammer or a baseball bat or the heel of a heavy boot. Whoever did this must have made one hell of a racket, but then he knew the neighbors were away. It's what allowed him to be so thorough.

Aiden's room, at least, had been spared. His bed was neatly made, his toys all dusted and put away. Had I left it like this? Or had my pet psychopath straightened up the child's bedroom to make a point? The point being what? That he wasn't simply deranged? That, unlike me, he had a moral code? Kids off limits, parents fair game? Or maybe he just had a particular fondness for Aiden. Because this was personal. Because this was someone who knew us. Someone like Paul.

I moved on to the master bedroom. More knifework. The bedding, the mattress, the pillows, the curtains, the clothes hanging in our closet—all cut up with deep thrusts and long gashes. If I hadn't felt so numb, I might have been impressed by the sustained effort. It looked like the work of a single mind carried out by a ten-man crew. More demolition than vandalism. Nothing nuanced about it. Nothing imaginative. Which made sense. I'd refused to engage with the LEGO restoration or the private film screening, so now I got raw, unbridled hate. This was my punishment for going off grid when the game had just begun.

*Time to call the cops, Teen.*

But of course that time was well past. Instead, I stood in the center of the living room and turned in a slow, tight circle. *"All the king's horses and all the king's men . . ."* Living here would never be the same. Maybe that had been true for a while, but it struck home now. Something else struck me: I wasn't scared so much as resigned. The end was near. It had to be. The room for escalation was running out. I found that oddly comforting. No more thinking two steps ahead. All I could do was deal with whatever landed right in front of me.

I leaned against what was left of the arm of the couch, took out my phone, and scrolled through my contacts. To my surprise, he answered on the third ring. Then I remembered I hadn't given him the burner number. I could picture the color dropping from his face when he heard my voice.

"Listen, Tina, I've been meaning to—"

"Forget it."

"The truth is I can't remember—"

"I don't have time for this, Desmond. I need a favor."

I needed him to call Paul, say there was some kind of computer-related emergency at the Foundation. A glitch before an all-important meeting, the tech guy out with the flu. Major funding in the offing. All was chaos without Tom. Would Paul please come down to the office ASAP? He had helped out before, under less trying circumstances. It was logical that Desmond would call him. Desmond didn't understand, but then he didn't have to. What mattered was that the request came from someone other than me. I couldn't ask Paul to meet me somewhere, then not show up. He'd know straight away. That is, if I was right this time. If it really was Paul behind the curtain.

"What do I say when he gets here?"

"Tell him you're so sorry to have inconvenienced him, but the problem resolved itself. Then buy him a cup of coffee."

"Is this some kind of prank?"

"Sort of. But you have to play the straight man. You can't let on that I'm involved, or you'll spoil the surprise."

"I don't know if I'm comfortable with this."

"Would you rather have a conversation about the night you say you can't remember? Maybe with your pal Detective Knowles?"

"Jesus, Tina."

"He's been looking for a concrete motive. I think if I were to tell him that you—"

"All right, I'll do it. I just want to know what—"

"If you knew, you'd blow it."

There was a pause. I pictured him hanging his head.

"Yeah," he said, "you're probably right."

"Wait ten minutes, then make the call."

I went back into the kitchen, braved the fetid lake, found Paul's spare key, which I'd always kept in the junk drawer, embedded in a mound of expired cottage cheese. I wiped it clean on a kitchen towel and slid it into my pocket.

Either my tormentor hadn't thought to destroy the clothes in our dresser, or his arm had given out from all that slashing. I put on a baggy, glitter-ridden sweater I'd held onto but never worn, an untouched present from a dozen Christmases ago—possibly given to me by Mrs. Davidson, I couldn't remember. Then I donned one of Tom's solid-color ski caps and pulled it down to my eyes. From squinting distance, I'd be just another piece of cityscape.

On my way out, I took a pair of latex gloves from under the sink and stuffed them into my pocket with Paul's key.

A chocolate car wasn't enough. I had to be sure.

CHAPTER

36

I WAS WATCHING FROM the bus shelter at the end of
the block when Paul exited his building and turned
toward the nearest subway station. His walk didn't give
anything away. No hesitation. No sideways glances.
Nothing to suggest he felt eyes on him. Nothing to say
he was the author of a day-old double homicide.

*Maybe that's because he isn't*, I thought.

I kept telling myself that this was just another of my
scripts. Paul wasn't the type to amass a body count. He
wasn't the type to park more than a foot from the curb.

*Only one way to know for sure.*

There was a lingering smell of onions and garlic in
the apartment. He must have cooked himself an omelet
once Aiden and I were gone. I called Paul's name even
though I'd just seen him leave. The ruins of my home
had barely shaken me, but now my hands were trembling. I started tiptoeing through the living room, then
caught a glimpse of myself on the widescreen TV and
saw how ridiculous I was being. No need for stealth. I
was in and out of here all the time. And if he happened to
come back early, I could invent a dozen different reasons

for being here now—I'd left behind my phone, wallet, car keys; Aiden forgot a book he needed for school. It's not like Paul would think I'd snuck back in search of evidence against him. Not unless there was actual evidence to find.

I put on the latex gloves, headed for his home office. I didn't know what I'd be handling—a thumb drive, a CD-ROM, an old-fashioned floppy disk. Something I wouldn't want to compromise with my own skin and prints. Most likely, though, the evidence I was looking for would live on his hard drive—the video of me rifling through Dumb Jake's pockets, memos addressed from Bickert to Tom, those webcam links. Any document mentioning Bill, Jeff, Lowry, my old man.

But then my finding anything at all was contingent on Paul having left without shutting down or logging out. I could navigate a hard drive, but only if somebody let me in first. I groped around the wall for an overhead switch, then remembered that Paul kept his study like a darkroom—a blackout curtain on the lone window, a door with a flap at the bottom so that the only light came from his computer screen. He said he needed to feel as though he were being sucked into his work, the way he wanted kids to be sucked into his games. In the event he had to read something on paper, there was a desk lamp—a model spaceship with a bulb in its belly. I managed to turn that on by feel, then sat down in Paul's swivel chair, pulled out the keyboard and tapped the spacebar.

A triptych of monitors lit up with a screensaver Paul had created for *Dr. Living Stone*, the astronomy game he'd been playing with Aiden. Now and again a rotund calico in a checkered vest flashed across the galaxy like a shooting star. I waited, then hit the spacebar again. The central monitor went blank. A millisecond later, Paul's face filled the screen.

I didn't scream so much as squeal. He seemed to be staring straight at me, cocking his head left and right as though he'd seen me before but couldn't say where. My first thought: I'd triggered some kind of security app, and he was watching me from his seat on the subway. I started to say something, but he cut me off.

"Hmm," he said. "You don't look like me. Try leaning in a little closer."

He scratched his chin, wrinkled his brow. His voice sounded campy and staged.

"Maybe you need a shave," he said.

Facial recognition software. No chance I'd be rooting through his email or his trash folder. Pre-recorded Paul kept on blathering. He turned suspicious, then threatening. The police would be called, charges pressed. Somehow, his face knew that I was still there. Then I noticed the little green light at the top of the monitor. I was being filmed. *Idiot.* Of course I was. I spun around, bolted from the room in one long stride.

I went into the kitchen, drank the dregs of Paul's coffeepot, took a minute to calm myself down. Foundation headquarters was twenty minutes away. Twenty minutes to get there, a half hour to be there, twenty minutes to get home. I had time.

Back in his office, I steered clear of the keyboard while I searched his desk for a disk or a thumb drive or any pages he might have printed out. Nothing. Every drawer was empty, every surface bare. I went into his bedroom, dug through his dresser, checked under his mattress, climbed on a chair and flashed my phone light through the grill of an air duct. More nothing. Nothing in his closet but a decades-long collection of T-shirts and hoodies that he ironed and hung up like business suits.

I moved to the bathroom, opened the medicine cabinet, inventoried his pill bottles and toiletries. Deodorant, ibuprofen, dental floss. An expired roll of antacids and a rusty pair of nail clippers. The kinds of items you'd find in any medicine cabinet across the country. I felt small and traitorous. This was Paul's privacy I was violating. The Paul who took in my son. The Paul who'd stayed glued to his father's side through those torturous final months. The same Paul who seemed to wake up wondering how he could make my life easier.

*You're a total shit, Teen.*

Or maybe I wasn't. At first, I thought I had to be misreading the label. How many single men keep a bottle of ipecac tucked behind their cough-syrup collection? How many people, period? As far as I knew, they didn't even make the stuff anymore. I pulled the bottle down, opened it, tilted it toward the light. It was a little more than half full. I sniffed at the mouth, then whipped my head away. The dull-brown liquid stunk like rotting garbage. Wouldn't Aiden have gagged, retched, spat it out? No milkshake was that potent.

I screwed the cap back on, set the bottle back on its shelf.

*Think, think, think.*

I drifted into Aiden's room, sat on the edge of the bed, and stared at the wall in front of me. A piece of artisan chocolate and a missing dose of vomit potion weren't exactly conclusive. The question I was fumbling around now . . . Why would Paul have poisoned Aiden? Say he was behind all the rest of it—burglary, blackmail, attempted murder, more blackmail, arson, actual murder, home invasion, and demolition. What could he have hoped to achieve by hospitalizing my son?

I told myself again that I was wrong. Way wrong. So much drama had my imagination on edge. A sweet tooth and a fear of toxins—that was as much as I'd proven so far. My old man was the one who wanted to destroy me. He was the felon, the one with ties to all the key players. But the doubt had been planted. I couldn't just shut it down.

Paul graduated from MIT. I wasn't going to find anything he could hide on a microchip or up in the cloud. I should have known better. But physical objects were another story. He'd left the ipecac and the chocolate out in the open, almost as though he wanted me to find them. If Paul commissioned the initial robbery, then he'd have something from Tom's safe. Something with substance and three dimensions. Paul had suggested more than once that the blackmail had to do with Tom's business. Was that Paul working in a bit of the real story? Some kind of document, maybe? A piece of paper with a signature or a seal. Or something a bit thicker. An old-fashioned ledger? A day planner? The most mundane option—photos of Tom with another woman; keepsakes from some quick-burning, carnal affair—seemed the least likely. Tom was addicted to his work, devoted to his son. When would he have found the time for a fuck buddy?

I checked my phone. A half hour had gone by. I should have asked Desmond to call as soon as Paul left. I started with the largely empty foyer closet, then worked my way forward.

It was hard to believe he'd lived here since before Aiden was born. Apart from the figurines and the twenty-third-century furniture, he'd hardly collected a thing. I found a Kindle but not a single book, an iPod but no CDs or vinyl. No dust either. That was one thing I remembered about Paul: even as a kid, he'd liked a bit of polish. He'd refuse to play in the family room because a basement could never really be clean.

There were maybe a dozen promotional posters for his games hanging throughout the apartment, all of them finished off with the same matte border and silver frame. Dizzyingly-busy images featuring live-action versions of the models from his shelves—cartoon goblins and trolls facing off on blood-red hills; basic math equations written across low-slung clouds; a sleek sports car sailing through the spray of a baroque-looking fountain. I shifted each poster, peered behind. No safe, no lockbox, no cubbyhole.

I double-checked under the beds, lifted up cushions, pulled back curtains and blinds. I rapped my knuckles along the sides of the coffee table, checking for hidden compartments. I rolled back area rugs. I ran out of obvious places to search. I went into his freezer, lifted the lid off a container of Rocky Road, picked up a package of pierogies and felt it for anything outsized or misshapen. I made mental notes, put every object back where I'd found it.

I leaned against the kitchen island and caught my breath. I felt desperate. Ridiculous.

Then I started to laugh. I was remembering something again. More accurately, I was remembering two things at once. One was funny and one wasn't.

The unfunny memory had to do with Bill and me playing hide and seek in that five-hundred-square-foot tomb on the Lower East Side. The apartment was too small for us to hide ourselves, so we hid things. Like an Easter egg hunt, but with whatever we could lay our hands on. Once, Bill hid a belt buckle in our parents' shoebox heroin kit. He'd found the kit under their bed, a space I didn't dare invade. Eventually, I gave up, and he had to show me. I slammed the lid shut. He opened it again. The collection of objects frightened me—especially the syringe and the lighter. I didn't know what they were used for, and I don't think Bill did then either, but laid out side by side they looked angry, poised for violence. Bill took up the lighter and played with it until he struck a flame. I screamed for him to stop. We must have been alone in the apartment. We usually were.

The funny thing I remembered had to do with Paul. It was something I couldn't believe I'd forgotten. The summer between his junior and senior years of high school, I stumbled on a batch of letters he'd received from a girl in Iceland. She'd been an exchange student in his class the year before. He'd complained it wasn't much of an exchange since no one from our school got to go there. They hadn't started dating until her year was almost up. The letters were more like targeted pornography. The girl was a budding dominatrix—her love object had to be on the verge of emergency care before she could climax. In flawless English, she wrote about standing on Paul's head while wearing stiletto heels and flaying his back with a cat-o'-nine-tails.

However Paul answered, it was enough to hold her interest; I only found the letters because she'd written so many. Paul had slid them into the backing of a framed *Clockwork Orange* poster he'd hung on his bedroom wall. By August, the backing started to look swollen. Then I noticed the corner of a page jutting out. I remembered willing Mrs. Davidson to find the letters too—a woman who wore turtlenecks year-round and canceled her subscription to a knitting magazine because it started running Victoria's Secret ads. Maybe she did find them and, like me, said nothing about it. Maybe, like me, she thought the thing she never would have said out loud: *Good for you, Paul.* Maybe, if one of us had confronted him, he would have quit hiding letters inside picture frames.

But he hadn't.

I found it tucked behind a poster that hung between the bathroom door and the hall closet. A thick stationery envelope with a single word written across the front: *Tom.*

# CHAPTER

# 37

*Dear Son,*

*As you know by now, the cancer has spread through my lungs and throat. I've never been one to wait, never been one to abide by somebody else's terms, and so tonight the cocktail of drugs they've given me will finish the job. Before I go, there's something I want you to know. I've put off saying anything, not out of cowardice, but because I couldn't imagine how someone of your temperament would benefit from the knowledge. I'm still not sure, but now I've reached the end, and there's no one else worth telling. It's your absolute confidence in your ability to distinguish right from wrong that has always made me hesitate. I wish I could respect it more, but given where I started, I only see it as a luxury you've been afforded by my willingness to cut corners—and throats, when needed, though always within the bounds of the law. Minus one exception.*

*You probably don't remember Jimmy Montgomery; you were a toddler when he and I parted ways. Looking back at what will soon be the full sweep of my life, it's clear that losing Jimmy is the closest thing I have to a regret. In the decade before your birth, we were inseparable. We grew up ten blocks apart but never knew each other as kids. It was only after Vietnam—we were discharged the same week—that we met. We worked together as housepainters for an outfit based in Rego Park. That was how we fell into real estate: ninety-something degrees with one hundred percent humidity in mid-August, and we were standing outside in overalls, painting somebody else's house for the benefit of somebody else's pockets.*

*We put our heads together and decided there had to be a better way.*

*So, we found second jobs; pooled our income; and, just a year later, bought our first property: a two-family home with a studio apartment in the basement. Jimmy and I roomed together on the top floor and rented out the other units. We'd both grown up in multifamily homes, but our parents were occupants, not owners. We thought we were King Shits. We weren't, of course, but we were on our way.*

*Eight years later, we each had homes of our own on the outskirts of Forest Hills. Not posh, but within walking distance. No mortgages. That had become a rule with us. If you can't pay in cash, don't buy it. I was married, with a kid. Jimmy was still taking applications for Mrs. Right, and he had no shortage of applicants.*

*As business partners, we'd come a fair way from the Rego Park multifamily. We had a three-story brick building with a restaurant on the ground floor, a business on the second floor, and an apartment we rented out on the third.*

We partnered in the restaurant with a sous-chef, from a swank Manhattan hotel, who was tired of being second in command. The restaurant alone brought in a nice income. French-American cuisine with a picturesque little courtyard out back. There wasn't anything like it within a dozen subway stops. The business on the second floor was ours. Evans and Montgomery Realty. Two young men who lived to work and took only the most calculated risks. We'd jumped a few rungs above middle class, but there was still a lot of ladder left to climb.

At least, that's what I thought. Jimmy, I'd soon find out, didn't see any need to keep climbing. He liked his life just as it was. He had everything he wanted, and there was nothing he loved so much as the work itself, so why tempt fate? Looking back, I'm sure the difference between us was you. Once you have a child, you start thinking in terms of generational wealth.

I'm telling you all this because I'm building toward something, but also because you should know your history. The fact that you've never shown the slightest curiosity only confirms for me how distasteful you find your family name. I don't suppose this letter will help.

An opportunity opened up. Waterfront property for sale in North Brooklyn. Barren warehouses just begging to make way for luxury high-rises with skyline views. The scope was beyond anything we could have done on our own, but we had a potential silent partner. Arran Tavish, a Scotsman who'd emigrated to New York and made a fortune in fashion and retail. In fact, the high-rises were his idea. He wanted a physical legacy, a literal piece of *his adoptive city with his name emblazoned above every entranceway.*

*But Arran wasn't young anymore, and what he didn't want was hassle. He was looking for front men. People to oversee the construction and run the place once it was built. He knew about Jimmy and me because a long-time friend of his lived in Forest Hills and ate most nights at our restaurant. Every great fortune begins with a spark of dumb luck. Arran did some research and decided Jimmy and I were a perfect fit—young and ambitious and capable, but not established enough to oppose his will should push ever come to shove.*

*All we had to do was raise ten percent of the down payment. That was the buy-in. Ten percent up front in exchange for ten percent of the profits plus a commission on every unit sold, not to mention our own westward-facing condos. I almost couldn't breathe. I saw my future all mapped out. I saw your future mapped out. I'd done the math. In the beginning, Jimmy and I would be stretched to our limits. We'd have to sell the restaurant, the business, and the building they were housed in. We might end up breaking our rule, mortgaging our homes. But the returns—both in lifestyle and profit—would be astronomical. And if we invested wisely, the returns on those returns would blow past the wildest numbers we'd allowed ourselves to imagine.*

*But as I already said, Jimmy wasn't interested. His stance was firm: Why jeopardize what you have in hopes of gaining more than you could ever spend? He was immovable, and contractually there was no way for me to sell my half of the business— not soon enough, anyway. I was gutted. I felt I'd* been deceived. Our attitudes were diametrically opposed. It had never once occurred to me that we'd arrived, that here was anything but a rest stop on the way to someplace better.

I told Jimmy that I would deliver the news to Arran, but then I couldn't bring myself to make the call. Day after day, I stalled. I stalled, and I fumed, and— unconsciously at first—I schemed. I was furious with Jimmy. It was as though he'd deliberately and spitefully shredded our winning lottery ticket. I'd have to live now knowing what could have been. Whatever measure of success I achieved, I would have to make constant peace with the fact that it should have been greater, that my one turn on this earth fell short of its potential. Because of him. I've been mean and angry all my life, but I've only tasted genuine hatred a handful of times. That was the first.

I simply couldn't let it stand. I couldn't let Jimmy keep me from my money. And I saw only one solution, one way for us to split our proceeds and part ways. It didn't take divine inspiration. Fraud predates the invention of insurance, and quite possibly the invention of fire. Today, those three elements—insurance, fraud, and fire— seem nearly inseparable. At least in the restaurant business.

Nothing is easier than staging a fire in a chef's kitchen. Everything you need is already at hand. Grease and oil, gas and flame. A bleary cook at the end of his shift leaves an apron on the stove, turns a knob three-quarters instead of all the way. The con is so obvious, and yet it's beyond me how investigators ever prove intent without a confession.

The difficulty for me came in ensuring our lone tenant was elsewhere. He was a reclusive old man, a retired accountant who never made any noise and whose trash bin filled up with empty gin bottles over the course of each week. He'd been in the apartment since well before we bought the building. His name was Mike Ohls, but we called him The Ghost because usually when you spotted him, you only got a glimpse. Soon enough, he would become my literal ghost. He had a sister, a twin, who lived out in Hoboken. He visited her on Sundays and stayed overnight. It was the one personal detail he'd shared with me, and I remembered it because the sharing itself seemed stilted and out of character, as though he were forcing himself to make conversation because he wanted me to know that, contrary to popular belief, he had a connection in this world.

So, it had to be Sunday night, after the restaurant closed. At nine PM, I climbed the stairs to Ohls's apartment and rang the bell. If he answered, I'd call it off, at least for now. I'd apologize for disturbing him, make up an excuse about faulty plumbing. I rang again. It wasn't the kind of bell you could miss. Loud, strident, sustained. It would have been a nuisance if he'd had regular visitors. Still, I switched to knocking, calling his name. No answer. I suppose I could have let myself in, made absolutely sure, but the thought didn't occur to me. I had no doubt he was in Jersey with his sister.

I went down one flight to the empty office, sat by the window with the lights out, and waited. The restaurant closed at ten on Sundays. At a little after eleven, I watched Tony, the chef, get into his Oldsmobile and drive off. I didn't hesitate. I thought it would look better to the arson investigators if the *fire started just after the staff had left. I entered the restaurant through the back door. It was as easy as I described.*

*Either Ohls was passed out drunk, or he was already dead. I'd like to believe the latter. A heart attack. A stroke. A fall. A bottle of pills. Any of the flash deaths that leave the elderly sprawled in their apartments, waiting to be discovered. If he'd been alive and sober and had simply chosen to ignore me earlier, then he would have heard the smoke alarms. He would have had plenty of time to get out—if not by the stairs, then by the fire escape. But they found him in the back bedroom, burned so badly that dental records were used to make the identification.*

*Even with our business gone, Jimmy wanted no part of the waterfront complex. My half of the payout got me most of the way there. For the rest, I sold our home, moved us into a tiny one-bedroom in College Point. We wound up stuck there for two years while the towers were being built. Your mother nearly divorced me. But, as you can guess, it worked out in the end. By the time I was forty, I owned a luxury high-rise all my own. Then another. And another.*

*I don't know that Jimmy ever suspected me. The prospect might have been too horrible for him to consider. We kept in touch for a while, then let ourselves drift. He's dead now. No wife, no kids. A bachelor until the end.*

*You can shred this letter or burn it or give it to the press. You can hunt down a distant relative of Mike Ohls and say that restitution is at hand. Or you can simply accept the fortune I'm about to pass on to my son. Go with the option that best suits whatever future you imagine for yourself. Maybe this letter is, in the end, a kind of test: once you've made your decision, you'll know beyond questioning who you are. You'll know if there's any of me in you.*

*They say you can't choose your family, and you've made it abundantly clear that you wouldn't have chosen me. I'm sorry we so seldom saw eye to eye. Nevertheless, I admire what you've been able to accomplish, even if you've never been willing to acknowledge the advantages that helped make your success possible. I hope you will cling to those advantages now. I hope you will make the wise decision, but I have my doubts. For my part, I am convinced the man was already dead.*

*I leave my legacy in your hands; it's of no more use to me. Don't forget to enjoy yourself once in a while.*

*Goodbye,*

*Dad*

# CHAPTER

# 38

IT WAS HANDWRITTEN on a thick, canvas-like paper.
The ink looked as though it came out of a bottle and
was applied with a feathered quill—more Declaration
of Independence than twenty-first-century suicide note.
I sat on Paul's futon with the pages balanced across my
lap. I felt sick to my stomach. I felt like being alive and
being sick were the same thing.

Sick, sad, stunned. Sad for Tom, for the secret he'd
refused to share, for the energy he'd spent righting a
wrong that wasn't his. Maybe that's what it means to
be someone's child. Tom's case was just extreme. Then
again, so was Bill's. So was mine. And Aiden? If the
events of the last few days were anything to go by, it
wasn't looking good. I felt stunned because I couldn't
make any of what Paul had done—or the fact that he'd
done it—real. I couldn't let go of the idea that fit so
neatly with what I thought I knew of my life: my old
man was behind every bad thing. But then there was
the letter on my lap. A letter that could only have come
from Tom's safe.

I pushed all the thinking aside. Paul might be home
at any moment. I had to make up my mind. There were

two choices: burn the letter or put it back where I'd found it. The first was tempting, but the second made more sense. For starters, disappearing the original wouldn't do any good: he would have a scanned copy squirreled away on his impenetrable hard drive. I had a quick thought about taking a hammer to the equipment in his office, having as much fun with his property as he'd had with mine, but I dismissed the idea for one very compelling reason: Aiden. Paul could do a lot worse than give Aiden a stomachache. I didn't want to panic him. Not until I knew for sure that I could end this. So I folded the letter into its envelope, then slid the envelope back where I'd found it.

My short-term plan hadn't changed: I had to make sure Bill was safe before I did anything else. I felt certain now. It might have been Lowry who knocked me into the side of Jeff's garage, but it was Paul who came back later and lit the match. He must have snuck out while Aiden was sleeping. He knew about Jeff through Bickert's files, the same way he knew about Lowry. Like me, Paul had been hunting for Bill. Bill was supposed to take the credit for Paul's sins, from burglary to blackmail to murder. Bill was a readymade patsy—the orphan junkie who resented his sister's storybook life—but he would have his own story to tell, and someone might even believe him. Better to have him off himself in a fit of remorse. That would tie everything up nicely. The addict's brain snapped. He stopped himself the only way he could.

And then a question that came at me like a thousand volts: had Jeff—drunk, bleary, and bewildered—told Paul where to find Bill? It was easy enough to picture. My movements turned automatic. I ran from the building, dialed Desmond as I jogged toward the garage.

"Did he leave yet?" I asked.

"He didn't get here yet."

"What do you mean?"

"He called maybe fifteen minutes ago. Said he was running late."

*Fuck.* Something had tipped Paul off. Either Desmond's performance on the phone or my performance that morning. Or maybe he'd just spotted the missing chocolate.

"What did you tell him? When you first called?"

"I said we had clients coming in this afternoon. We needed a 3-D model off Tom's computer, but I kept getting an error message when I tried to open it. I was pretty convincing. I sounded—"

I hung up, punched in another number. Aiden's school. The principal's assistant answered—a hardcore administrator without a shred of warmth. She was perfect for my needs. Reasons didn't matter to her, only procedures. She put Paul on the no-fly list without asking questions, promised the change would take effect immediately. Yes, she was sure Aiden was in class—she'd have been notified otherwise. I added two authorized guardians: Chief Vetrano and his wife. Aiden knew them and liked them. He'd even spent a weekend with them at their time-share in Vermont. When he thought of them, he thought vacation. If I couldn't make it back by the final bell, I knew they'd come through. The tricky part would be explaining to Chief Vetrano why he couldn't tell anyone he was watching my son, why he couldn't mention Aiden's name at the station house. I was still hoping to remove those webcams before anyone caught sight of them.

*The webcams.*

Something clicked into place—the answer to a question I'd been asking myself nonstop since I found the ipecac: *Why make Aiden sick?* Because Paul knew I was headed to Ferril Lake, and he knew who I'd find when

I got there. Jeff must have talked. If Paul could install a camera, then he could install a tracking device. He hadn't had a chance yet to drive upstate himself. He was on Aiden duty. He had to maintain appearances. So he kept tabs on me. If I got to Bill before he did, he'd lose his scapegoat. When he saw I was on my way north from Ossining, he poisoned Aiden to make sure I'd come running back.

I sprinted the last hundred yards to my car, got on my knees and ran my hands under the bumper. I lay on my back and used my phone's flashlight to search the undercarriage. Eventually I found it tucked up inside one of the rear wheel wells. A tiny black box with a magnetic backing. I yanked it off and crushed it under my heel. Not that it mattered now. Paul already had his head start.

I turned the key in the ignition, started to switch gears, then stopped myself. *For the love of God, Teen,* I thought, *just call the cops.* A simple welfare check. Have an Orange County patrol car swing by 8055 Ferril Lake Road on the grounds that the occupant threatened suicide. If I was right, and Paul was on his way, the police could still get there ahead of him. Best-case scenario: they'd scare Bill off. Worst-case scenario: they'd pick him up on a possessions charge, then find his name flagged in relation to a homicide investigation. But at least he'd be safe.

I googled *emergency services orange county new york*, then clicked on the number and hit "Speakerphone." An operator answered as I was pulling out of the garage.

"What's the location of your emergency?"

"8055 Ferril Lake Road. My brother. He said he was going to kill himself. Please hurry."

I lied my way through a half-dozen questions about Bill's mental state, then hung up before she could take my information. I felt slightly less anxious now that the police were involved. Still, I wasn't about to turn around. Whether it was at the cabin or the local jail, I was going to find Bill. Maybe I was going to find Paul too. I'd deal with that when the time came.

Meanwhile, my mind was spinning, struggling to fill in the blanks. I needed to know why Bill had run, what had happened in that squat, what he'd remembered in Alden's armchair, why he'd gone to see our old man. I wanted desperately to know that Tom was wrong, that Bill had nothing to do with the robbery, the blackmail. I wanted to hear from my brother that he hadn't killed Jeff and Lowry. There were still dots I couldn't connect, places where I couldn't make Paul fit. I had to have all the information gathered and processed before I turned it over to Knowles. If there was one thing I believed about Bill, it was that, face-to-face, I could get the truth out of him. Why didn't I believe that about Paul?

It was one of the questions I kept circling back to during the stop-and-go drive. If I was honest with myself, there'd always been something about Paul that kept me from getting too close. A feeling I couldn't pinpoint. I figured it had something to do with his goodness: How do you talk to an angel? But maybe my instincts had been telling me something else. Something I'd refused to hear. There must have been signs. People don't just crack. If this was Paul, then there had to have been some monster in him all along. A monster I'd missed.

But then, had I really looked? I'd been on the cusp of puberty when the Davidsons took me in. I'd just lost my family. Nothing seemed real. Everything came at me shrouded in haze and distance. I'd felt like I was trapped inside a television, looking out, and the only way I could shatter the screen and break through to the other side was to allow myself to get very, very angry. Not at someone or because of anything. There was just a well of anger I could tap into anytime I liked. Now and again, Mr. Davidson had to talk me down. Mostly I let loose when I was alone—I was aware enough to know how well I'd landed. I taught myself to scream without making a sound. When that didn't work, I'd beat the shit out of a pillow. The rest of the time, I just bit my lip and held my breath. Mrs. Davidson wasn't fooled. I remembered sitting in a diner, looking up from my banana split to see her mouthing a single word: *damaged*.

A handful of years later, I was away at college, and I only ever thought about Paul for as long as it took me to read the postcards he sent. I was almost surprised to find him at home when I came back for long weekends and breaks.

Still, he was an unlikely suspect. Motive belonged to my blood family. Tom bullied Bill into exile. Tom looked down on Bill. Bill saw Tom as an appendage of me. That made me a traitor. My old man's motives were timeless: revenge, hatred, money. Why should the daughter who'd abandoned him get to live the good life while he fought for his sanity in a metal-and-concrete cage? But Paul, on the other hand . . . He and Tom were close. He had plenty of his own money. He adored Aiden. He'd never said an unkind word to me.

Every question led to more questions, chief among them: *Why? And why now?*

My mind was all out of synch with the day. The sky had looked ready to burst when I left the garage, the clouds hanging so low they felt more like ceiling than sky. Now, there was nothing overhead but blue and the contrails from a 747. The traffic, too, had cleared. I might have been playing hooky, speeding toward the shore of a mountain lake, taking a nice, quiet weekday to reconnect with nature, swap out the soot in my lungs

for fresh, country air. Except that I couldn't stop thinking. About Paul, Bill, Desmond, Tom, Jeff, my old man.
The unknowable parts of them. Their secrets, small and
large.

The Manhattan skyline was fading from my rearview mirror when my phone rang. I glanced at the
screen. Unknown number, Orange County, New York.
The operator must have traced my call. I thought about
letting it go to voicemail, but what if the police had Bill
in custody? Or worse . . . What if they'd taken him to
the hospital? Or the morgue?

I tapped "Speakerphone." A tinny male voice shot
through the car.

"We sent officers out to 8055 Ferril Lake Road. They
didn't find anyone at the premises. Are you sure that's
where your brother was calling from?"

"Positive," I say. "Or at least I'm positive that's what
he told me."

I half listened to the rest of his spiel, waiting for my
opportunity to say thank you, then goodbye. Whether
the police had found him there or not, Bill was at that
cabin. I knew it. Or at least I felt it. Maybe he ran out a
back door and watched from the woods until they left.
Maybe he'd hiked into town on a supply run. But he was
there. He had to be—it was the last place left for me to
search.

CHAPTER

# 39

I WAS PULLING OFF the highway when my phone rang a second time. A number ran across the GPS map. The hospital. Always before, it had been me calling them. I hit "Speakerphone." It was Laura's voice on the other end.

"He opened his eyes," she said.

Rumble strips saved me from swerving onto the shoulder.

"Is he alert?" I asked. "Does he know where he is?"

I was shouting. I couldn't seem to control my own voice.

"He isn't talking yet. But yeah, his eyes are focused. He seems aware of his surroundings."

"Thank you, thank you, thank you . . ."

"I can let you in to see him, if you want. Professional courtesy."

"The thing is, I'm not . . ."

I stalled. What excuse could I give for not rushing to my husband's side? I had a sudden vision of Laura on the witness stand: *"She said she felt herself coming down with the flu."* And then the prosecutor: *"That's funny, because she was caught on a toll booth camera in the Hudson*

*Highlands."* It was a strange thing to think of just then, but I didn't want to put Laura in that position.

"It's okay," she said.

Whatever it was she thought was okay, I left it at that.

"When I can," I said. "I'll be there as soon as I can."

Something I'd been taking for granted from the start: Tom would wake up. It was a fact that had allowed me to become preoccupied with less obvious questions, like who was this man I had married, and what would our future look like once he was whole again? So much had to be cleared away before we could begin to find answers. Right now, only one thing mattered: he'd opened his eyes. I could picture that much. I could see him lying in his hospital bed, the swelling beginning to subside, the scars a little less angry, a host of monitors blinkering in the background. I could feel his hand fighting to grip mine.

*       *       *

The lake was there ahead of me, its water a shade of blue I thought only existed at alpine elevations. I was passing through a self-proclaimed town that looked more like an outsize visitor's center, the shops and restaurants all named for local attractions: Bear Mountain Brewery, Ferril Lake Souvenirs, Ferril Lake Camping Supplies, Ferril Village Store. I kept reading Ferril as Feral.

The GPS told me to turn left at the lake. My adrenaline was reaching toxic levels. The driver behind me had to hit his horn when the light changed. I felt alternately like I might go soaring through the roof of the car or pass out at the wheel. I had no doubt I was about to find Bill—I only doubted the condition I'd find him in, and who I'd find him with.

I drove past a long stretch of eateries and boat rental shops, and then the property turned residential. The homes were set back from the road and fronted by trees, but you could see enough to know there'd been a recent real estate boom. The weekend cabins of old had been knocked down and replaced with vinyl-sided, faux-Georgian McMansions. It looked like architect Tom's final ring of hell. If Jeff had lived, he'd have made a pretty penny. At least it was the closest he'd have come to collecting all the purses he missed out on. I wondered if some prohibition against felons had kept him from selling the place already.

I'd circled halfway around the lake before the addresses reached the 1800s. I read the numbers on the mailboxes but still managed to drive past the Henriksen family getaway three separate times. Unlike the gated affairs on either side, the Henriksen driveway was unpaved and untended, with rotting leaves and branches masking the entrance. There was just enough space between the trees for a midsize vehicle to scrape through.

A few yards in, the timber frame cabin from the newspaper photo became visible. It hadn't been in great shape when the photo was taken, and it hadn't aged well since. The porch out front was sloping badly. The weathervane up top was solid rust. The entire property looked battened down. No lights in the windows, no smoke rising from the chimney, no laundry hanging from the line. No vehicle parked in the weeds, which meant either Paul hadn't arrived, or he'd already come and gone.

I stepped out, sucked in some lake-front air, shut my eyes and listened. A small stream ran behind the cabin, the water churning just loud enough to serve as a pleasant white noise. If Bill was stirring inside, I couldn't hear him. Maybe he hadn't heard me pulling up either.

There was a single, porthole-style window cut into the roof sheathing, where I guessed the loft must be. As I had at Jeff's garage, I kept willing Bill's face to appear. I wanted him to wave and smile as though nothing were wrong, as though I were a normal sister who'd just driven up from the city to visit my textbook-normal brother.

*No time for this shit, Teen.*

I started forward. There were two doors to choose from: one on the front porch and one at the side of the cabin. I wasn't convinced the porch would hold my weight, so I walked around to the side. The mesh screen was torn and hanging loose. The door itself was ajar. I didn't think that meant anything. I wouldn't have been surprised to learn it had been ajar since Papa Henriksen's last visit. I gave it a hard knock. I called Bill's name. No one answered. I pushed the door all the way open with my foot, peered inside.

The place was dark, but I could make out the essentials: sparsely furnished living space, coal oven, rope ladder leading up to the loft. A duffel bag lay at the center of the floor, its contents spilling out onto a tattered area rug. Against the far wall, a slim vertical strip of light shone through a crack in the doorframe. I stepped in. The floorboards made a sound like violin strings breaking. I stopped, looked up at the loft, still half expecting to see Bill's eyes staring back. The air stunk like a campground outhouse. Cleanliness was never his thing— unless maybe he was bleaching a crime scene.

The stream seemed somehow louder from inside the cabin. I moved to the center of the room. Then I realized it wasn't the stream I was hearing. There was a faucet running somewhere close by. Bill filling a bathtub? I walked toward that thin strip of light, feeling my pulse beginning to calm. There were plenty of things I'd imagined my big brother might be doing when I found him, but bathing himself wasn't one of them. It seemed so innocent—like a kind of baptism. I knocked lightly on the door, called his name. No answer. I gave my knock a little more force.

"Bill?"

I looked down, saw I was standing in a puddle. I flung the door open, found Bill lying in an inch of water on the tile floor, wearing nothing but boxer shorts, the top of his head pressing against the tub, his hair soaked from the runoff, his body crammed awkwardly into the space between the toilet and the door. There was vomit in the bowl, spattered across the lid, dripping down the sides. A needle and a trio of empty dime bags lay in the sink. No spoon, no lighter. I leaned over, shut off the faucet, then dropped to my knees beside him. He was conscious, shivering and sweating, eyes staring up at me through what looked like a film of egg white.

"It's going to be okay, Bill," I said.

He gave his head a feeble shake. He looked so fucking scrawny. So pale. I wiped sweat from his brow with the back of my hand. There was a tat on his chest I didn't know he had: Celtic spirals I could tell he'd drawn himself. I felt my jacket pockets, my pants pockets. *Shit.* I'd left the Narcan in my kit. My kit was in the trunk of the car. Bill lifted a hand, tried to grab my wrist. The hand fell away when I stood.

"I'll be right back," I told him. "You just hang on."

He tried to say something. Then he shut his eyes and gave up. I spun around, started a sprint, nearly fell forward with the effort to stop myself. He was standing there, maybe six feet away, backlit by what little sun made it through the porch window. Paul.

"Afraid I can't let you go, *Teen*," he said.

# 40

H E STOOD WITH his arms crossed at the wrists, holding the gun so casually that it might have been any
object at all—a hat, a bouquet of flowers, a rolled-up
magazine. He wore a pair of latex gloves like the ones I'd
found in his kitchen.

"Are you going to shoot me, Paul?"

He looked down at the revolver as though he'd forgotten all about it.

"It's not even mine," he said, gesturing toward the
bathroom. "It's his. He must have taken it off Jake Bickert.
If he'd been carrying it when I walked in, this might all
look very different. But he was asleep, sprawled out on the
rug like a dog. The gun was lying on the side table."

Paul stepped back, waved me over to the couch, then
sat across from me in a duct-taped armchair. I felt that
familiar mix of terror and rage roiling up.

"What have you done?"

He shrugged.

"Does it matter? I didn't change anything. I just
sped things along."

"Sped what things along?"

"You think Tom's secret wasn't going to come out? You think a man like Jeff Henriksen was going to meet a good end? And Bill. Wasn't his life always headed exactly here? We can alter the path, but we can't change the destination."

I told myself this was a scene I'd been called to. Before I could treat the patient, I had to disarm the man with the gun.

"Maybe," I said. "But we can change what's happening right now. Let's walk outside together. I'll get the Narcan. You drive away. I'll say I found him like this. That will buy you enough time."

"Time for what? To discover some tropical island, open a daiquiri stand on the beach?"

"You can go wherever you want."

"But I don't want to go anywhere. I don't need to go anywhere."

"If you stay, they'll—"

"A junkie kills himself with dope—but the distraught sister who found his body? The paramedic who lost the patient she'd spent her life trying to save? With her husband lying in a coma and that tragic backstory always haunting her? She might use a gun. The same gun her brother used to murder a former cop."

"There will be an investigation," I said. "The truth always comes out."

"No, the story that makes the most sense always comes out. The story with the fewest loose ends. The story the cops can sell to the DA, and the DA can sell to a jury, and the media can sell to the public. I don't fit with that story. I'm not on anyone's radar. But you're front and center. Your suicide will look like a confession. Either you were in on it all from the beginning, or you did some very nasty things to cover your brother's crimes. You said it yourself: Bill's the only family you've got."

I'd been so fixated on my old man, but I saw now how it must have started.

"Tom confided in you on one of your binges, didn't he?" I said. "He told you about his father's letter."

"I couldn't have stopped him if I'd wanted to. He went on and on about how it would ruin him if it ever became public. He'd be the philanthropist whose fortune was built on an arson-homicide. No one would do business with him. He'd become a pariah. He might even end up in prison. And yet he couldn't bring himself to destroy the letter. Instead, he kept it locked away in his safe. Almost like he wanted his little world to implode."

Paul might have had the idea to blackmail Tom, but he wouldn't have known how to execute it. Someone helped him. Someone with experience.

"Bickert was working for you, wasn't he?"

"And for Tom—at my recommendation. Of course, Tom had no idea that Bickert was a double agent. The man would have done literally anything for money. I paid him to set up the robbery and blackmail. Tom paid him to find the stolen suicide note and put an end to the blackmail. Bickert was only too happy to investigate his own crimes."

"He was the one who installed those webcams?"

"He jammed the station's cable signal, then went in posing as a Fios repairman."

"Why?"

"After Bill skipped on Hawthorne, we all thought he'd come running to you. Tom felt more convinced than ever that Bill was behind the blackmail. Bickert and I needed to find Bill so that we could finish framing him. But the webcams turned out to be unnecessary.

Bickert tracked Bill to that squat on his own. We could have wrapped things up sooner, but Bickert wanted to squeeze one last payment out of Tom. Unfortunately—"

"Tom figured out it was you?"

Paul nodded. I remembered the phrase Aiden over-heard: *"This will kill her."* It had been Paul on the other end of the line.

"Bickert insisted we shut the operation down imme-diately, that night, before Tom changed his mind and called the cops," Paul said. "I asked Tom to meet me at the Foundation. Bickert and Lowry went to the squat. According to Lowry, Bickert got careless. Bill wrestled the gun from him. Lowry managed to grab the letter on his way out the door. He sold it back to me later."

"And then you incinerated him."

"Lowry was an animal. He got Bill's location out of Jeff while I watched. It wasn't pretty. Afterward, Lowry became the last loose end—the only person besides me who knew the whole story. I was paying him a small for-tune, but he'd already started to demand more. I never would have been rid of him."

I shook my head.

"I ran straight to you with Tom's computer."

"Of course you did. You've never seen what's right in front of you. You're too busy staring backward. It's like your life stalled out twenty years ago. You keep revving the engine, but nothing much happens."

"A lot has happened. I have a son. A husband. A career."

"Yes, but do you *see* them? Or do you only pretend to see them? You go through the motions, but you aren't actually here. That's one thing we have in common—we're two of the world's great fakers. But at least I lift my head out of the sand long enough to get my bear-ings. If you'd ever really seen me, you'd know that what's happening right now—us sitting across from each other, with your brother OD-ing in the next room—has always been inevitable."

"You're talking in riddles."

"When I speak plainly, you don't hear me."

"What is it I haven't heard, Paul?"

He leaned forward, lowered his voice to a whisper.

"Me," he said. "My guilt."

"It's coming through loud and clear now."

He waved the gun at the room.

"I don't mean *this*."

"What, then?"

"Dad. Mr. Davidson, as you call him."

"What are you talking about?"

"You think he was a saint. He was so good to you that you never noticed how he treated me. How he treated Mom."

"How did he treat you, Paul?"

"He bullied me. He belittled me. Or else he pretended I wasn't there. He couldn't love me because I wasn't broken. Not like him. Not like you. I had a mommy and a daddy and a swing set in the backyard. He resented me for it. He hated me for it."

"That's not true. He—"

"Mom saw it. That's why she's kept my secret. Why she'll keep it until she dies."

"What secret? What did Mom see?"

"The scratches on my forearm where he clawed at me. I must have wanted her to see them. I must have wanted her to know."

He looked at me like he was waiting for it to sink in.

"You're saying that you—"

"It wasn't my idea. I refused at first. But he kept hammering at me. He called me a weakling. A coward. A sniveling little shit. He said he was glad he wouldn't live to see the man I'd become. He said he'd rather have no legacy than me. All those months I'd spent at his side reading to him, feeding him, mopping up his spittle. They meant nothing. Nursing him only made me more pathetic in his eyes. 'You want to help,' he said, 'but you can't. I'm already dead. No one can call this living.' He was lying in the hospital bed in the back room. Mom was asleep upstairs. 'Goddamn it,' he shouted, 'look at me.'

"It was true—there was hardly any of him left. I doubt he weighed a hundred pounds. He was shivering, even wrapped in all those blankets. He dragged the pillow out from under his head. Just that much effort winded him. 'Take it,' he said. 'I'll fight you, but that's only instinct. This is what I want.' I stood there, paralyzed, tears streaming down my cheeks. 'Go on,' he said. 'Prove me wrong. Show me you have it in you.'"

Paul was crying again now. He was back in that moment, reliving it with me as witness.

"Dad fought like he said he would. I felt his nails digging into my skin. I heard him screaming into the pillow. But now he was the weak one. I clamped down and didn't let up until his limbs quit thrashing. Then I slipped the pillow back under his head, folded his arms over his chest and fixed his hair. I was afraid, but also exhilarated. I'd done something that couldn't be undone. It was a new kind of power.

*"You showed mercy,"* Mom told me later. *"He's at peace now."* And then she never said another word about it. I'm the reason she moved away. It had nothing to do with you. Now that she's getting older, she doesn't want me near the plug. At the time, though, she must have been grateful. She tried to kill herself once, when I was an infant. Dad never forgave her for it. He reveled in not forgiving her. He hid that side of their marriage from

you, which was no hard task. He tried to hide it from me too, but I spent half my childhood with an ear to the wall. The things he'd say to her behind closed doors. *"You need me. You'd never survive on your own. Who else would take you in? Look at yourself. You've doubled in size. You're a shit mother. You spend your life crying in a corner. The biggest mistake I ever made was calling 911. Go ahead—give it another try. I'm begging you."* That kind and gentle man you believe saved your life—he was one more great faker."

Something was shifting in me. I felt the fear subsiding, the anger winning out.

"Maybe he was a fake," I said. "What he did to you is unforgivable. No father should put his son in that position. But Mr. Davidson didn't burn anyone alive. He didn't stick a needle in anyone's arm. He didn't lie in wait and then hit the gas."

Paul sat up straighter. His hold on the gun tightened.

"I never meant for those things to happen," he said. "It wasn't supposed to go that far. I never thought Tom would pay the ransom. I wanted to expose him. I wanted—"

"To hurt me? Why? Because you thought a shiny new big sister would swoop in and rescue you? Is that it? I let you down?"

He shook his head.

"I thought we'd rescue each other. But you barely noticed me. You kept me on the outside, and you made sure I felt it. Bill, on the other hand . . . the junkie. Your brother by blood. You'd have given your life for him. But the thing about being on the outside is that the bigger picture comes into focus. You see the patterns. You see who people are. You see where they're headed. And that gives you an advantage because the people on the inside have no idea. Proximity blinds them. They go around thinking they can change each other, make all the pieces fit before the clock stops ticking. You don't love Bill—you love the idea of being the one who saves Bill. And the Tom you think you love doesn't exist. I had to make you see that. Not so things could change, but so they could end. So I could start over. I've spent my life stuck in other people's stories. When Tom told me about that letter, I saw my way out. I saw how my story could begin."

"And what's your story, Paul?"

He smiled like we were just now getting to the best part.

"I'm going to be the hero who steps in and raises his orphaned nephew," he said. "Me, who was never really your brother. Just an object that sometimes obstructed your view. I'll be the one feeding him breakfast and picking him up from school and tucking him in at night. I'll chaperone his first prom. I'll drive him off to college. And when the time is right, I'll tell him all about you. How you killed yourself because you were a coward. Because you couldn't face who you were. How he wasn't enough—not nearly enough to live for. I'll make sure he has a strong sense of the people he comes from. Grandma and Grandpa and Uncle Bill. Maybe I'll give him his first taste of heroin. Call it a rite of passage."

It was the blow that might have broken me if I hadn't remembered Laura's call.

"None of that will happen," I said. "Tom's awake. He's talking."

"Bullshit."

"I got the news on my way up here. The police are with him now."

"You're lying. Tom's done. I was there. I felt the impact."

"Call the hospital. They'll tell you. Or I can call, and you can listen in."

He stood up, then came bolting forward. He stuck the barrel of the gun under my chin.

"You're a liar."

"I know the number by heart. We might even be allowed to say hello if the detectives have finished. In which case, the cops are already looking for you."

"Shut your mouth."

"It was Lowry who took that video of me, wasn't it? But you're the one who gave me a private viewing. You're clever, Paul. But you have to see that it's over now. You have two choices: you can either run or turn yourself in."

He backed away, started pacing in tight little circles, gnawing at his bottom lip and whispering to himself. I thought about the mace in my pocket, then thought better of it: even if I blinded him, he'd still have hold of the revolver.

"Run while you can, Paul. Drive to the airport. Get on the next flight out. I'll tell them you were headed for Canada. That should give you all the time you need."

He stopped short.

"I've got a better idea," he said. "First you, then me."

He raised the gun, aimed the muzzle at my forehead. I told myself to lunge. I saw myself hurtling toward him, flailing for the barrel, but I couldn't make my legs move. I couldn't utter a sound, and yet I felt sure that it was my own voice I heard screaming.

"Don't—"

Bill was on his feet. He'd lifted a butcher's knife off the kitchen counter and was staggering toward Paul. Paul pivoted. Bill lost his footing, reached for something to grab onto, then collapsed. The knife skidded onto the area rug. I leapt from the couch, grabbed the gun in

both hands, and used my bodyweight to tear it free. I
went careening into the wall beside the fireplace. Paul
picked up the knife, started after me. I set my feet. The
first bullet hit him in the shoulder. He reeled but kept
coming. I fired again.

# 41

I FLUNG THE KNIFE up into the loft, then crouched beside Paul and felt for a pulse. Nothing. No breath either. His eyes were shut, his mouth hanging open. I stood, slipped in his blood, landed hard on my side. I couldn't think of what to do next. I might have lain there until someone found us if I hadn't heard Bill moaning.

I dropped the gun on the armchair, ran over to him, then rolled him onto his back. One side of his face was badly skinned. There were splinters from the unvarnished floor lodged in his cheek. His lips had gone blue and his breathing was shallow.

"You hold on, Bill," I said.

I sprinted out to the car, grabbed my kit from the trunk, then sprinted back. His eyes were open, but I couldn't tell for sure if he was conscious. I pulled out the Narcan, fumbled with the packaging.

"Here we go now."

I sprayed, rubbed his chest, sprayed again.

"You hear me, Bill?"

I gave him another round.

"Bill?"

His pupils swam for a beat, and then I could see the world coming into focus for him.

"What's so funny?" he asked.

I squeezed his hand.

"I'm crying, you idiot."

"Why?"

"You're going to be okay, Bill."

I sat him up, wiped his cuts with iodine, covered his cheek with gauze.

"Let's get you some clothes," I said.

I found jeans and a sweatshirt crumpled up inside his duffel bag. Stale, but clean.

"Can you stand?" I asked.

He nodded. I took hold of his wrists and pulled him to his feet. I was pretty sure he weighed less than I did.

"There's something I can't remember," he said, stepping into his jeans, holding onto my arm for balance.

"It will come to you," I told him. "Just relax now."

With his arm around my shoulders, we made a slow exit, neither of us daring to look back. I got him to the car, sat him down in the passenger seat, then walked a few yards off and called 911.

"Where are we going?" he asked when I climbed in behind the wheel.

I reached across, took his hand.

"We're just waiting," I said.

It wasn't long before we heard sirens in the distance. Bill yanked his hand from mine. He seemed to look everywhere but at me.

"There's something I've got to tell you," he said.

He wasn't bothering to blink the tears away.

"Easy, Bill. Take a breath and—"

"It was me, Teen."

"What was you?"

"I killed her."

I thought he had to be talking about Bickert. Then the *her* registered.

"Me," he said. "Not Dad."

\* \* \*

Bill finished telling me right as the overgrown driveway flooded with emergency vehicles. My first thought: Alden hadn't resurrected a memory so much as planted one. My second thought: our old man had planted it. But that was just my mind stalling until the truth could take hold. Bill's story was too convincing, the details too precise.

The bit about the last dime bag was true, only it was Bill who'd smoked it, our mother who was searching for it. Bill stood watching from our bedroom doorway as she overturned furniture, knocked pictures off the walls, dropped to her knees and crawled across the patchwork rug, patting down every fiber. Then she got up, cursing, and ran into the kitchen. Bill heard silverware ricocheting off the floor, plates shattering, cabinet doors opening and slamming shut. He came out of our room, inched his way up behind her. She didn't see him. She was trembling, sweating, clawing at the skin on her arms. Bill called to her. She didn't hear. He said he would help her look for whatever it was she'd lost. She turned on him.

"*You piece of shit,*" she said. "*Where the fuck is it?*"
"*What?*"

She grabbed his face in one hand, squeezed so hard he tasted blood.

"*Tell me.*"

"*I'm sorry. I didn't—*"

She knocked him to the floor with a backhand. He landed on a bed of silverware, felt metal tines breaking his skin.

*"What the fuck did you do?"*

She pinned him down, beat on his arms while he covered his face, then slid her hands around his throat and squeezed. Bill didn't think—he grabbed a knife and swung. Then the world went blank until our father came home and lifted him to his feet.

"I wanted to confess," Bill said. "When I left Hawthorne. I still want to. But he made me promise. You can't say anything either, Teen. Not to anyone."

"No," I told him, "I won't say anything."

Because if I did, then the last twenty years of our old man's life would have been for nothing.

"Did he tell you why he did it?" I asked.

But I already knew. My old man saw an opportunity—a chance that wouldn't come again, and he saw what would happen to him if he didn't take it. To him and to anyone he cared about when he was sober enough to think straight. More pain. More blood. More scorched earth. Until eventually it was him with a knife in his neck or a needle hanging from his vein.

"You had no choice, Bill," I said. "I'd want Aiden to do the same."

\* \* \*

A uniformed cop put me in the back of a squad car, told me to wait. I watched a pair of EMTs jab an IV into Bill's arm and drive him away. More and more people arrived. Vanloads of forensic technicians in their landlord-white spacemen outfits. An ancient-looking medical examiner. Some kind of sheriff in a tricked-out SUV. A series of unmarked cars. They were going to have to start cutting down trees to make room. Before long, two spindly kids in lab coats wheeled Paul out on a gurney. I turned my head until I heard the doors to the ME's van slam shut.

It seemed as though the Ferril PD had forgotten about me, and for my part I returned the favor. I was stuck in a decades-old scene, trying to see it through Bill's eyes.

*Our mother?*

I couldn't dial in a clear picture. I couldn't dial in any picture at all. Bill wasn't the only one who'd wiped swaths of his hippocampus clean. I realized that I'd never really thought about her—only about who she might have been. Afterward, and for a long time, I'd obsessed about the chances I thought our father had stolen from her. The chance to purge the junk from her veins. The chance to reinvent herself. The chance to be a mom. I remembered in a vague way that she'd liked to sing. As a kid, I used to imagine myself watching from the wings while she belted it out on stage, the spotlight glinting off her sequin dress. But even then, she was a faceless figure—a portrait I'd started but couldn't complete.

A detective stuck his head in the squad car and asked if the two-door green Chevy parked at the boat launch across the road belonged to Paul. I told him I didn't know. He turned and walked away.

Later, at the station, they gave me a residue test, took my fingerprints, and swabbed for DNA. They confiscated my belongings and my clothes and dressed me in a plastic jumpsuit. All for the purposes of confirmation and exclusion, they said. When they were done, they put me in a room with no windows and no clock and left me alone again for what felt like hours.

I tried not to think, but the effort only made my mind race faster. All those years with my father as the ogre, the bogeyman. Every ugly thing his fault. All those memories I clung to just so I could keep on hating him. Were they real? Could it have been my mother that dealer shoved up against a wall? Or was it nobody? How much had I invented? Lifted from books and television and the kids at school? How could I feel sure of anything when I'd been so wrong? About my old man. About Paul. About Bill.

A woman stuck her head into the room and asked if I wanted coffee. I said no, but could I please call the hospital. My husband was in intensive care. Tom. His name was Tom Evans. She said she'd call for me, then return with an update. But when the door opened again, it was Knowles who entered. He looked solemn, or like he was trying to look solemn. Always in his windbreaker and jeans. He sat down opposite me and set some files and a notepad on the table between us. I was almost glad for a familiar face.

"Have they given you anything to eat?" he asked.

I nodded, even though they hadn't. I trusted Good Knowles less than I trusted Bad Knowles.

"I'm not here to interrogate you, Mrs. Evans. I understand you've had quite a day. At this point, I just need to confirm a few things."

Translation: *"Let me take one more stab at catching you in a lie."*

"I came here straight from Brooklyn Methodist. Tom gave me a statement. He says—"

I nearly flew out of my chair.

"Tom's talking?"

Knowles looked at me like it was my fault I didn't know already.

"Full sentences?" I asked.

"For the most part."

"Any slurring?"

"Some. He's groggy, but he's with it."

"I need to see him."

"Soon, Mrs. Evans."

Knowles had to be kicking himself—Tom's health wasn't where he wanted my attention.

"How soon?"

"You can head back when we're done here."

"Then ask me your questions."

I might have been the first person ever to smile in that dank little room. Tom's mind was whole. Whatever happened to me, Aiden would have his dad. I felt sparks shooting all around my circuitry.

Knowles pushed back in his chair. From then on, he did most of the talking. Tom had told him about the robbery, the blackmail, his old man's suicide letter.

"A secret he kept even from you."

But not from Paul. Like I suspected, Tom had unburdened himself during a particularly high-octane bender. He'd been so far gone that for a long time afterward he didn't remember saying anything. But then a phrase in one of Paul's blackmail notes brought back the whole drunken conversation. Tom figured out the rest. Paul setting up the robbery. Paul recommending Bickert. Tom went out that night thinking he could protect me. *"This will kill her."* But the Paul Tom knew, the Paul he'd hoped to reason with, didn't exist.

"I spoke with your brother too," Knowles said. "His version of what happened in the cabin matches what you told local PD."

"Because it's not a version," I said. "Paul was going to kill us both."

"Bill confessed to shooting Bickert too. Also in self-defense, which is probably true—I doubt Bickert had any other motive for being at that squat. Still, there's tampering with a corpse. Your brother should have called us instead of hiding the body."

"An addict with a record? You wouldn't have believed a word he said. You wouldn't believe him now if it weren't for Tom."

Knowles surprised me with a grin.

"Is that what you told Bill when he called that night?"

He was handing me one more opportunity to deliver the truth.

"I didn't tell him anything," I said.

# CHAPTER

# 42

*Six months later*

As Knowles suggested, and with a little help from Tom's legal team, Bill's role in Bickert's death was ruled self-defense. Bill plead guilty to the tampering charge: a class E felony—probation, no jail, and court-mandated rehab. This time, a center in Long Island City. Bill's choice.

I visited him there. It wasn't swank like Hawthorne, but it wasn't shabby either. More Bill's speed. We sat at a desk in an unused classroom while he showed me some of his latest drawings. The cabin, Ferril Lake, a tree fronting the stream out back.

"I thought I'd lose my shit living alone in the woods," he said, "but I kind of liked it."

He'd switched from his little black pad to a nine-by-twelve-inch sketchbook. I hoped the larger dimensions meant he was finally taking himself seriously. He definitely looked healthier. He'd put on weight. His cheeks had filled out. He even had some color. When he reached the first blank page, he set the sketchbook flat on the desk and pulled a pencil from its spiral binding. I didn't mind—doubling as Bill's model felt like a return to normal.

"You left those drawings at the squat for me to find, didn't you?" I asked.

He nodded without looking up.

"Why'd you run from me, Bill?"

"Jeff said I'd be making you an accessory."

"Did he say anything else?"

"Yeah, he did."

"That it must have been Tom who sent Bickert?"

"Tom thought I robbed you. Then I split on Hawthorne and left him holding the tab."

"And Jeff convinced you that telling me where you were hiding would be the same as telling Tom?"

"I'm sorry, Teen."

I shook my head.

"It's me who should be sorry," I said. "Paul was right about one thing—I have a gift for being oblivious. I had no idea that Tom threatened you. And Paul was the last person I—"

"It's okay, Teen. I'm glad shit happened the way it did. Knowing's better than not knowing."

"You mean about Mom?"

"Yeah. At the end, it was like she had no idea who I was. I see her face now and think, *That can't be me.* You know? I can't let that be me."

"It won't be," I said. "It isn't. It never was."

"It wasn't her either. That's the point."

"I know, Bill."

We went quiet for a while. Quiet has never been a problem with Bill—models aren't supposed to talk in the first place. I watched him etch in my bangs, shade the mole on my right cheek.

"Things are going to be different now," I said.

"Does that mean better?"

I hesitated, then said, "Yeah, I think it does. I think this is finally us standing on the other side."

"Yeah?"

"It has to be, right?"

He kept his eyes on my portrait.

"Anything's possible," he said.

\* \* \*

I took leave from work, spent long hours with Tom at a different kind of rehab, standing by his side, chiming in with moral support as he braced himself on the parallel bars or read a story out loud to his speech therapist. He needed a quad cane just to get from his bed to the toilet, and every third word tripped him up, but his memory was solid. He told me about his father's suicide, quoted verbatim from the letter. I didn't have to ask, which was something.

Whether or not the police will open an investigation into a thirty-year-old arson-homicide remains to be seen. But even if they do, Tom and I will be all right. It's too soon to know how, or how much of us it will take, but I'm confident we'll be okay. He needs to heal first. Physically. Once he's whole, the work can start. Little by little, we'll let each other in again. I can't imagine either of us walking away.

Aiden asks about his uncle Paul. He wonders why when one person returns to him, another leaves. And he's still convinced that Daddy's accident happened in the course of a mission. Aiden comes with me to rehab sometimes. He's seen the scars, watched his father take slow, agonizing steps. He's heard his father's voice catch and stumble over simple, everyday phrases. His conclusion: *"Dad must be the bravest man alive."*

\* \* \*

"There won't be a funeral," Mrs. Davidson said. "What would be the point?"

I pictured her staring out her living room window at a long block of streamlined adobes, waving to the community security guard as he cruised past in a golf cart.

"I'm sorry," I told her.

"For what?"

I couldn't say, exactly—it was more like an expression of general remorse, two words meant to bridge the gap between now and the end of the call: I couldn't imagine there'd be another. Neither could Mrs. Davidson. She saw this final exchange as an opportunity to correct the record.

"You think I kept you at arm's length," she said. "The truth is you never let me anywhere near you. Your eyes went dead when I walked into the room. You spoke to me in little grunts. I remember saying, 'You can call me Mom, you know?' and you answering with 'Yes, ma'am.' You didn't want a new mother, any more than I wanted a daughter. But Alan thrust us together. He always got his way. Not that I blame him, really. For anything. He was one of those foster kids you read about. Locked up in basements. Burned with cigarettes. Stuff you can't believe really happens."

I heard myself asking, "Why didn't you want me?"

"Because I had nothing to offer you. Your being there was a constant reminder that I had nothing to give."

She took my silence for a prompt.

"It's sad, isn't it?" she said. "You were a child. What you knew of the world was so violent and unpredictable that you accepted it all as normal."

"Accepted all what?"

"Me locking myself away for days on end. Alan treating me like a stranger or else humiliating me, berating me, bludgeoning me with the past. Then there were those little trips I'd take just to get away from him. To think things through, which is next to impossible when you doubt your own mind. Of course, I always came back. And Alan worked so hard to keep our battles secret. From you and from your social worker."

Her voice had a waxen, unreal quality—not at all like she was talking to the person who'd killed her son.

"Are you going to be okay?" I asked.

"You mean because I'm not weeping and gnashing my teeth?"

She waited, but again I kept quiet.

"I expect I'm in for some very bad nights," she said, "but it hasn't been as much of a shock as you might think. I've been prepared—not for this, exactly, but for something like this—for so long that part of me is relieved. I was always afraid of my son, you know. Outwardly, he was so well behaved, but there were signs. Signs that he was overcompensating, that there was something in him he couldn't understand or accept. When kids picked on him at school, he never got angry or scared—just confused, like he was trying to figure out what they sensed in him, because he sensed it too. Still, I wasn't sure there was anything actually wrong with Paul until Alan got sick."

I'd gone back over Mr. Davidson's final months again and again. Even knowing how it ended, I couldn't find any hint that Paul had been anything but a guardian angel.

"What was it you saw?" I asked.

"A fascination, mostly. He wasn't caretaking for Alan—he was transfixed by a gruesome end. He masked it as best he could, but there were clues. I came home once to find the thermostat up at one hundred degrees and Alan covered in blankets. There were scratches on his arms. Paul claimed they were self-inflicted, which was entirely possible. Alan was so out of it then. When I asked him, I couldn't get a coherent answer. Another time, I found him wearing a pair of garish bright-yellow sweatpants. Paul claimed he'd wet himself while he was asleep. It had happened before. But there were red marks around both of Alan's wrists, as though he'd been tied down."

"Paul told me Mr. Davidson was ready to die. He said he begged for it."

"He told me that too. And I wanted to believe him. Almost as much as he wanted to believe it himself."

"If you thought Paul was dangerous, then why didn't you say anything?"

"I told you: I didn't trust my own mind. And I didn't think anyone else would trust it either. There was always the chance I was wrong. And if I was wrong, then I was the dangerous one."

But she hadn't been wrong. Neither had Paul when he accused me of reveling in my own trauma. I'd arrived at the Davidsons', taken one look at the manicured lawns and the mailboxes lining the curb, and told myself there was nothing more to see. I could forgive myself for that much. I'd been a kid. But how had I kept on believing in a big-hearted boy who pushed away his own pain in order to help the people he loved? He hadn't been capable of love. He hadn't pushed away anything—he'd been hoarding, waiting for his best chance. And I'd handed him my son.

Mrs. Davidson responded as though I'd been thinking out loud.

"Don't blame yourself," she said.

I was about to ask *for what*, but she'd hung up. It wasn't the worst note to end on.

\* \* \*

My father gets out tomorrow. The decades-long punishment for his one good deed will finally be over. He'll move into a halfway house designed and built by his son-in-law. My old man will meet his grandson. And he and I will meet too. That's how I have to think of it: a clean slate for both of us.

I testified at his hearing—just not the way I'd imagined. I said he was a changed man. Rick Morgan, aged fifty-three, was brimming with kindness, compassion, and love. He was haunted, yes, but also hopeful. He was the man I first saw in Bill's sketchpad. I didn't know how much of it was true—I only knew that he was innocent of killing my mother and that he'd sacrificed himself for Bill.

I still can't quite picture it—Tom, Bill, Aiden, and my old man gathered around the same holiday table. So many things could go wrong before that happens. A relapse. A parole violation. An affair. A secret indictment. A plane wreck or a blood clot. But I'm trying hard to believe what I told Bill: *This is us, standing on the other side.*

# EPILOGUE

THE DAY WAS almost too perfect. Cloudless sky, foliage hitting full bloom, the occasional kite above the Hudson, deer grazing along the side of the highway. Mother Nature's apology for winter. The stuff of travel brochures and pharmaceutical commercials.

The mansion looked even shinier this time of year, as though the spring sun had given it a fresh waxing. I rang the bell and waited outside the cathedral doors. It was Alden herself who opened them. The purple highlights were back in her bangs, a midlife resurgence of her goth alter ego. As we shook hands, something hit me that should have been obvious from the start: Alden was recovering herself. Post-traumatic addiction therapy began with her own core trauma. I wasn't sure if that gave me more or less faith in her therapeutic powers, made me more or less confident in my decision to drive up here.

She led me straight back to her office. No small talk. No hint that she'd read the papers. No asking after Bill. That last omission felt deliberate: this was my time, and how we filled it would be up to me. I started to sit down at her desk, but she shook her head, gestured to the leather recliner instead. The texture of it surprised me: it didn't support my weight so much as meld with my body. I thought of Bill sitting here. I thought of Aiden's visit with Dr. Menendez. And I felt suddenly hollow, as though I were trivializing their experiences by suggesting that there might be anything at all buried inside of me.

I wanted to run, but the chair kept sucking me down, and Alden had a hand on my shoulder. Her touch was gentle, warm. I remembered Aiden's description. *"It's different than regular sleeping. It felt like a bath."* Without being told to, I shut my eyes.

"Let me know when you're ready to begin," Alden said.

# ACKNOWLEDGMENTS

I'm forever grateful to my agent Peter Steinberg for believing in this novel; Toni Kirkpatrick for rescuing it from oblivion; Kara Klontz for a cover that makes readers want to look inside; Rebecca Nelson for shepherding the book through the production process; Madeline Rathle and Dulce Botello for working hard to make sure people know *Not by Blood* exists; Yezenira Venecia and Jill Pellarin for catching the mistakes I missed; and Elliot Reed for his stellar web design.

And, as always, I want to thank my wife, Nina Shope, for her endless love and support, and for being my coconspirator in all things.